THERE'S NO 'F' IN WONDERFUL

Praise for
There's No 'F' in Wonderful

'Bill Broady's voice is unique in British fiction. His new novel, *There's No 'F' in Wonderful,* continues a high-serious comic tradition that is now otherwise close to extinction.' —DAVID ROSE

'Here the human drama in the uncertain days just after Punk is brought to life in an X-rated screwball comedy set in a Northern casino - told with Broady's unique gift for extravagant but just-right simile, for twisted romance, and for unexpected pathos.' —RICHARD PRICE

'Bill Broady's *There's No 'F' in Wonderful* vividly resurrects an all but vanished world of smoky casinos and Northern Soul discos, bringing to life a ribald, unique suite of oddball characters who stay in one's mind long after the novel is finished. Shot through with tenderness and humour, Broady's ability to evoke time and place - 1970s Yorkshire - with sublime melancholia and brio at once is unparalleled.' —JEAN MCNEIL

'A novel of rhythm and hope, set in a Leeds instantly recognisable to anyone who experienced it, Broady works with broad Northern humour, neatly shot through with brains, all held together with writing that's subtle, sometimes beautiful, sometimes raw, to create an unforgettable story.' —CHRIS NICKSON

'*There's No 'F' in Wonderful* is a pulsating and dreamlike literary romp. Viscerally hilarious and riven with electric prose, Bill Broady has written another truly memorable novel.'
—RICHARD OWAIN ROBERTS

'A rambunctious, laugh-out-loud royal flush of a novel. The rocking, cheap suits, Cinzano and furs world of 70s Leeds clubland that Bill Broady depicts with such characterful detail and cinematic relish may no longer exist, but it will live on forever through the pages of this hilarious, joint-jumping, rug-cutting read.' —PIERS TORDAY

ALSO BY BILL BROADY

FICTION
Swimmer
Eternity is Temporary
The Night-Soil Men

SHORT STORIES
In This Block There Lives a Slag

BILL BROADY

THERE'S NO 'F' IN WONDERFUL

SALT

CROMER

PUBLISHED BY SALT PUBLISHING 2026

2 4 6 8 10 9 7 5 3 1

Copyright © Bill Broady 2026

Bill Broady has asserted his right under the Copyright, Designs and
Patents Act 1988 to be identified as the author of this work.

*This book is sold subject to the condition that it shall not, by way of trade or otherwise,
be lent, resold, hired out, or otherwise circulated without the publisher's prior consent
in any form of binding or cover other than that in which it is published and without a
similar condition including this condition being imposed on the subsequent publisher.*

This book is a work of fiction. Any references to historical events, real people
or real places are used fictitiously. Other names, characters, places and events
are products of the author's imagination, and any resemblance to actual
events or places or persons, living or dead, is entirely coincidental.

First published in Great Britain in 2026 by
Salt Publishing Ltd
12 Norwich Road, Cromer, Norfolk NR27 0AX, United Kingdom

GPSR representative
Matt Parsons matt.parsons@upi2mbooks.hr
UPI-2M PLUS d.o.o., Medulićeva 20, 10000 Zagreb, Croatia

www.saltpublishing.com

Salt Publishing Limited Reg. No. 5293401

A CIP catalogue record for this book is available from the British Library

ISBN 978 1 78463 380 6 (Paperback edition)
ISBN 978 1 78463 381 3 (Electronic edition)

Typeset in Neacademia by Salt Publishing

Printed and bound in Great Britain by Clays Ltd, Elcograf S.p.A.

To Jane and Mignon with love

ONE

ALTHOUGH there were three interviewers the two women had so far remained silent. One was looking encouraging, the other distinctly underwhelmed: every minute or so they would exchange expressions. They must have been twins: only by their hair would you have been able to tell them apart.

"Do you have a bad temper?" The man in the middle enquired.

"No" - I resisted an urge to take him by his scraggy throat - "Why do you ask?"

"We've found that most redheads are on a very short fuse."

"That's not red" - the bottle-blonde pointed - "It's auburn."

"Pale gold," I corrected.

"He's a ginger!" The brunette jeered. "And all gingers are nuts."

"Everybody has a temper," the man continued urbanely. "So when did you last lose yours?"

I stared at him. His name was Gray - after the colour of his teeth.

"Well," I said at last, "My mother claims that I used to throw the toys out of my pram."

As if in response the fluorescent light above us flickered then went out.

I had been seated next to the wheel of a roulette table in the middle of the empty casino. My interrogators were lined up across the baize. Although the air was teeming with dust motes the dark wood gleamed, and the metal shone.

"Can you smile?"

"I think so."

"Well, go on then."

I obliged.

"No – so we can see your *teeth*."

I bared them and growled.

"That was nice. Do you *need* to wear dark glasses?"

I took them off and everything swam.

"How tall are you?"

"Eighteen hands – Two yards – Six feet."

"You look taller," said the blonde suspiciously.

"Six – one actually but it seems a bit lame to add the inch."

"Why has your jacket got zips up its sleeves?"

"I bought it from a man in a pub," I said. "He said they're for wing attachments."

I was good at interviews – I almost always got the nod. It was the jobs that followed that were the problem. If only I could make a career out of being interviewed, like Sir Peter Ustinov. He was my hero: I once ran into him in a Dublin bar and – struggle though I did – I just couldn't prevent myself interviewing him.

"We open at two in the afternoon, but most shifts are from eight until three – or four, if you're cashing up." Mr Gray's teeth disappeared when he smiled. "Would that be a problem for you?"

"No." I really didn't care what I did so long as it was by night.

"OK!" They sprang to their feet. "Take off those rings and let's see what you can do!"

Gray tossed me a £50 cash chip which I scooped up on the half-volley.

It was a beautiful thing – not plastic as I had expected but of inlaid, tiger-striped wood. I walked it rapidly through my fingers, across the knuckles and back again then with my thumbnail flicked it up so high that it almost reached the ceiling and caught it without looking, flat on the back of the other hand. I had perfected this during my childhood, using my lucky King George V florin, in the hope that – like George Raft in *Scarface* – it might give me a dangerous air.

Gray pushed a pile of baby-blue chips towards me.

"Try to pick these up with one hand."

I obliged.

"Now cut them into fours."

By some instinct I accomplished this in what turned out to be the regulation manner, employing a hooking forefinger as the gauge.

"And knock the top one off to prove the stack."

"OK," said the blonde. "But can you do that with your *left* hand?"

I could, but more slowly.

"Try it with both" – the brunette was sweeping two more stacks across – "And with your eyes shut."

"And no peeping!"

I flailed blindly around, sending the chips flying towards them but they had already taken evasive action.

"Good," said Gray. "If you'd pulled that off we'd have known you were a plant."

Next, we simulated a game in which they attempted to cheat in every possible way.

"No bet!" I kept saying, "No bet!" as I threw the errant chips back into their grinning faces.

"Whatever happens, keep that wheel spinning!" Gray shouted. "If it ever stops it'll be the end of the world."

At last they resumed their seats. "Excellent!" said the blonde.

How could she know that my natural aptitudes never lasted long? I took to most things like a duck to water until I became self-conscious – realizing how ridiculous I must be looking, a man pretending to be a duck – and promptly sank like a stone.

"Those nails will need cutting," said the brunette. "Not to mention keeping clean."

"Well, you're in" – Gray concluded – "Subject, of course, to references and police checks, under the 1960 Betting and Gaming Act."

I had not reckoned on there being a security check that would entail a visit to my home. The police were the very reason why Ed and I had recently moved to this city.

Despite our reputations we were not master criminals – merely obsessive dopers who had drifted into social dealing only to be caught up in the ineluctable logic of the thing. It was just a game to us: all dressed in black we would swish around the campus or beckon from shadowy entryways. Policemen were merely plastic figurines we fished out of our play-boxes.

We had never dreamed that these phantasms could actually harm us, so I was shocked when Ed got himself caught. It was not simply for possession – he had been apprehended breaking into a dispensing chemist. While the coppers were chasing him an accomplice was slipping out of the back with what had turned out to be an empty DDA Cabinet: despite the threats and beatings he had resolutely refused to name this man.

Serious jail time had seemed inevitable but instead he walked free with a £50 fine, while the university declined to send down or even suspend him. A regiment of celebrity dons and Catholic priests had been marched through the court, explaining how this brilliant but unworldly youth – arguably the most promising English student of his generation – had been led astray by malign influences. Everyone glared at me but there was little they could do: I had graduated long ago. It was now that I discovered that Ed's dad was a Home Office Pathologist and his mum a highly regarded Justice of the Peace. As we left, the drug squad boys were kicking lumps out of the walls.

I had always prided myself on playing things cool but now I realized that we had merely been pushing our luck. An off-duty cop warned me in the pub that it was now my turn. Ed could evidently shoot the Queen Mum and get away with it so they would be doubling down on me. Although my gaff was always clean they were going to make sure that the next time they raided they would find what they were looking for. "'ElIo-'Ello-'Ello!" – I could almost hear the thud of those bulging bags of Class A goodies as they dropped on my bedroom floor – "What 'ave we got 'ere then?"

Ed was exhibiting worrying signs of paranoia.

"They're always following me," he said. "It's a good job they don't know where we live."

"Leeds is the place for us," I told him. It was only thirty miles away, but North and West Yorkshire were like two different worlds. "I know some people at the Art College and there's a great club scene and you can score anything down Chapeltown way."

Within a week we had packed up and gone. After painting our new flat – brilliant white gloss even on the ceilings – I went looking for work while Ed would drive his 450 Ducatti back and forth for lectures and seminars. He did not tell even his tutor about his move. We had determined to give up dealing and confine ourselves to judicious recreational use. It was amazing just how easy it was to change your life.

So the last thing we needed was to be brought to the notice of the local force. I was just about to turn down the job when a letter from the casino informed me that I had been cleared to report next week for the induction course. Evidently all those checks and references had been purely nominal: as usual, I had gone through on the nod.

Late on Friday afternoon, however, as I sat in the kitchen, about to eat breakfast, a Police Inspector called. Just as I lifted the fried egg sandwich to my mouth, I became aware that a large dark form was blotting out the light.

"I just happened to be passing," it chuckled. "and thought I'd drop in."

Neither the front nor the back door had squeaked: it was as if he had silently emerged from our empty fridge.

I squinted to make out his features while he continued to scan the very depths of my soul.

"Well," he drawled at last, "You don't look much like the shadowy mastermind of the Yorkshire drug scene."

"I'm not." I put down the sandwich to steeple my fingers together like Doctor Fu Manchu.

"There's egg on your shirt." He sat down opposite and opened his pocketbook.

"Yours is a name that keeps on coming up. 'Observed in

conversation with' . . . 'A known associate of' . . . 'A regular visitor to the property' . . . and so on."

"Perhaps it's because I used to wear a ponytail," I suggested. "People tend to notice you more."

"Most of these sightings were between two and six a.m. . . . When there's not a lot of folk around *to* notice."

"My eyes are hypersensitive to light," I explained. "So my days and nights are back to front."

"I know what you mean." The voice shifted alarmingly from bass to counter-tenor.

"'To see God only I go out of sight

And to 'scape stormy days I choose

An everlasting night.'"

"It's familiar," I said, "But I can't place it."

"Aren't you supposed to be the one with the English degree? It's John Donne's 'Hymn To Christ'."

How typical of Fate to send me a metaphysical rozzer! Now I could see that his chin was shaped like a saddle's pommel, chalk white and dotted with blue stubble. He pulled down his cap-brim but I could still feel his eyes moving across my skin.

"Where's Bike-Boy, then?"

"Ed? He'll be at college."

"Blaggers' College, is that? They tell me he's a genius but he's one of the thickest-looking blokes I've ever seen."

"Like Socrates," I said. "The two often go together."

"That moustache: don't tell me it's real."

"Not just waxed," I said, "But wax."

"One thing I don't get is why some people call him The Star."

"After Edwin Starr, the soul singer. You know – 'War' . . . 'Time' . . . 'Pain'."

"A neat summary" – he wrote down the name – "Of the human condition."

"My own favourite is 'Girls Are Getting Prettier'. You'll like that one."

With a flourish he produced a small, tightly rolled joint but
instead of dropping it on the floor he shook it, licked it, stuck it
in his mouth, then raised a quizzical eyebrow and struck a match.

"Don't mind me," I said.

He took a deep hit and passed it over. It tasted like pure resin,
foul-smelling like Thai stick, probably sprayed with something or
other. My sinuses were trying to punch their way out of my face.

"How much would boots like that cost? Are they proper snake?"

"I bought them from a man in a pub," I said. "He walked home
in his socks."

I returned the one-skin: this time he sucked in the smoke with a
dreadful gurgling sound, so deeply that it might re-emerge through
the eyelets of his mirror-polished Size 14s.

"It is my unfortunate duty to confirm your suitability for employ-
ment as a trainee croupier in accordance with the Betting & Gaming
Levy Act." He exhaled with a reverse gurgle. "But let me give you
a word of warning" - the face twisted itself to perfectly replicate
Gray's freezing smile - "Watch out for the manager."

"Don't tell me," I said. "He's not as nice as he looks."

"You're obviously a decent lad," he said, after he'd finished laughing, "So why are you getting mixed up in this dirty game? They're
nothing but leeches, preying off human weakness. They even make
. . . drug-dealers look good."

"It's the hours," I said. "You know I don't like daylight."

"Well, if it's the night you're wanting my brother-in-law owns a
24/7 garage in Beeston and he's looking for a supervisor. All you'd
have to do is sit in the cabin with a baseball bat on your knee. Most
nights you wouldn't even need to hit anyone."

"It sounds wonderful," I said, "But where's the catch?"

He took a final toke and then levered himself to his feet. I
feared he might now drop the roach and arrest me but instead he
just popped it into his mouth. The cardboard was still glowing,
but he showed no discomfort, swallowing it straight down. He had
evidently decided that it was not yet my turn.

I escorted him to the front door, although he had paused by the fridge as if about to leave by the way he came. Halfway down the path he turned round.

"Has it ever struck you that you might be playing for the wrong team? Why don't you join the force - before you get yourself into some real bother? The Lord loves a reformed sinner - just read *The Golden Treasury*."

"What?"

"Bottom right in that bookcase - Voragine, between Villon and Voynich."

His feet made no sound on the gravel as he walked away.

My sandwich looked as if it had been congealing since the Ice Age. With a horrible clang I tossed it into the bin. I had just cracked our last egg when there came a loud hammering of boots and fists brutally testing the hinges of the door.

I was done for: my new friend had been toying with me before sending in the heavy mob. I did not even bother to flush away our meagre stash: I would take my condign punishment like a man.

Now two figures were at the kitchen window. Although distorted by the stippled glass they were evidently not policemen. One blur was pinkish, the other baby blue. They had fled while I was prising the window open but now came hopping back into view. Youngish women that I did not recognize: the foxy faced one looked like an Avon rep while her blockish friend could surely only be a Jehovah's Witness. Perhaps the two organisations had merged? The world was certainly ready for a new religion - we'd been thinking of starting one ourselves.

"Is Ed in?"

Neither looked like his type - or mine. "No," I said.

"What about Willikins?"

I did not like the way this was shaping. The prettier one was standing on one leg, flamingo-style, while the other flexed her neck muscles. In one of our previous flats the "Watchtower" gang had smashed the front windows - we never did discover why.

"That's me," I conceded. "How can I be of assistance?"

"No, not YOU, silly," trilled the Avon Girl. She was brandishing a sheaf of vellum inscribed like some medieval codex in that unmistakable hand. "We're looking for Ed and Willikins – the circus dwarves."

"Oh them," I said, "They're living upstairs. I'm afraid the circus is out of town but I'll tell them you called."

"They saw our notice in the paper and wrote us the most wonderful letter. What are they like?"

"I don't see much of them: they're very shy. Some nights I hear them singing – Schubert, I think – in counter-tenor and castrato."

"Here's our number" – she scribbled on the back of a deckle-edged card – "Tell them to ring us the moment they get back."

Off they skipped, chattering away. The larger one had a disconcertingly deep voice. Lori and Lorna: it wasn't hard to guess which was which.

This curious episode had not come as a complete surprise.

"We should be in proper relationships," Ed had announced, a few days ago. "With grown-up women, not with girls – not something permanent, you understand, just a bit less . . . provisional."

"Yes," I agreed. "It would be nice to break that three-week barrier."

"I aspire to three days," he said.

"But where are you going to find them? Everyone we meet in the clubs just vanishes without trace."

"What about putting something in the paper? You know – the lonely-hearts' column."

"'Drug dealers with rubber fetish seek bondage slaves. No time wasters.' I can't see them printing that in *The Mercury*."

"We'll have to make ourselves sound . . . interesting but normal," he had concluded.

The dwarf gambit was evidently his idea of this. At least he had responded to an existing ad rather than tendering one of his own. What on earth could he have written to Lori and Lorna? That letter had been at least six pages long.

I wondered if he really did think of himself as being a dwarf. He was extremely sensitive about his size – even at twenty-one grimly insisting that he was still a growing boy. Every week I had to chart his progress up against the door frame while he tried to cheat by standing on tiptoes. Last time I had discovered that he had concealed a copy of *Hudibras* under the carpet. He mortified himself with agonising stretching exercises and staggered around in six-inch stacks which rendered his dancing almost static. Yesterday he had been trying out a new walk – brisk, springy and long-striding, as about to deliver leg-spin. He was the same height as my father: pre-war he would have been on the tall side.

I had never understood such things – what did it matter so long as you were visible? – but then I was gifted six feet on entering my teens.

When Ed finally arrived, he was carrying a box of eggs of which two were broken and a soft white loaf that had been flattened into a cast of his own backside.

Although everyone called him Ed – for Edwin – he spelt it Ead – or Eadwyn – after the sixth century King of Northumberland. During his reign, according to the Venerable Bede, a woman carrying a newborn babe could cross the kingdom from sea to sea without the least mishap.

"Lori and Lorna!" he cried, hugging himself and lurching round the room. "Are they sisters?"

"They didn't say but I've never seen two women less alike."

"How tall are they?"

"Lori's about five-five. Lorna is the same but . . . stockier."

He glared. "You didn't scare them off, did you?"

"Of course not – but if you'd warned me, I could have opened the door standing on my knees. I told them you were away with the circus, and they left their telephone number."

"Did they seem interested?"

"They were avid, keen as mustard – transported, reeling from Cupid's darts, consumed by hitherto unacknowledged desires."

"Thank God!" He cut a clumsy caper. "We're on!"

"Why did you tell them we were dwarves?"

"I don't know." He made a strange but characteristic gesture, as if he was donning a hat. "I thought it might" - he adjusted the invisible brim - "pique their curiosity."

With a triumphant yell he fell upon my discarded breakfast, consuming it in a couple of bites.

"Most women," he continued, "Don't really go for those Warren Beatty types. It's Woody Allen or Dudley Moore, Kissinger or Onassis that are fighting them off."

"They're not dwarves, just little men and they're rich and power-ful and make people laugh."

"Picasso was a dwarf - so was Alexander Pope and so is Anthony Powell."

"No he isn't. I've seen pictures of him - he's a hulking great patrician-looking bloke."

"He lives in our village - he and Violet are among my mother's dearest friends. Photographers always pose him in a special sitting-room of scaled-down furniture. His one mistake was being shown stroking his favourite cat: this appeared in 'William Hickey' as proof that he was keeping a puma as a pet."

He licked the grease and bike-oil off his fingers.

"It's a deep psychological thing with women. Midgets remind them of babies, of course, but also of cocks, large, tumescent and magically freed from their previous owners. They fantasize about being able to give birth and fuck at one and the same time. For social reasons, of course, they choose normal-sized partners, but they never really give them their hearts. We, however, now have an edge: after my letter we will always give off - if only subliminally - the irresistible aura of midgetry."

He had evidently been giving this a great deal of thought.

"What exactly did they say in their ad?"

"Sporty but serious but fun."

"Count me out," I said.

For the next two weeks I would be getting up when I had formerly been going to bed: training was from nine to five. While crossing the park on Monday morning I was almost vaporized by a shaft of morning sun.

Training was not at the casino itself but in a closed down club on the outskirts of town. With its crumbling orange brickwork and perforated tin roof it had evidently been shelled during the Great Casino Wars. None of the heating worked and only the main room with its roulette tables was lit. The rest of the place was Stygian: we had to use the walls to find the way. Our shoes would squelch as we crossed the mossy carpets, leaving footprints that slowly filled with water. The ladies' toilet opened on to a foul-smelling void, while the gents had been blocked with concrete: we had to share the facilities of the recording studios next door. These were infested by silent, shaven-headed kids in black romper suits, perpetually crawling among the cogs and coils of disembowelled Bentley drum-machines. In the whole fortnight these did not produce a single sound. Sometimes, when the wind was in the right direction, we could smell the bread rising at Bray's Bakery far below.

We were a motley crew: rather like *The Dirty Dozen* except that we were only five – one woman, four men – and our instructor was not Lee Marvin but Ellen, the weary-looking brunette who had interviewed me.

"You should be six," she told us. "We've got this superstar off the cruise ships – some bloke called Chris – who's supposed be jetting in for a refresher course."

What would a 'Superstar Croupier' be like? I wondered if every profession – plumbing, teaching, banking, embalming – now felt obliged to give itself such ridiculous airs.

"Why so many men?" I asked.

"Actually, we employ twice the number of women but there's a higher turnover with your lot. Most can't take the pressure but the few that do just shoot up through the ranks: Inspector in two years, pit-boss in four, manager in ten. Do you remember Sally at the interview? It took her twelve years to get to pit-boss: we're the only ones in West Yorkshire - and we'll never go any higher."

"Why's that?"

"No-one likes seeing a woman in charge: 92% of our punters are male."

The punters! I had not given them a thought. Who were they, these curious creatures who, drawn by the lights, would cluster around the green baize to - quickly or slowly - throw all their money away?

Our solitary female was short and squat. Through a thick mane of hair that crackled with static electricity two dark eyes could sometimes be glimpsed, alternately sparkling with merriment or malice. She could have been any age: one of those people blessed or cursed never to be young or to grow old. Her name was Gigi - or maybe G-G, as in Gypsy-Girl.

All the men had freakishly long arms - but now it struck me that mine were just the same. Perhaps they had grown since I had taken the job?

By that first lunchtime we had bonded tight. We were croupiers, we were croups, a group of croups. While waiting for The Super-star to arrive we had provisionally dubbed ourselves The Filthy Five.

Alan was a wide-eyed ex-postman, every part of whose body - even the ears - appeared to be double-jointed. How the dogs must have hated him, vainly leaping and snapping as he slam-dunked into their letterboxes without even opening their garden gates! We called him Octopus - because of the way he sprawled across the table - which soon morphed into Pussy, setting off wild mewing whenever he opened his mouth.

I guessed that Dominic was a Christian even before I saw the silver crucifix at his neck. Tall, square-shouldered and flaxen-haired, he reminded us of Freddie out of *Scooby Doo* and so - by extension and antithesis – he became Shaggy, although it was hard to imagine anyone more carefully groomed.

"Does your mother choose your clothes?" Helen enquired but he merely nodded and smiled, rather proudly. It was impossible to wind him up but once you'd cracked that bland exterior, he could be helpless with laughter for half an hour at a time. I'd observed that Christians either can't stop blinking or never blink at all: he belonged to the latter category – his eyes remained wide open even when he was weeping with mirth or sneezing, a quite remarkable trick.

Rhys was mono-browed and bow-legged with big flat feet. He was dubbed Benny: not only did he sound like a Welsh version of Top Cat's sidekick, but he also carried in his knapsack – along with his unvarying cheddar and pickle sandwiches – an orange Umbro rugby ball.

As for me, I was now Arfa, as in *The Crazy World of Arthur Brown*. When I protested that I had recently seen his new band Kingdom Come, with Brown crew-cut and clean-shaven on one side of the face and wildly hirsute on the other, they explained that it hadn't been down to any physical resemblance but because I was so obviously off my head.

On the two faded practice tables we simulated endless games, taking it in turns to deal or bet. If we had been using real money I would have been set up for life, but I was under no illusions that my luck would last. I was a born beginner, fated to keep on beginning over and over again.

"That's the way! Get in there!" Helen would enthuse whenever the ball chanced to hit zero on the wheel, as if it was like a dartboard bull's-eye to be aimed at. This zero was what gave the house its edge: without it presumably no-one would ever win or lose. The colours and the odds and evens would double the stake, the columns and the splits would pay twos and the thirty-six numbers thirty-five to one . . . but zero – that thirty-seventh slot, neither odd nor even and neither red nor black but white – would blow every stratagem to pieces. You could always bet on the zero, of course, but apparently very few punters did.

"They're afraid" said Helen. "They think it belongs to The Devil."

A third, unused table featured at its extremities both a zero and a double zero. Had this been a failed prototype? Or had they hoped that nobody would notice? If they had got away with it would there have been a third and then a fourth and so on until the house cleaned up on every spin?

We were shown how to place the ivory ball inside the wheel's inner rim before flicking it hard against the direction of rotation. This was harder than it looked: whenever Alan tried, the ball would come shooting back out again. Once he actually hit the ceiling so that it pinged back down to plug itself into the twelve slot.

"Number twelve, black," he announced. "I'm getting the hang of this."

Rhys would flail among the stacks of chips like Godzilla levelling a city. Just the back-draught of his great dark paw would set the wheel whirring like a propeller. He had no sense of balance, listing alarmingly whenever he raised his heel. Quite unable to pivot – he seemed to have no hips – he would slowly shuffle into each required position, his stomach growling the while.

"What's so funny?" he kept asking.

On Wednesday a pigeon got in. Gigi caught it on the wing and with unexpected gentleness cradled it between her hands while we stroked its head and breast. After this it appeared daily for elevenses, bolting down the bourbon biscuits, watching us play for a while, before exiting through a tiny hole in the cornice.

Alan would sleep during lunch breaks, while Dom read his tracts and Gigi knitted what appeared to be a bulletproof vest but Rhys – having donned a white sweatband like his hero Merv 'The Swerve' Davies – would take his ball outside to play. Now he was transformed, sure-footed and quick, but unfortunately a rugby ball is not like a soccer one: it won't come back to you when you kick it against the wall. There was something touching about the way his shoulders sagged as he retrieved it from the puddles so that I found myself out there in the drizzle, fumbling his spin-passes, ducking his head-hunting tackles. Soon I began to enjoy the way the laces of the ball bit into my instep and the discovery that I could kick it twice as far and twice as high than ever I did in my rugby boots. I had spent most of my school days ducking games even though I secretly loved to play them but when things are compulsory what choice is there but to refuse?

We even had music while we worked, for Dom had brought in his tiny tinny transistor. Its dial was stuck on Radio One and the signal came and went: he had to keep adjusting its three-foot aerial. Tony Blackburn, Dave Lee Travis, Johnny Walker: it was mainly rubbish, confined as they were to the playlist, but there were a couple of decent and recurring tunes. The Four Seasons' 'Who Loves You?' and The Drifters' 'There Goes My First Love': we would all sing along, our voices getting higher and higher until they passed into ultrasound and only the pigeon could hear.

What we really enjoyed, however, were the appearances of Arnold, Blackburn's dog. Whenever he barked, we would crease ourselves laughing – and some mornings he would bark over fifty times. Dom was sure that he was a spaniel while Rhys said a corgi and Gigi a lurcher, whatever that might have been. Alan, who had a wider experience of dogs, identified it as a German shepherd. I knew that he was correct for this was my old friend, 'Alsatian barking in a farmyard (five seconds)' from the BBC Sound-effects LP which had provided – along with *The Kinks Kontroversy* – the soundtrack to my childhood.

"Isn't it clever," said Rhys, "The way Arnold always barks on cue?"

"But he's only a jingle," I blurted out. "Blackburn presses a button. Listen: it's always the same double bark, flat then sharp, with a bit of echo on the second one."

"What?" Rhys' lip was quivering. "Do you mean that Arnold isn't really in the studio?"

"Don't tell him about Santa Claus," said Alan.

By the end of the week I almost loved these people. Everyone I had met since leaving school now seemed like noisy and grotesque puppets, with me the noisiest and least substantial of all. The truest friendships lay in shared adversity: reduced to peddling our golden youth for twenty quid a week not one of us had shirked or whined but stuck to the principle that you must dutifully fulfil your tasks while having as much fun as possible in the process.

Even in my meanest holiday jobs I had always driven myself, lashing like a galley-master at my own back. No-one was ever going to be able to say that I had not earned my crust. In this spirit I would always arrive early and leave well after time: from the first day my new colleagues had done the same.

Helen had the good sense not to attempt to assert her authority, realizing that our euphoria made us ideally receptive to being taught. After just five days the changes were startling. Dom was Mr Hips, sweeping and swooping like a tango dancer. Alan had stopped falling over, Gigi had straightened up and opened her eyes wide, then wider still and even Rhys' rampaging now possessed a weird delicacy – what the left hand destroyed the right would raise up again. As for myself, I was if anything slower but more deliberate: Helen seemed particularly pleased with this, as if her initial suspicions had been allayed.

"What's happened to The Superstar?" I asked her. Halfway through the process, the mysterious Chris had still not appeared.

"I don't know." Her tone implied that she didn't much care.

⁂

I really did not want to have the weekend off, for fear that the spell might be broken: as if to compensate, Al and I spent most of that time out in Club Land.

This was the best time for Northern Soul: when it was no longer just a cult but had not yet developed into a fully-fledged scene – before the gauleiters were assigned to the decks and defrocked

Jesuits began enforcing a rigid dress code of no nudity, no industrial footwear or stiletto heels, no denim jeans unless creases had been ironed in. The city was full of top clubs - The Precinct, The Ritzy, The Miners' Arms, The Mojo, The Black Diamond - plus scores of unlicensed others that floated between increasingly unlikely venues. Out on the street you wouldn't hear a thing but the moment you opened those doors the sound would hit you like the fists of God. One night The Turk-Noise - with its nauseatingly oceanic light show - materialized in a Roundhay church, carbonizing its scarlet brick, sending mosaic tiles rattling across the floor and only closing when the yawning priest and congregation turned up for matins.

It was fun, all right, but we always had the feeling that we were missing out on the real thing. All the really legendary characters - the Siamese twin sisters, the speed freak who could dance with himself, the boy with a pet rat asleep beneath his fedora - continued to elude us. They were always a couple of clicks ahead on the circuit. Sometimes we would catch a burning, choking smell - brimstone, presumably - that indicated that they had only just left.

"You should have been in here last Thursday," people would tell us.

"But we were," Ed hissed in my ear, "And they definitely weren't."

For three consecutive nights we had planted ourselves in The Central Social, generally considered to be the hub of the wheel. The faces kept on changing but our quarry never showed. The bouncers and bar staff were suspicious: didn't we realize that the whole point was to keep on moving? It was as if every club was another station on some ancient pilgrims' road.

Ed had noticed that people only ever spoke of *Northern* soul. In Cockermouth or Newcastle they did not modify it to North Western or North Eastern and not even the Brummies had mutated their own Midlandish strain.

"And how about London?" We asked a barman, "What are they calling it down there?"

"They're not calling it owt." The man's jaw jutted out over

the counter. "No bugger south of Watford has even *got* a soul."

On the Saturday night we ended up in another of those peripatetic clubs: it actually called itself The No-Name. All the music was hi-tempo but out on the floor everyone was shuffling as if they were three weeks into the dance marathon in "They Shoot Horses, Don't They?" Unfortunately, Susannah York and Jane Fonda were not in attendance.

As usual, we started dancing with each other. My own style was cool, minimal and boring – I had been taught by experts – but Ed's was more eye-catching, flailing and arhythmical, unrelated to whatever was playing. He claimed to be hearing the music of the spheres: if so, the universe was in dead trouble. Dressed all in black – silk shirts and suede trousers with short vinyl jackets – we already stood out among the Ben Sherman boys. They stood around looking daggers but never quite dared to attack. They couldn't work out just what we might be. Presumably these "Queers" that they kept growling about would resemble themselves, only smaller and weaker, with slightly higher voices.

"Lads shouldn't be too good at dancing," one of the two girls who had now inserted themselves between us was shouting in my ear. They had braces on their teeth and brawny, blue-veined arms: beneath their make-up they were glowing with health. They also seemed to disapprove of our clothes and claimed not to understand a word we said.

"You're not from round here, are you?"

I was, having been born a mere ten-minute bus ride away, but I knew that geography was not what she was talking about.

As we left together, they were holding their noses, while miming pulling a toilet chain. It was hard to see why they were bothering at all.

They accompanied us to the park near our home but then refused to walk any further. Most of the bushes and parterres were occupied by writhing but still fully clothed bodies, as if we had just missed a mustard gas attack.

"You're them Satanists, aren't you?" The more talkative one enquired.

"No," I protested, "I'm a croupier."

"And I'm a scholiast," said Ed. "An exegete."

"My boyfriend's a soldier." Her friend spoke for the first time. "He could beat you up."

"I bet he couldn't," I replied.

"Could!"

"Couldn't!"

The others joined in but on opposite sides.

"Could!"

"Couldn't!"

This went on for a while until we were all pressed up against the flanks of a garden statue of the nymph, Pomona.

Although my girl was lightly dressed, her bra proved to be immovable while her knickers boasted the strongest elastic I had ever encountered. It felt as if I was trying to reset a mousetrap. I couldn't even tell whether I was inside her or not but she reached an immediate climax . . . then her friend joined her and they both just stayed up there. Could anyone really sustain a ten-minute orgasm? I certainly never came and I don't think Ed did either. Something kept nipping at my inner thighs – I thought it was her fingers until I registered that both her hands had locked across the base of my spine. On the other side of the statue Ed appeared to be attempting to climb his partner like a ladder, his eyes rolling up towards the moonless sky, while her teeth had clamped on to his moustache to keep him on the ground. I wondered whether Pomona might join us, like in some Watteau painting, but her face remained stonily averted. There was something oddly innocent about encounters like this: each time I felt that I had become even less experienced than before.

At last my girl broke away.

"That was nice, but we've got to be at work in an hour."

"What sort of work are you doing on a Sunday morning?"

"Milking."

"Would that be cows or sheep?"

They put their heads together. "Pigs!"

We pointed out that no buses would be running but they knew about the all-night taxi rank below the university tower.

"What are your names?" Ed asked, but they pretended not to hear.

"See you at the club," they said but we knew they would not be there: perhaps we would run into them again one day in Mecca or Jerusalem?

As their taxi was pulling away its back window rolled down to allow a silver-nailed hand to wave goodbye. It was polydactylic, with an extra middle finger.

"Wait! Wait!" We chased after them. "Come back!" – but the car shot the lights and was gone.

Next morning I looked out of the window to see Ed in the phone box across the road. Yet again he was trying Lori and Lorna's number: it rang and rang but no-one ever answered.

"You must have freaked them after all," he complained. "They've given us a number that doesn't exist."

"If it doesn't exist it wouldn't be ringing: they must be going out a lot."

"Maybe they're deaf." He hadn't even met them yet but he was already getting jealous.

"Don't worry," I reassured him. "They're probably praying – or visiting the sick."

After a dozen further attempts, he gave up.

When we had finished breakfasting – on eggs, of course – he surprised me by refusing to accompany me to the pub. He had set himself to learn by heart all twenty-two of the Harley Lyrics, for no other reason than to see if he could. I had always been in awe of people who could actually remember stuff.

As I was leaving, he appeared in the hall and fixed me with what I realized was intended to be a meaningful look.

"I've been thinking," he said. "What if Lori and Lorna really did give you a made-up number but then it turned out to belong to two other girls who are even nicer than them?"

"That, sir, will almost certainly prove to be the case," I replied, in Jeevesian fashion.

He did not respond, merely closed his eyes.

"Ready I stand for death to smite.
Done is my every deed.
May God above us give us light
That of saints we may have sight
And heaven as our meed!"

I could still hear him all the way down the street. The voice was very high, at once tremulous and declamatory, like those ancient recordings of Tennyson or Yeats. The judge at his trial had not been wrong: Ed was indeed a most unusual young man.

TWO

WHEN I arrived on Monday for the second week of training I knew at once that something had happened. The street door now opened easily, and the vestibule was flooded with light from no discernible source. Someone must have got the heating started: the carpets had dried out and those mephitic lavatories were offset by a sweeter smell.

No sounds of conversation issued from the gaming room but when I entered all my colleagues were already there, sitting up straight on their high stools, staring in silence at what appeared to be a small bear or an enormous dog. While its body's short-napped hair was light brown striped with black that of its head was coppery-orange, long and flowing. The creature's back was towards me but then its stool began very slowly to turn.

It was as if I registered an image of the face a split second before I saw it. Whether this was through premonition or some long-buried memory I could never subsequently decide.

No, it wasn't a dog or a bear or even a man but a youngish red-haired woman wrapped in a long coat of some unfamiliar fur.

"This" – Helen's eyes were slitted and glittering – "is Christine."

"Call me Chris." The voice was clear but curiously hollow and distant, as if after a game of hide and seek, when everybody has finally given up, she was calling out to us from the bottom of a well. Her hair was truly red: next to her I must have looked like an albino.

She gave a little wave, looked into my eyes for about three seconds, then blinked like a camera shutter.

"I'm sorry I missed last week: I only got in yesterday morning."

She took off the coat, folded it and then laid it reverently along the radiator where it was to remain obediently for the rest of the day. Underneath she was wearing a low-cut grey silk top with a matching long skirt, slashed almost up to the right hipbone. I wondered if she had come here on the bus.

My arrival seemed to have broken the ice.

"Where are you staying, Chris?" Dominic asked.

She arched an eyebrow. "They've put me in The Station Hotel."

"That must be nice."

The eyebrow descended. "Not really."

Her perfume came at us in waves, teasing and tickling our noses then clutching and choking our throats, like a cherry orchard on fire.

"Where are you from, Chris?"

"Miami."

"No, originally – I just can't place your accent." Like Professor Higgins, Dom considered himself to be an expert dialectician and grammarian. "Is it Irish?"

The head shook vigorously but the hair remained perfectly in place. Although the light was behind her I could not descry one single split end.

"Welsh," growled Rhys. Wrong again – a gleaming wing swept across the left cheek before tucking itself away behind her left ear.

"Is it maybe West Country?" Twin curtains closed over her face then opened again.

"She's a Geordie." Gigi's eyes were even narrower than Helen's.

"West Hartlepool," said Chris, brightly. "And I'm never going back there – not even in a box."

Now the hair was just rippling, like water held in suspension. It did not appear to be lacquered or even cut in any definable style but nevertheless every last follicle appeared to be perfectly content with its place in the general scheme of things.

Helen rose without a word and made for the practice table, to spin the wheel and start the serious business of the day. Her hips appeared to have widened over the weekend, and she moved in short scuttling steps with head tilted forward like a barnyard fowl looking for grain.

"Well, Christine," she gritted, "You need to make up for lost time. Perhaps you'd like to show us how it's done."

We took our places opposite, assuming the usual bomb-headed expressions to indicate our temporary punter status.

In an instant, using both hands, she had unerringly pushed across to us our pretend stakes – two stacks of chips apiece. I was watching her face, of course: a cold smile had flickered on and off for each of us in turn.

I had been wondering just what to expect from a Superstar Croupier. Would they be accompanied by a sixty-piece orchestra or cutting fancy ballet moves? Would levitation or even ectoplasm be involved? . . . As it was, I had to admit to being disappointed. Her movements were merely efficient – mechanical, unshowy, utterly dull. Where was that verve, panache and brio to which Dom and I aspired?

After a while, however, I adjusted to this new rhythm, realizing that although it might seem torpid, she was three or four times faster and twenty times more accurate than we were. She seemed to be making time stop before starting it up again, speeding it up or slowing it down at will. At one point, while she was looking down the table, I sneaked a late bet on to zero only for the chips to come flying back into my lap. I had not even seen the hand that moved.

Her session went on and on. Everyone was frozen by this revelation that it is possible for a body to be in constant motion while also remaining perfectly still.

The face was only lightly made-up and unlined, but she was evidently much older than the rest of us – twenty-nine, at least. No freckles showed but I was sure that her hair was not dyed: she had a redhead's features, strong and well-defined. My father would have approved. "Now *that*" – he might say, flashing back to his old boxing days, "Is what they call a *safe* jaw."

I was fascinated by how her skirt, as if anticipating her movements, kept shifting its vent from one hip to the other. Her décolletage also varied: at one moment dropping alarmingly low, the next vanishing altogether. She was accompanied by a crisp rustling sound, as if there was a layer of tissue paper next to her skin. I had known a couple of girls who spent significant time and money on their appearances but there had not been this uncanny element in the impression created. And this was merely her Monday morning look: what on earth would she be like if she was going out somewhere and decided to make an effort?

At last Helen signed for me to take her place and Dom remembered to switch the radio on.

"What a horrible racket," said Chris, then covered her ears as we swelled the chorus of "Who Loves You?" Nor did she share our enthusiasm for Tony Blackburn and Arnold: "Can't you turn it to Radio Two?"

I didn't like to tell her that even their morning DJ, Jimmy Young, now had his own push-button sidekick, a quacking duck called Raymondo.

"What's the recipe today, Jim?" It would helpfully enquire. Much had changed since Chris had quit these shores.

At the mid-morning break she declined coffee or tea, instead helping herself to a glass of boiled water into which she dropped two red and blue capsules which did not dissolve.

"What's wrong with the Station Hotel?" Helen finally blurted out."

"It's got long white corridors like a hospital" - the silver-nailed ring finger stirred her glass - "With thudding sounds going round and round. When I open the door there's no-one there: I think it must be rats."

"Rats are light-footed," growled Gigi.

"Probably mice," suggested Alan.

"Or plumbing," said Rhys.

"Mice in the pipes," I announced, "Or rats in the slats."

Once more, those huge eyes focussed on me then blinked – more slowly this time.

"But rats don't thud," Gigi persisted: Chris went into the kitchen and poured pills and water down the sink.

For the next two hours, while we were taking turns to fumble on the table, her expression never changed. As a punter she played no obvious system but was the only one of us to finish ahead. Twice she piled her chips on zero and both times it obliged. Whenever I tried to catch her eye, she tossed her head and turned away.

I was quite happy being ignored but at lunchtime I became aware that she had leaned forward to stare fixedly at my left ear. When her eyes finally flicked over to appraise the other it felt as if the face between them had been obliterated, as if I was just a pair of disembodied ears, floating in suspension. I did not look at her again, but our eyes sometimes met in those cracked and fogged mirrors lining the walls.

It was a relief to get outside but Rhys' heart was not in our game: all fingers and thumbs, it was as if he had never seen a rugby ball before. His eyes kept shifting towards the filthy windowpane through which we could see Chris on the sofa, crossing and uncrossing her legs. Her skin was giving off a curious glow: I suspected that even in total darkness it would be doing the same.

When we returned Dom had seated himself next to her.

"Were you in hospital, Chris?" he was saying.

"No" – She scratched a golden kneecap –" A clinic. I had a total mental breakdown: whatever you do, never go mad in the West Indies."

Chris was the first back up at the table: if anything, her movements were even more unerring than before. As far as I could see, the only flaws in her technique lay in her announcements. She kept saying *"Rien ne va plus"* instead of "No More Bets" and sometimes when she called the numbers her locution became indistinct, so that "twenty-four black" came out as "enny'or'bla" while "fifteen white" was "itee'whi'." In contrast, I could not stop myself booming away like Todd Slaughter in *Murder in The Red Barn*: everyone kept begging me to tone it down.

"Do you have any tips, Chris?" Dom asked when he took her place. "Is there anything I'm not doing right?"

"All of you are pretty good, considering. But there are one or two points. Breath" – She pressed her hand flat against his chest – "You're not breathing deeply enough. Take the air in very slowly through the mouth, not the nose. Now hold it – count up to six – and exhale – to a count of eight or nine."

Dom had complied. His eyes were almost starting out of his head.

"That's right," said Chris, "but try and do it more quietly. Now . . . Posture. Up on the toes and raise your right hip – no, just a little – that's it. Now you can pivot from wheel to board and back again. When the ball's spinning, shift to the other one, then on to the left when you call. Keep those feet moving: it'll stop you cramping up."

Now it was Gigi's turn. Chris put a forefinger under the chin and canted it upwards. The effect was alarming: she appeared to have grown by more than a foot. Rhys was set to hopping about like a rabbit in order to loosen his neck muscles, producing a sound like gravel in a mixer. To correct Alan's ball insertion, she placed her own hand on the back of his: I could have sworn that they had actually fused.

She had no advice for me. Either I was perfect or that rats and mice crack had put me beyond the pale.

As we were clearing away, Chris took up a £50 wheel chip and blurred it through both sets of fingers then clasped her hands as if in prayer. When she slowly opened them again the piece had disappeared: as she was capping her view to scan the ceiling, the fingers of the other hand nipped it out from between her breasts. Everyone applauded but I did not feel that she had done this for our benefit.

At ten past five I followed her out of the building. I was hoping to see her jumping on a Number 52 but instead there was a minicab, waiting with its engine running. The driver hit his head in scrambling out to open the back door then almost emasculated himself on his nearside wing-mirror. His face was long and deathly pale and his eyes were crossing, having glimpsed those long brown legs scissoring across his back seat. As he returned to the wheel, he had trepanned himself again.

I watched their erratic progress up the hill. It was fortunate that the new one-way system would carry them straight to The Station Hotel.

How could you drive with your eyes crossed? How could you ever come back from a *total* mental breakdown? Surely Chris must have been exaggerating: perhaps she had taken that year off just to perfect her tan? It seemed strange that anyone would drop such a thing into a conversation with people she had only just met. When I was at school, we used to spout that stuff about madness being the true sanity, sickness the true health. "He who cures a disease commits a crime" – Laing and Artaud had been our heroes until we watched our friend Andy drifting off from a bad acid trip into full-blown psychosis. After he was taken to The Bin we no longer discussed such things.

Home . . . be it ever so humble there's no place like it. I always took a different route back, ducking into doorways, breaking into a run whenever I turned a corner until I was sure I was not being followed. This was not due to our recent brushes with the law: I had been doing it ever since I learned to walk.

The passage behind the house was so dark that I blundered into Ed's bike, still warm from its journey from the Groves of Academe. He kept it immaculate – all the grease stayed on his hands and clothes.

Home . . . is where the heart is. When that grey door creaked open, I always experienced a flood of joy as if returning from exile or a war. Within the hour, however, I would be dying to be out of the bloody place once more.

Unusually, no music was playing but from the front room there emanated sounds that could only be described as thudding, as if the rodents of the Station Hotel were extending their domain.

Naked, except for purple y-fronts, Ed was cavorting in front of the curtainless window. His right hand flourished a conductor's baton, even though the dusty 78 on the turntable had ceased to revolve. Rimsky-Korsakov's "Scheherazade": he was straining to hold in the air the fading echoes of the violin's long final note.

"Orryanora!" It sounded as if something was stuck in his throat. "Orryanora!"

After a while I established that Lori and Lorna had at last picked up their telephone and he had somehow persuaded them to meet him tomorrow night – downtown, in a newly-opened wine-bar.

"A what?"

"A wine-bar."

"I've heard tell of bars of yummy chocolate and bars of shiny gold" – My head had tilted in a yokellish way – "And now it be woine . . . Whatever will they be a' thinkin' of next?"

Ed tossed away his wand. "You drink in Yates's Wine Lodge, don't you?"

"Arrr" – I double-tapped the side of my nose – "But lodges bayn't bars!"

"But woine is still woine."

"Not if you be a'drinkin' of it in 'alf-pint schooners it bayn't."

Ed was pulling on his trousers. "You *are* coming with me, aren't you?"

"You're the one who answered the ad." I handed him a denim shirt, its sleeves bleached and stiffened by sweat. "And I think they noticed that I wasn't a dwarf."

"No, no, they said you were fun! Now what am I going to tell them?"

"Say that our trapeze act went wrong and I dropped into the lion's jaws. Orryanora! Tell them I died with their names on my lips."

He followed me into the kitchen. "Well, how was *your* day?" There was a note of condescension in his voice.

"Strange," I said, "Very strange."

"Every day is strange to you – even the ones when you never get out of bed."

"Especially those."

Not only had Ed not been shopping but he had also consumed an entire drum of Meridian peanut butter.

"Let's go to the pub," I growled.

He shook his head. "I've got to work out what to wear."

"I don't think they'll care in The Newlands."

"No – for Lori and Lorna."

"What are you going to do when they see that you aren't a dwarf?"

"Don't worry." He consulted his watch. "I've still got twenty-five hours."

"Why don't you sit in the bath in your court suit then let it shrink on you? If that fails, you could try cutting off your legs."

While he was still considering these possibilities I left, slamming the front door behind me. We were starting to resemble a long-married couple in some dreary sitcom – *George and Mildred*, maybe, or even *Terry and June*.

The Newlands was unusually quiet. Instead of mounting the pinball machine I carried my pint into a corner to sit and meditate on Destiny. The three or four other solitary topers were evidently doing the same.

"I don't have a destiny," Ed would often say. He seemed to believe that you had to be over six feet tall to qualify for one. Surely it was regulation issue for the voyage, along with heart, tongue and brain and fork, ditty-box and spoon – why, you might as well start doubting the existence of the soul itself!

I had always known that one day – probably tomorrow or at worst next week – Fate would take a hand. There would be no mistaking that moment: a brawny arm would come plunging through the clouds to bear me away to unknown other worlds or to deposit in my path something – or, more likely, someone – utterly unexpected.

Oddly enough, I had never met another man who would admit to sharing this belief, whereas every woman would insist that Mr

Right, the perfect partner created just for her, was waiting around the corner. They had all been equally certain that I was not him.

I had to admit that whenever I closed my eyes and tried to visualize the shape that my own destiny would take, I could not get beyond a blinding white light that emanated from an unmistakeably female form. I reassured myself that love or sex, marriage or children would be incidental to what subsequently transpired. I was pretty sure that – once I had grown accustomed to that light – a second Eve would be stepping forward holding the key to a New Eden in her outstretched hand.

Had I been saying any of this out loud? None of the other customers were looking at me but I distinctly felt that I was being observed. It was as if Chris was still coolly appraising me: perhaps I would let my hair grow again to cover my ears. There was certainly something unsettling about her but I was pretty sure that the woman in my dreams had been slimmer and ash-blonde.

I wondered if not having a destiny might be the rarest and highest destiny of them all. Living moment by moment, sinking ever deeper into the present, utterly impervious to fate and chance – how good would that feel? Wouldn't you have become some sort of God?

Having bought another pint I went over to the pinball machine and put my last coin into the slot. That would suffice: I would play for as long as I wished on the replays I'd won and then sell off the rest before leaving. This time I decided to keep my eyes shut and go by sounds, vibrations and instincts alone – rather like Tommy, except that Roger Daltrey had been deaf and dumb as well.

Next morning all my comrades had smartened themselves up. Dom was wearing a three-piece suit of grey-blue mohair: he made sure that we did not miss the label on its inside pocket –

CHARLES R BENTLEY – BESPOKE TAILOR –
OF BRADFORD

Alan's hair had been flattened down but within the hour those familiar peaks and crevasses had reared up again. Rhys appeared to have been dry shaving without a mirror: even the bulb of his nose was nicked. As for me, I was sporting a cap-sleeve T-shirt of a cartoon mole in beret and shades blowing notes out of a tenor saxophone.

We had not given Chris a nickname: we just stopped using our own. Helen had never called her Christine again, only 'you' or 'she' or 'her'. Gigi, with newly plucked eyebrows and a midi-skirt that hung like a tablecloth, was fixing her with the evil eye. Chris just stared back until she looked away – rendered strabismic, like the chauffeur.

Dom was smitten: hadn't his religion warned him against women like this? We discovered that his radio was no longer working, its aerial having retracted into its guts. He had evidently sacrificed it on the altar of Chris.

Back at the table she was getting faster and faster. She was like an emissary from another world where different physical laws applied. If she had ascended to the ceiling, hooting like an owl, I would not have been one whit surprised. Helen, as if hypnotised, let her keep on dealing – on and on – until we were stripped of every chip.

Chris returned to the sofa and crossed her legs, then nodded to Dom, as if to indicate that she was ready for more questions.

"Why did you decide to come here?"

"I didn't decide" – she gave a sudden, dazzling smile – "I was sent."

"But why here? Why not London?"

"London is an easy place to get lost in and they want to keep an eye on me. They say they've got big plans – why does nobody ever have any small ones?"

"Will you be going back to the cruise ships?"

"I hope not: I'm through with the sea. Maybe Las Vegas – I was at The International learning to deal stud poker. At the end they stuck me on the top table for a week."

"What was that like?" Helen couldn't help sounding impressed.

"Like swimming underwater" – the smile flickered – "Without needing to breathe."

"Have you ever been to Monte Carlo?"

She nodded slowly, twice.

"Chekhov said that their casino was like a sumptuous water closet."

She glared at me. "A *what?*"

"A big toilet," I said, "but a very clean one."

"It wasn't *that* clean." Had she winked as she swung her head away?

When I got home Ed's bike was already outside but there was no sign of the man himself until I tripped over his crash helmet in the kitchen. The rest of his clothes – even the socks and the purple knickers – were strewn across the greasy floor. It was as if they had slid off his body while he wished himself smaller and smaller until he vanished altogether.

He had forgotten to shop: there would be no squashed bread and broken eggs for tea. The sink was clogged with black hairs and oil: he had been expanding his moustache to Nietzschean proportions but had now evidently pruned it back and re-Dali-fied it.

There was no note to tell me where he had gone. Although I had often upbraided him for treating me like a parent, I felt aggrieved when he did not. Presumably he had joined L&L in their Bar of Wine: I imagined them dandling on the palms of their hands his tiny naked form.

The front door slammed behind me: I didn't need Ed. I could always rely on running into someone who knew me or at least acted as if they did. I waved to Pomona as I crossed the park but she did not acknowledge me. I wondered whether Chris's stone would be softer to the touch.

After crossing Woodhouse Lane I paused before descending to the valley below. Chapeltown: Nighttown, Dis, stew of sulphurous repute. Half-West Indian, half-Irish – all sin. Abandon hope all ye who enter: surely that was Virgil over there, pissing in a shop doorway on St Marks Road.

Down in the Kozy Kafe, while I was wolfing down a meatball

bhuna, I got talking to a couple of brawny psychiatric nurses who were fortifying themselves for the night shift. They showed off the padded gloves they would use to pacify the residents and sniggered about the sedated young women who were awaiting them. When we got outside, they decided to take me in charge, frog-marching me towards those great spiked gates until I managed to trip them up and flee.

The Skinners Arms was packed with shouting, red-faced men: Guinness and Beamish and Murphys were all on draft. I was not surprised to see my Uncle Bert wedged against the bar. He was as voluble as ever, holding forth on the intricacies of crown-green bowling – a sport that I would definitely not be taking up – until I realized that his voice was modulating into Strine. In an ever-thickening Aussie accent he recalled his adventurous youth in the outback – breaking brumbies, stuffing jumbucks into tucker-bags, saving grateful sheilas from rabid kangaroos. I was pretty certain that he had never in his life ventured south of Skibbereen.

"What's a brumby?" I tried to ask him, but the words would not come out. I suspected that those nurses had spiked my lassi with something. Such things happened more often now: it was evidently a fad. Everyone was doing it: bishops, dustmen, chartered accountants, cabbies and kings and queens – all trying to blow each other's minds.

Without Ed I did not fancy the clubs: only psychos and women arrived on their own. A poster on the door of the WMC announced that it was Jazz Night – featuring a US TENOR SAX LEGEND of whom I had never heard.

The place was small and almost empty: the band was late, having got themselves stuck in a hotel lift, so most people had given up waiting. I must have dropped off at my table for a while because the next thing I knew the five of them were up on stage, all playing different numbers. The Legend sounded a bit like Ben Webster, my dad's favourite – that is if Ben Webster was being sucked down a plughole, his mouthpiece locked between his teeth. Then the drummer soloed at length, while his colleagues shared a bottle of

Courvoisier: the man's wig, black and shiny, kept sliding across his head like an omelette in a pan until – at the polyrhythmic climax – it finally dropped off, to land with perfect timing on the splash cymbal.

I had been joined at my table by a barrel-chested man with a black beard that completely obscured his mouth. I could not understand the noises that he emitted but after a while he managed to convey, through an elaborate mime, that he lived around the corner, he had lots of drugs, and he wanted to share them with me.

Now The Legend had donned a deerstalker hat and begun to declaim some poetry that was almost as bad as my own. Either he was lying flat on his back, or I had levitated and was viewing him from above.

I came to in a candlelit room. Magic must have whisked me there because I could not have managed the stairs. There was my new friend, cross-legged on a prayer-rug, rolling a twelve-skin spliff. Something green and slimy was writhing on the papers: hurriedly, he sprinkled tobacco over it, then buried it under what looked like iron filings. He lit up then passed it straight on to me. The taste was surprisingly mild, almost mentholated.

Only now did I become aware that a skeletal woman was sitting in a rocking chair by the window. Although it was hard to imagine anyone looking less pregnant, she appeared to be knitting baby clothes. The hollows in her face deepened with each knit, purl and drop-one. Her breathing was loud but painfully irregular, like the wind blowing through an Aeolian harp. Then I saw that a harp was indeed set on the sill although the window behind it was closed. Rather to my relief, she declined the joint so I returned it to her husband who took a huge drag. Burning debris was starting little fires in his sweater but he did not attempt to beat them out.

At last, she – or the harp – formed comprehensible words.

"You want to fuck me, don't you?"

"I don't think so," I replied.

"And you want him to fuck you" – she pointed a needle at the mouthless man as he rocked around the floor, legs locked in the lotus position – "Don't you?"

"No," I said, more decisively. "No thank you."

They were like ogres from some evil folk tale: I was waiting for their unborn baby to proposition me from the womb. Fortunately, I would only have to clap my hands three times to make them disappear.

"That's all right then." The needles were embarking on what appeared to be a third arm or a third leg. "We were just testing you."

"Testing me for what?" I asked but they did not respond. Once again the joint was between my fingers, flaring like a blowtorch: the more we smoked it the longer it grew.

A grey dawn was scorching my eyes like a hundred exploding suns. In Bray's Bakery the loaves and baps of the morning were rising: that heavenly smell revealed that I was still on earth.

I was lying in someone's doorway – I hoped it wasn't the one in which Virgil had been relieving himself. When I tried to move, I rattled: my pockets were crammed with bottles of pills – kaleidoscopic and unlabelled – enough to spike the entire city. My cock felt sore, but nothing seemed to have been done to my arse. I had neither pissed nor soiled myself and there was no blood or vomit on my clothes. My wallet was still there: whatever I had done during the last few hours had been free – in fact I appeared to be a tenner up.

So much fun! So much excitement! So many strange adventures! I had to admit that I was growing bored of the whole thing. I was like Philip Marlowe investigating some dark, unfathomable mystery – except that I had no idea what crime had been committed and I never got paid. Last night had been like a familiar movie that I had watched and enjoyed only to find, as the curtain came down, that I had already forgotten it. I was evidently looking for the wrong things in all the wrong places.

I was still laughing when I realized that the face of a demon – scarlet and shiny, its cheeks running with blood or sweat – was leering down at me. Something about the eyes reminded me of Helen.

"You're early," it said. "Are you OK?"

It was Helen! Either I had made my way to – or been deposited outside – the old casino.

"Fine. What about you? You look a little . . . hot."

"It was a busy night – I didn't finish cashing up till half past four, so I went on to The Steam Packet."

"Is that a club?"

"No, it's a sauna – on Buslingthorpe Lane. There's always places open if you know where to go."

"Do you live round here?"

"No, Ellen's working in Manchester, so we got a place halfway between – up by Booth Wood reservoir, where there's nothing but mountains and six lanes of the M62."

"How often do you see each other?"

"Hardly ever, but in our game you have to take what you can get." She helped me to my feet. "What's that sticking out of your nose?"

I extracted – or, rather, unscrewed – a piece of black wood, like a miniature chess piece . . . most likely a rook. Perhaps one day an explanation would be presenting itself.

My reflection in the mirror was no different from usual but Rhys, Alan, Dom and Gigi, as they arrived, double-took and started giggling. Chris was observing me with disgust mixed with a sort of grudging admiration: I could feel my eyes beginning to cross, so I turned my head away.

Helen, of course, stuck me straight out there on the table. Everyone was expecting me to collapse but I found myself dealing far better than before: my motor functions and co-ordination worked best when fully disconnected from the brain. I relaxed and watched those numb but nimble fingers moving through the murk.

At break Chris sat down next to me.

"How old *are* you?" She demanded, as if this had been the subject of some contention.

"Twenty-one." I was really twenty-two but I did not like to admit to being only three years off that age when – on David Bowie's authority – I would be too old to stay alive. "What about you?"

"Thirty-two," she announced. "Thirty-three in March."

I was surprised that she would so readily admit to this: weren't women supposed to lie about their age? I wondered if this apparent candour was a diversionary tactic to draw attention away from her real secrets – although her recent insanity was evidently not among these.

She returned to Dom but did not lower her voice.

"I had a *total* breakdown." She laid a hand lightly on his wrist. "I thought I'd died and gone to Hell. It was like being cooked in boiling oil along with a thousand screaming parrots." She glanced over at me. "Should you ever decide to go mad, don't do it in the West Indies. ZZT! ZZT! ZZT!" She rolled her eyes and jabbed her fingers into her temples as if to simulate some voodoo form of ECT.

"It's not hard to get over these things" – it was as if she had read my mind – "They just stick all the bits back together and then screw them down even tighter than before."

Dom's Adam's apple was bobbing up and down. He was shadowing her as if waiting for a fissure to open in the earth so that he could pull her back to safety. The only way I could imagine him protecting her was if she were to take him by the feet and employ him as a club.

Back out on the table, his right hand was still trembling from her touch. The rest of his body grew stiffer by the minute, as if embalming fluid was running through his veins. Whenever she leaned forward to place a bet he would emit an audible groan.

At the end of the day, as he was helping her on with her coat, he could no longer contain himself.

"Chris," he blurted out, "I think you're . . . wonderful."

Her expression did not alter. Without farewells, she turned on her heel and marched straight out.

"Don't worry," I said. "I don't think she heard you."

We watched as she crossed the car park. The chauffeur's dilated pupils, as if magnetized, were converging at the bridge of his nose.

Wonderful: it was a curious word. As a child I had taken it to be the beginning of some alternative counting system: "One-der-ful" instead of "one-two-three." Then my cousin Pam had taken me to see Cliff Richard in *Wonderful Life*: whenever Hank Marvin appeared on screen she would pinch my legs, very hard – a taste of things to come.

When I returned to the flat *Scheherazade* was playing but it sounded slower than before. Ed was evidently in a pensive mood.

He did not enquire where I might have been for the last thirty-six hours.

"Aren't you going to ask how it went with Lori and Lorna?" he demanded at last.

"No."

He sighed. "It was all a bit strange."

"What do those two *do* exactly? Don't tell me – the fat one is an exorcist and the thin one sells perfume."

"Of course not" – he gave me an old-fashioned look – "They're teachers. Lori's primary, Lorna's nursery."

God alone knew what damage they were doing to young and impressionable minds.

"Did they mention me?"

"Yes – Lori said you were cute but that you obviously hadn't yet come to terms with your situation."

"What situation?"

He shrugged and returned the needle to the record's outer rim.

"You told them I wrote that letter, didn't you?"

"No," he said. "Not in so many words."

"What did they do when they saw you?"

"They said hello and then went into the ladies' together. Ten minutes later they came out and told me off for pretending to be a dwarf when I was really" – he gave a Dom-style gulp – "a hobbit."

"Shouldn't you have curly hair? And bigger ears? And even furrier feet?"

He shrugged again. "I was wearing that brown tweed suit."

"If you're a hobbit what do they think I am?"

"Lori says you're a sort of grumpy elf – like Elrond – but Lorna is certain that you're an orc."

"I didn't know women liked *Lord of the Rings*," I said, "There's nothing but men in it and besides it's the most fearful tosh."

"There's Arwen Evenstar . . . and Galadriel" – he was counting them off on his fingers – "And Eowyn the warrior maid and Rosie Cotton at The Green Dragon."

"To say nothing of Shelob, the giant spider."

"I sang 'Worldes Blisse' to them and they thought it was Elvish."

I was not surprised: Ed would start a song as a baritone but finish as a counter-tenor.

"I suppose they're both of them . . . *religious*."

"Not really. They do go to church but only so they can sing in the choir."

"What was your wine bar like?"

"Warm and quiet: it made a nice change. We were there long after closing time. They kept it open especially for us."

"What on earth did you talk about?"

"The soaps, mostly – you know, *Coronation Street*, *Crossroads* and the rest."

"But we haven't even got a television set."

"I know, but the longer we talked the more I realized how much I already knew without seeing a single minute of any of them. It's as if they're archetypal, deep inside us, part of the collective unconscious, like in Jung."

"More like smallpox – airborne germs you can't escape. Or maybe you can pick them up from a toilet seat."

He shook his head and smiled indulgently. "It felt good to be doing what everybody else does. I've been different ever since – calmer, more content. When I got back I slept for eight hours straight."

His eyes were still red-rimmed but there was indeed something unusual about him.

"You know, you're looking taller, even with your boots off."

When he stood against the pencilled wall-mark we discovered that he had grown by over half an inch.

"I don't get it. I weighed myself at college today and I'd lost a couple of pounds."

"At this rate you'll be three stone and nine feet tall by Christmas. You'll have to tell the girls that you're really a ring-wraith."

"Lori warned me not to get any taller," he said dolefully.

"At least things are happening," I reassured him. "And magic is still magic even when it gives us exactly what we don't want."

❧

On Friday, our last day, the atmosphere in the Old Casino was subdued. We did essay a ghostly chorus of 'Who Loves You?' but our hearts weren't in it. Dominic no longer enquired into Chris's past, and she had reverted to acting as if she was the only person in the room.

The hours passed all too quickly. At lunchtime no sooner had Rhys and I got into our up-and-under routine than we were called back inside again. The others had remained seated in silence around the table, dropping breadcrumbs on to the baize. The pigeon did not flutter down to eat them. In the afternoon we were all fingers and thumbs except for Chris who now seemed to be stacking up the chips even before the ball had descended to its slot.

Why couldn't we just keep on training forever? I recalled those American astronauts team-bonding through their weightlessness exercises and machine-drills until that glorious day of lift-off.

"What rocket?" – they had cried – "What the hell do you mean – Outer Space?"

We knocked off early and presented Helen with her farewell gifts. The Four Seasons' Greatest Hits . . . a balsa wood box of sugar-dusted Turkish delight . . . a Variflamme cigarette lighter with RENO stencilled on its side. She started crying, as we had known she would. Her toughness was all a pose: if she ever did make it to Hell, the demons would all be queuing up to be nice to her. Without a word, Chris took off her Hermes scarf, folded it and then handed it over.

"It's lovely" – Helen raised it to her face – "What is it, this perfume of yours?"

Chris stared at her. "Connect," she finally said. "Connect is the only scent I ever wear."

Dom nearly fainted and I could see his point. She was just so classy! What was this brave new world where mysterious women spoke in low tones not of perfume but of scent?

"Let's go for a graduation drink," suggested Alan.

Helen declined: she was going home if she could remember where it was. She had wrapped the scarf around her head like a bandeau, but it insisted on slipping down over her eyes. Chris, however, much to our surprise, dismissed her attendant car and followed us.

Down the street I had observed a huge pub of sticky black stone but when we arrived it was all boarded up. I suspected that they had seen us coming and got busy with the hammer and nails.

A double-decker bus came toiling up Melville Road, like an ancient elephant heading for the mountains to die.

"If we get off this before the university," I said, "We can cut through the park to my local."

Chris did not follow the others up the stairs. "I like to sit where I can watch what the driver is doing," she explained.

I recalled Annie Ross's classic song – "Twisted" where a neurotic hipster on her analyst's couch displays a similar aversion to our dear old double-deckers.

Chris's eyes were fixed on the back of this driver's neck which turned red, then redder still: I hoped he wasn't going strabismic on us. His conductor had gone upstairs: when he descended he did not approach us for our fares.

We were all of us laughing and chattering away as we crossed the park, arm in arm – except for Dom who was regarding me in a most unchristian way. He presumably thought that on the bus I had been forcibly preventing Chris from joining him. Although it was still raining the leaves had somehow contrived to stay nice and dry in order to produce a satisfyingly loud rustling sound, like wire brushes on a snare.

A red handprint had been outlined on Pomona's left breast. The perpetrator was evidently sinistral and very short: they had needed to reach upwards, not down or across. Over her left shoulder I could see that our kitchen window was dark: Ed and I were not at home.

We were hearing The Newlands long before it came into view. At weekends – summer or winter, stormy or calm – those double doors were always wedged wide open. What sounded like the groans and whistles of a frustrated soccer crowd alternated with bursts of distorted music, all underpinned by a ground-bass of grinding and shunting – railway sounds, even though the nearest tracks were almost two miles away.

Pausing on its threshold Chris tightened the cinch on her handbag, then removed necklace, watch and rings to slip them down between her breasts. It was evident that she had been in such places before.

"Double Campari, please" – she handed me a fiver – "With soda, just a splash, and no ice."

"I don't think they'll have it."

"OK" – she put a hand on my shoulder as if to steady herself – "anything that isn't whisky or beer."

There must have been upwards of a hundred souls in there but most of the tables were still free. Approaching the bar I was confronted by the usual roiling scrimmage: Ed had identified it as a Northern equivalent of the Eton Wall Game. Fortunately, my father had taught me how to handle such situations: at the Moses Walk – a wide-legged stumping with the left hand raised as if hoisting an invisible staff – they parted like The Red Sea.

Much to my surprise there was indeed Campari: the barmaid

even slid a slice of lime – fresh lime! – round the rim of the glass. I saw that Chris, having folded her fur to wedge it behind her back, was now lighting a very long white-filtered cigarette with a tiny gold lighter which she then stowed with the rest of her hoard. When she exhaled a succession of perfect smoke-rings ascended – always an ominous sign in a cowboy film.

Alan, Rhys and Dom were all Tetley Bitter-boys while Gigi had ordered a double Powers'. Her eyes were keen: that bottle of Irish, its label obscured, had been at the far end of the topmost shelf. When I picked up the tray my left shoulder locked where Chris had touched me so that I sloshed the drinks: she had surely intended this to happen.

As I turned, a loud roaring – like a pride of hungry lions encountering a tribe of testy elephants – issued from the games room beyond the bar. Rhys and Dom both flinched while Alan jumped out of his seat. Gigi had ducked below the table: only the smoke-rings did not waver.

On first encountering this phenomenon Ed and I had rushed in to find that it had merely been the dominoes players, crouched intently over their boards, silent once again.

To the left of the neglected dartboard sat the old men, nursing pints of dark mild. They were shabbily dressed but ramrod-straight: some even had Pip, Squeak and Wilfred – campaign medals from The War to End All Wars – pinned across their breasts. Their eyes glittered ominously: I recalled the legends of those buried armies of Barbarossa and King Arthur, still awaiting their last apocalyptic call to arms.

To the right were the women, most of them young, packed in tight around their tables. They played at high speed, slamming their counters down with a dull clacking sound like the horns of fighting rams. All had purchased a soft drink which they then never touched. They were crop-haired and heavily-booted and wore no make-up: one resembled Jean Seberg but I knew better than to try my luck.

You would have thought that these two groups might combine

for an occasional challenge match, but they appeared to be totally unaware of each other's existence. Their games evidently had different rules: the girls would knock – loudly – before picking up from the bone-yard while the old boys merely *nodded*.

Ed maintained that their loud sporadic cries must be orgasmic, the result of some unfathomable sexual connection between them. "Dominoes and submission," he opined. It did smell wonderful in there – a heady fug of Auld Kendal Shag and sinsemilla.

"So you *are* a smoker, after all!" I presented Chris with her drink.

"Only when I go out". They were Pall Mall exports in a soft primrose pack.

"Is this going out?"

"Well" – She sniffed suspiciously at the Campari – "It's not staying in."

"Cheers!" I raised my glass, but nobody wanted to clink with me.

"What's it going to be like on Monday?" Dom groaned.

"Maybe it will be fun." Al sounded like a condemned sinner at the portals of Hell.

"I can't remember" – Rhys' right arm was making convulsive movements – "I can't even remember how to cut the chips."

"You don't have to remember," said Chris. "It's like swimming: once your body knows what to do that's the end of it."

I didn't like to mention that on a recent visit to the Lido found that I had indeed forgotten how to swim. This might have been due to a combination of Mandrax and mescaline, but I was pretty sure that the waters really had turned into blood and then congealed.

Gigi's face had retreated into her hair, while the boys huddled together, their eyes darting about as if anticipating a blow: Chris had not reassured them either. The bar was now shrouded in greenish mist through which livid faces twisted and gurned; the ceiling descended, and the walls were closing in – by some strange contact high – or low – I saw how The Newlands must appear to them.

A tall woman strode past to join the dominoes players. She

was wearing a short winceyette nightgown over green rubber wading-boots. This was a look that the Sisters favoured: somnambulistic trout fishing was evidently another of their leisure pursuits.

"Hi!" Another new arrival, a man with the big square teeth and forgiving eyes of a donkey, paused by our table. "I hear you've been dallying in Chapeltown again" - he said to me - "best get yourself an exorcist and a penicillin shot."

My friends watched him go: a model aeroplane had been glued to the top of his head.

"What the hell was that?" Rhys enquired.

"A Dornier 247, I think."

"No, no - him!" - they pointed - "Him! Him!"

"Oh, Ian - he's an artist."

"You mean a piss-artist."

"No - he's exploring the fields of robotics and auto-destruction. He does these anatomical drawings in red chalk like Michelangelo then shreds them with his machines."

"So he's a con-artist, then?"

"Maybe - but next year he's exhibiting in Brussels and Berlin."

Ian and I had been at school together. It was odd to think that when we first met all we could talk about was cricket. His arrival seemed to have gingered up the crowd: fists had begun to fly. The Black Flag anarchists were discussing tactics once again.

"I never wear black" - Chris managed to be audible without raising her voice - "They say it doesn't show the dirt but mud is brown and dead skin is white."

"And coal dust is silver," said Rhys, unexpectedly.

"No," I sighed. "You just can't get good black dirt anymore - not even for ready money."

"None of these women are wearing make-up," Al complained. "What's the point of a barmaid without lippy and slap?"

"The boys at the bar are making up for it" - Chris shook her head - "I've never seen so much kohl and mascara in my life."

Gigi's own eyes were growing wider and wider. They were focussed on something behind me: I knew even before I turned that it could only be The Luria Boys.

There were three of them: a father and his two sons. They were always dressed identically in shit-brown too-tight suits, grotesquely short in the arms and legs, cream shirts, snot-green neckties and huge heavily pocked brogues. Their hair had been shaped by the same pudding-bowl. I had heard that they were in and out of the asylum on a seasonal basis, admitted and discharged together.

"Hello," said The Dad.

"Na'then?" said Eldest Boy.

"I'm gonna kill yer." Said The Littl'un.

"Don't worry," I told my friends, "He's always saying that."

Chris's eyebrow arched. "I suppose they're artists as well?"

"No, artistes: they're topping the bill at The City Varieties, the last hurrah of the music-hall."

"What do they call their act?"

"The Three Wise Men."

Pa Luria was even better than my dad at getting served: even the anarchists recoiled. He returned with four pints of snakebite wedged between his swollen fingers and he and The Eldest sat down at the next table and began to drink. They were in perfect unison, like human pistons, raising the glasses to their lips, loudly slurping and swallowing, then slamming them back down only to raise them inexorably once more. They never exchanged a single word. When Pa went back for refills his son's right arm would keep pumping away, ferrying the emptied glass to and from the slackened mouth. The barmaids shunned their table so the stack would rise and rise until the two men disappeared behind ramparts of foam-streaked empties.

The Littl'un did not sit or drink. He stood in the centre of the room with his back to the others leaning forward, feet wide apart, as if braced against a gathering storm, and conducted an argument with himself. No-one had ever established what the source of this contention might be. When the chin reared up the voice rose to a scream and when it rested on that barrel chest there issued from the back of the throat a blood-freezing growl.

The term "traumatic aphasia" did not begin to cover them: here were neuropsychological mutations far beyond the classifications of the Luria - Nebraska Test. Ed and I had been speculating about the absent Mrs Luria, eventually concluding that she must resemble Audrey Hepburn and be presently wintering in Biarritz.

"I don't like it in here," said Alan.

"You're the one who suggested going for a drink."

"Do you call *this* going . . . for . . . a . . . drink?" He lowered his voice. "These people . . . they're all . . . *strange*."

"I can't stand students," said Rhys and the rest nodded in agreement. I doubted that a single soul in here was enrolled in further education, although a few were yet to notice that their grant cheques had ceased to arrive.

Chris finally broke the silence - "Same again?"

The others had barely touched their drinks: spiking them might have been a good idea.

"Does anybody want to watch me playing pinball?" I enquired. "It's quite a sight, even if I do say so myself."

There were no takers. I put The Four Seasons on the jukebox, but they sullenly refused to sing along. Behind me The Littl'un sounded as if he might be giving it a shot. He had begun to twirl like an ice skater, three turns clockwise then three turns back.

Dom went off to the lavatory, giving the bar a wide berth, only to return almost immediately, claiming that he had just been propositioned. Evidently the lights were out again for he had been unable to identify the culprit.

"This evil voice came out of the darkness."

"What did it say?"

"It said" - His Adam's apple bobbed again - "'Hel-lo'."

Holding the tray high above her head, Chris had returned with the drinks. Her teeth were clamped on to her lower lip to keep herself from laughing. Snatching up her Campari she returned, snorting loudly, to the bar.

I thought I had succeeded in keeping my own face straight, but Dom had not been fooled.

"It wasn't me," I spluttered, "I've been here the whole time."

At this point the final straw blew in: Ed.

Last week he had driven his bike right up to the bar and then, when everyone ignored him, dismounted and sheepishly wheeled it out again. Tonight, he was still making something of an entrance – stamping imaginary snow off his boots with his visor still down and his muddied leathers squeaking as if infested by mice.

He bowed to the Lurias and then grabbed my pint to dribble beer down his smoked glass face. When he did remove his helmet the internal build-up of heat caused the well-oiled moustache to emit a rancid stink. Slowly he unwound his white silk scarf to display the two vicious hickeys on his throat.

"This one's Lori" – he pointed – "And that one's Lorna."

As he moved to the bar he passed Chris, staggering as she stuck out a leg.

"I reckon he bit himself," said Gigi.

"How can anyone bite themselves on the neck?"

"Perhaps he's double-jointed."

"No," Chris's fingers were snapping like castanets, "he'd just take his teeth out."

When Ed returned, he was mimicking her tray-balancing and sashaying walk which confirmed my suspicion that he had been watching us for some time. Apart from the Campari he had got the drinks all wrong.

"Well" – he cracked his knuckles – "Don't you want to hear the gory details?"

"No." I had always hated men talking about sex.

"Well," he continued, "Lori and Lorna live way out in Alwoodley – very classy. It took some finding: whenever I stopped to ask directions the people ran away."

He appeared to approve of these reactions.

"They've got this big penthouse flat that belongs to Lori's dad. You could see right across Eccup Reservoir to Harewood House. There wasn't a single book in the place, except for cookery ones. In the kitchen there was a spice rack as big as a ship's wheel and whole drawers full of slotted spoons and spatulas. Why would anyone need five wooden steak-hammers? And the fridge was full of stuff that I didn't even recognize."

"I believe they call it food," I said.

The Littl'un's screams and growls had gradually faded: the lips still moved but no sound came. This was the time for action: he began to slap his own face - left palm to the right cheek, right palm to the left.

"Homo philosophicus," Ed said fondly. "The dialectic method at work: perhaps at such moments his mind is perfectly calm, in equilibrium and infinitely wise."

At this, the Littl'un clenched his fists and began punching himself alternately in the stomach and the mouth. When he spat the blood was bright scarlet and broken teeth were rattling across the floor.

"Don't worry," I said, "It' an old wrestling trick - Tic-tacs and blood capsules."

This did not seem to reassure my colleagues.

"Does he take up a collection at the end?" Chris asked.

"He probably will - if he ever gets there."

"Lori and Lorna" - Ed was resuming his tale - "have got the biggest TV set I have ever seen. We were watching the telly: it was great. At last, I have seen *Coronation Street*."

"What was it like?"

"Like some Russian science-fiction film - utterly incomprehensible. When it ended both the girls ran upstairs. I could hear them locking their bedroom doors."

"What kind of people would put locks on their own bedroom doors?"

"Sensible ones," said Chris.

"When they finally returned, they'd put on these little baby-doll nightdresses but I could see that they were still wearing under-things.

"They started rubbing against me, licking my ears and clawing my back but whenever I tried to kiss them, they clenched their teeth. Then I touched Lorna's bottom by mistake and they both started screaming blue murder. I was halfway down the stairs when they came jumping out of the lift and dragged me back again.

"They couldn't get over the discovery that I was wearing two pairs of socks. When I explained that my feet were between sizes, they started calling me 'Mr Eight-and-a-Half'."

Chris's eyes were dancing but the others remained stony-faced.

"When I finally did leave, they wouldn't return my socks: they said they wanted them for trophies. So, I drove back with my boots cutting me to pieces" – he wrenched off the left one to reveal damage that was not readily apparent – "I should have gone barefoot or even naked, like Peter Warlock did."

"Warlock was also an ex-Etonian," I explained. "Composer, musicologist, nude motorcyclist, black magician, killed himself."

Ed began to sing: that eldritch voice always lifted the hairs on the back of my neck.

"The bailey beareth the bell away –

"The lily, the lily, the rose I lay."

The Littl'un had fallen flat on his back. He appeared not to be breathing but then his eyes flicked open to observe our reactions. In a few minutes he would spring back to his feet and start the whole cycle again.

"I think Lori and Lorna might be seeing other men," said Ed, gloomily. "Their telephone kept ringing: they took the calls in their bedrooms and when they came back they said 'Wrong number'."

"The paper is still running their ad," I said, "They must be going through a selection process . . . but however you look at it, biting can only be a good sign."

"I hope no real dwarfs turn up" – he glanced at Rhys – "Or I'm done for."

Gigi was regarding him with unconcealed horror.

"What do YOU make of them?" he enquired. "Dwarfs, I mean: speaking as a woman would you say that you were broadly pro or anti?"

She stammered and flushed scarlet. "My eldest sister . . . is very . . . small."

"Wow!" – he slapped the table – "I'd really like to meet her."

"It's funny to think," he continued, when she did not respond, "That in the seventeenth century male and female dwarfs were the highest-paid prostitutes in Europe. The Gonzaga Family were obsessed – they blew their entire fortune on them. Imagine flogging off Mantegna's *Triumphs of Caesar* just to be able to shag a dwarf."

At this, Gigi tucked her handbag under her arm and bolted into the ladies' toilet.

Whatever had happened to my new-found friends, my comrades-in-arms, my oppos? They looked as if they were trying to swallow their own mouths and were visibly ageing, like a time-lapsed film. At this rate they would be decomposed by closing time.

Even in the shallows of The Newlands they were out of their depth. I gave up trying to engage them and feigned an interest in Ed's precise mapping of L&L's gussets.

After ten minutes Gigi had still not returned: I prevailed upon Chris to go in search of her.

"The toilet window was wide open," she said, when she came back alone. "There's a long drop to the back yard: I hope the poor girl hasn't broken anything." Her voice was positively dripping with unconcern.

"That's a shame" – Ed was polishing off Gigi's whisky, even licking the insides of the glass – "I rather liked her."

Yet again, Dom was fighting back tears. I viewed him with a mixture of envy and contempt: how must it be to have feelings like that? Whenever he tried to talk to Chris she merely nodded absent-mindedly: when he moved his chair closer she moved hers away.

Alan's eyes rolled at everyone that passed. I was shocked by his censoriousness for I had always thought that Posties were broad-minded folk. Just think of all the pornography and drugs, summonses and final demands that he must have been stuffing through the letterboxes of Gipton, Gledhow and Green Hill!

Someone – I suspected Ed – had hooked Rhys' ball out of his holdall for now the anarchists were throwing it about with unexpected élan. I waited for Rhys to be up punching heads but he just sat there, deathly pale and biting his lip not even reacting when they began to hymn – in execrable Welsh accents – the exploits of the Pontypool front row. When the ball did emerge from the mêlée it struck Littl'un's head and bounced back in again.

I had not seen Chris leaving her seat, but she suddenly appeared, leaping high above the pack to effortlessly pluck the football out of the air then handing it on for the barmaid to stash away out of sight.

Dom muttered something under his breath then repeated it in an even lower tone.

"What did you say?" I asked, although I had heard him the first time.

"You're The Devil."

I wanted to answer but my tongue was stuck to the roof of my mouth. So I was not, as I had feared, some minor fork-carrier but Satan himself!

Dom was tugging on the little silver crucifix round his neck. His shoulders were shaking – but not with sobs nor yet with mirth. This was my first-ever sighting of Righteous Indignation. There was no relief to be had from the other two: the faces of Al and Rhys were registering milder versions of the same.

"You only brought us here to impress Christine."

Over his shoulder I could see that she and the barmaid had embarked on an arm-wrestling contest over the beer-soaked counter.

"She doesn't seem very impressed," I said.

"So why does she keep watching you?"

"I'm sitting on her coat: she's checking I don't run off with it."

Chris had tired of toying with her adversary and with a mighty shrug pinned her arm to the wood. She did indeed glance in my direction but her eyes were out of focus.

"You set it up," said Al. "This place, these people – you knew exactly what would happen when you brought us here."

"OK, I admit it." I held up my hands. "I planned the whole thing right down to the last detail. I had this pub delivered this afternoon – flat-pack assembly off the back of a transporter. And all these" – I made a sweeping gesture – "are merely players, a job lot from 'Spotlight', resting actors and artistes. I stuck aeroplanes on their heads, kitted them out in fishing waders, put them all on a bar tab. I paid them to beat themselves up, steal your footballs, hit on you in the gents'. It's all been an illusion – the street, the park, the city itself. I magicked them here just to piss you off. My name is Prospero, rightful Duke of Milan: welcome, mortals, to my faery realm!"

"I'm Ariel," Ed fluted then growled, "No – Caliban."

"Now see what happens when I do *this*!" I clicked my fingers three times: I was rather relieved when nothing did.

"As for impressing Chris, I've got a couple of crocodiles outside ready for me to rescue her from. I'll swing down on a rope, whipping my knife from my loincloth, then beat my chest" – I essayed a Tarzan cry but it came out as a Jimmy Saville gurgle – "Dom, your God never stood a chance."

"You think you're clever. You think you're better than us, don't you?"

"No." I did not like to tell him that from the start I had considered the four of them to be – in all the ways that mattered – infinitely superior to myself.

"Everything you did and said at training was an act, wasn't it? Then you'd go home and sit around with all your sick friends, laughing at us. I bet you even did impersonations."

"Oh, he did, he did," said Sick Friend Ed, helpfully. "He does it with everyone but they all end up sounding like Noel Coward."

"I have never put on an act," I said in the inimitably clipped tones of The Master. "I merely open my mouth and watch the words fall out. What more can anyone do?"

They did not reply to this question. I took a deep, deep breath and slowly counted up to ten.

"Gentlemen, gentlemen," I wheedled. "This is getting silly. What we need is a change of scene. If you don't like it here we can go somewhere else. All across this city the clubs are opening – let's make a night of it. There's The Vortex – they've got dry ice and strobes – or The Purple Pit – Friday nights are reggae and ska – and then there's Ennugi's down by the canal – it's new, they'll probably be paying us to go in."

"Will any of these people be there?"

"Anarchists don't dance, and it'll be too dark to see. Drink up, lads – Chris won't mind, I'll tell her where we're going."

I stood up but none of them moved.

"How far is it?"

"Will it be expensive?"

"Will there be any blacks there?"

I sighed: I had at least tried.

"Not very far" – I stretched out my arms – "Vortex ten minutes that way, The Pit twenty minutes the other . . . But if you've got a taste for the exotic" – My voice was rising – "and don't mind venturing a little further afield" – I cracked my knuckles, loudly – "There's Betelgeuse" – Now I was screaming – "only six hundred light years away!"

As one, they sprang up and ran.

By the time I gained the door they were going flat out down the hill, in quite the wrong direction for the buses. They were evidently taking no chances with those crocodiles around. Alan was in the lead, closely followed by Dom with Rhys a poor and puffing third. I would have expected them to have been in the reverse order.

"About Betelgeuse . . ." Back inside, Ed was lining up their unfinished pints. "It's actually six hundred and forty-two light years – six-forty-two-point-five."

"They've gone," I said. "I have absolutely no idea what all that was about."

"Just go into the gents'" – he downed the first glass – "and take a look in the mirror."

I shook my head: "The lights are out."

The Littl'un was now curled up under the Luria table, trying to force his right fist into his mouth.

"You've really upset him now" – said his dad – "With all your bloody shouting."

Chris rejoined us, tossing Rhys' ball from hand to hand.

"Those girls say I need my conscience raising but I keep telling them that I haven't got one."

"I think they mean consciousness – either way, you're better off without."

"Where are the others?"

"They've gone."

"That's a shame." Her nails were digging into the orange leather. "He's left his toy."

"I suppose you'll be off as well."

"No" – she surveyed the room – "I'm OK here."

"I suppose it makes a change from Mayfair and Vegas: a little touch of Old Bohemia, a guided tour of *The Lower Depths*."

"*A Voyage to Arcturus*," suggested Ed.

"*Travels In Arabia Deserta*."

"*A Journey To The End Of The Night*."

"Not really" – had she winked? – "It's just nice being out again."

"Is this out?"

"Well" – she paused – "It isn't staying in."

After seeing The Newlands through my colleagues' eyes I was savouring it with a new intensity. Everything that ordinary people shunned was OK with me. *'J'ai seul la clef de cette parade sauvage'* – I had the key all right but, unlike Rimbaud's, it was way too small for the lock.

Arm-wrestling Chris was now all the rage. The ladies from the Games Room were lining up to try their luck. There were a surprising number that I had never seen before. With much groaning and wringing of hands, she contrived to throw the occasional bout, but the doughtiest opponent grew pale at her touch. A chelonian head came poking round the corner, then another, until the domino men were filling the doorway. There was no doubt about it: Chris was actually registering in their visual field!

When it came to pinball, however, she was rubbish. She addressed it elegantly enough, hips and shoulder-blades rolling in perfect co-ordination, but she never got close to a replay. Then I realized that she was playing blind, her eyes never leaving the scoreboard. It was miraculous that those flippers were hitting anything at all.

She was complaining of hunger pangs that even crisps could not assuage. Although this was definitely The Pub That Did Not Serve Food, the barmaid rustled up a stack of white bread doorstep sandwiches. The meat was unidentifiable and the mustard-and-cress looked to have been scraped off the walls, but Chris wolfed them down regardless. I ripped open a tenth packet of salt-and-vinegar: my teeth were already so caked with the mush that I couldn't taste it anymore. After all those years of drink and dope, this was my one serious addiction, while the only monkey on Ed's back appeared to be PG Tips – cut with Gunpowder and Tippy Assam.

At five to eleven the landlord arose from his bed, called time and then returned to the Land of Nod. Only half a dozen people left, exchanging hearty farewells in the street before creeping round to re-enter by the fire-escape. I never understood this ritual because the front doors remained open the whole time. From now to Monday lunchtime The Newlands would never really close.

Chris was shaking out her coat.

"Shall we get you a taxi?"

"I could take you on my bike, if you want," Ed offered.

"I know you boys live round here." Her hands were expertly adjusting her collar. "I don't want to go back to my hotel. Could you put me up tonight?"

"Where we are . . . it's not what you'd call . . . salubrious."

"I wouldn't call anything . . . salubrious." She had left a gap between each syllable of the word.

We followed the Lurias outside but as usual they vanished on hitting the air. I was shocked to see Chris hopping on to the back of that awful motorbike. I consoled myself with my mother's maxim that really good clothes would never get dirty.

How I feared and hated that machine! How could Ed be so lacking in confidence in every other area while so nonchalantly mastering all those cc's? It should have been me – why could I never be the bad, bold boy on the bike?

Now Chris was working her way up the pillion, leaving space for me behind. Her arms encircled Ed while I primly gripped the steel bar at the rear.

"Don't worry!" He yelled over the engine. "The White Helmets team can get eight up – five of them juggling!"

It felt unstable until we picked up speed and then it got considerably worse.

"Lean! Lean!" Ed kept shouting but he never specified which way. Chris went left and I went right.

"Stick your legs out! All of them!"

We lived less than a mile away, but he had chosen the scenic route. Flat out down to Burley Road, an extravagant wheelie round the YTV car park, then back up to zigzag through cobbled alleyway and snicket. At least, this *felt* like the way we were going – my eyes remained tightly shut throughout. I wondered if we had passed the partially-eaten bodies of Alan, Rhys and Dom.

At last, we arrived, and Ed swept off his helmet: the face wore a blissful smile and the eyes were crossed. I imagined how Chris's heat had been penetrating that jacket.

"I thought you'd been burgled" – Chris was contemplating the chaos inside – "You boys really are serious about this, aren't you?"

"Serious about what?"

"About not being" – again she ticked off the syllables – "Sal-u-bri-ous."

Warily, she opened the fridge: it was empty, save for six cans of Special Brew and eight boxes of dates.

"You can have those if you want," said Ed. "I only use the juice."

"He rubs it into his moustache."

"Why?" It was nice to see her at a loss.

"That's what Dali does."

She blinked twice then gulped, Dominic-style.

"You know – Salvador Dalí, the Surrealist: Ed's a big fan."

"No I'm not," he protested. "His paintings are shit but you can't beat that moustache."

"You can have my bed." With a courtier's bow I indicated a ripped and stained mattress that appeared to be crawling up the wall.

"Oh no" – Ed seemed ready to fight for the privilege – "She can have mine."

"This looks nice." Chris had somehow discerned that under the piles of books, comics, bin bags and discarded clothes, a couch was concealed.

In less than a minute tidiness reigned: all our clutter was cowering in the corners of the room. She stood by the window, taking off her dress. She had not even tried to close the curtain, as if she knew that the rail might fall on her head.

"Why would anyone be watching?" She carefully draped the garment over a cane chair that I did not realize we possessed. "Don't you think people have got better things to do?"

This was what I had always said but I felt that different criteria might apply to Chris.

She was reaching round to unfasten her bra. It was surprisingly plain: light grey, cross-seamed but heavily under-wired, like something Howard Hughes might have designed for one of his starlets – beyond fetish or fashion, a problem in hydraulics elegantly solved.

Ed was entranced by the clatter of glittering objects that landed at her feet.

"Danae!" – he hissed – "And the shower of gold."

Before she could turn, I had enfolded her in my grubby white *Psycho* bathrobe. Its right breast bore the legend: 'BATES MOTEL, FAIRVALE CA96259'.

She insisted on seeing our shower but was surprised to find it behind a grease-spotted curtain in the kitchen.

"Good" – she said valiantly – "I can scrub my back and watch the toast at the same time."

I turned on the water: the shower-head coughed and jerked before ejaculating a few chilly drops

"Is there a toilet?"

"Out in the yard but I wouldn't recommend it. There's a proper one next to the communal bathroom on the top floor."

Although she was barefoot it sounded as if the goon squad was charging up the thinly-carpeted stairs.

"Do you think she wants us to . . . screw her?" Ed whispered.

"Why do you ask?"

"On the bike her breasts were pressing into my back"

"What else could they have done? If she's interested, I'm sure she'll let us know."

"That's what I thought." He sounded relieved.

Now she was stamping along the top landing. Her laughter sounded like a braying donkey with silver bells hanging round its neck.

Ed and I changed into our club wear. Despite appearances we were both 40 chest/30 waist/8–9 shoes. It was like having two wardrobes, except that he drew the line at my leather stuff and I at his hooded black cloak.

"That's the biggest bath I've ever seen!" Chris had returned, her hair pinned up and wrapped in a towel.

"We heard you laughing: there's an echo like a cathedral dome."

"Every door I passed opened and a face came popping out: always the same: square and bald with big round eyes."

"There are nine of them," said Ed. "The other tenants: we call them The Hydra. According to Apollodorus, Hercules killed it by cutting off all its heads, but it obviously survived and crawled back here."

"Resettled with a secret identity – or identities."

Chris was looking askance at the cloak. "You're not going out again, are you?"

"Just for a while: come with us – it's still Friday night."

"Once I'm in, I'm in." She lay back on the sofa which seemed to be shifting its contours to accommodate her form. "And, besides, I'm all" – she counted off the syllables again – "disassembled."

Her face looked thinner, the flesh settling on the bones, as if she had let some air out of her tubes. The dagger-nails had been peeled away to reveal fingers bitten down to the quicks; her eyes were watery and bloodshot as if the false lashes had been filtering the light. The irises had changed from green to khaki: up until now I had refused to believe in the existence of contact lenses. Without make-up she seemed younger – unpocked, unfreckled and unlined. Her skin seemed even darker, almost black under the chin and that mouth was redder than the lipstick that had been wiped away. It was as if she had been making herself down rather than up.

"Well, you've certainly got some books." She ran a forefinger along the multi-coloured spines, inclining her head as if expecting an ensuing chord.

"This will do for me" – she had plucked out *Death on the Instalment Plan*." I like thrillers."

Settling back, she drew the volume up in front of her face. The pages began to turn at unlikely speed: when we left she merely grunted.

"She's in for a shock with that Céline," said Ed. "I reckon she'll be gone when we get back."

"Oh, I don't know – my mum really enjoyed *The Naked Lunch*."

"I hope she stays," he sighed. "It'll be like *Snow White and the Seven Dwarfs* – except that there's only two of us."

"And we're not dwarfs."

The rest of the night was a blur. A roaring noise kept drowning out the music and even after the strobes had blown up my eyes were still slipping in and out of focus. I was being kissed by sloppy mouths tasting of Pernod and blackcurrant but when I stretched out my hand there was nobody there.

I lurched and jigged but my heart wasn't in it. I couldn't stop thinking about my colleagues, lined up there in The Newlands - their pale faces, those trembling lips sipping the over-salted beer. I needed to talk to Dominic - right away or at least before Monday - but I had no phone number or address. I knew that his parents lived near the football ground but I couldn't remember his surname - I was no longer sure about my own. I wanted to tell him that everything he said had been true. I was clever and nasty and I hated ordinary people. I was The Devil and I had desperately, desperately wanted to impress Chris.

Ed kept jabbering away in Middle English or maybe in tongues. We seemed to be teleporting from club to club without negotiating the streets. My throat was constricted, sharp pains shot between right arm and sternum and I was limping heavily - first on one leg, then the other. I reassured myself that I wasn't going to die, that the liquid pouring down my face wasn't blood but sweat or snot or amniotic fluid. Perhaps all our acid flashbacks were beginning to run together? Soon we would no longer be needing drugs - we would be running off flashbacks . . . of flashbacks . . . of flashbacks . . .

One image kept recurring: that flowing movement - up and over the head - of Chris's velvet dress. Even at the time there had been something uncanny about it, as if a waterfall had suddenly reversed its flow. It struck me that I had not registered her bottom or her breasts but focussed instead on the outline of the neck and head as if she was a natural phenomenon, some distant peak that was looming on the horizon. Had I really offered her my bathrobe? Surely it had flown across of its own accord, settling on her shoulders as the belt snaked up to knot itself at her waist? And hadn't it been an invisible hand that raised the collar, while another freed that shining hair to descend like stage curtains over her impassive face?

Now we had lost the clubs and wandered into a long, dark low-roofed tunnel, silent except for the echoes of dripping water. After a while a faint grey dot appeared, growing larger and larger until at last we found ourselves standing opposite our house. The lights in the front room were still burning. My watch read six minutes to six.

We crossed the road, then crouched to peep over the windowsill. Chris was still reading on the couch, with a pair of plastic NHS specs perched on the end of her nose. The floor was littered with empty straw boxes and date-stones. The soles of her feet were as tanned as the rest of her body.

By the time we entered the glasses had vanished and the book had been turned upside down.

"This is even better than Wilbur Smith," she said. "It's not just a story – it's the way things really are."

Even the skin between her toes had been toasted: I imagined her being slowly dipped into a bubbling vat of TanFastic.

"How can a man know such things? I used to work with a girl called Céline."

"His real name was Destouches," said Ed. "Dr Destouches. He was wounded in the Great War. When he returned, with a steel plate in his head, he chose to practice in the poorest district in Paris."

"Aha!" She clapped her hands. "I used to know a doctor like that."

"Céline welcomed the Nazis when they invaded France. If he hadn't fled to Denmark the allies would have hung him. He remained a fascist and anti-Semite to the end of his life."

"He couldn't have been," said Chris. "He was just pretending."

"Why would he do that?"

"My doctor wanted to heal the whole world. He cared so much that he started to believe that everybody's injuries and illness were down to him. He was a drunk – so mean and cruel you'd have thought he was worse than my dad – but he would always come on call. Céline's like that: he makes you hate everything then gives you a little nudge and you realize you were loving it all along."

"What happened to your doctor?"

"He crashed his car into a tree." She closed the book. "I used to have a handbag by Céline of Paris – beige leather with gold clasps."

"What happened to it?"

"When I got out of the madhouse it was gone."

Ed went off to throw up – or 'chunder', as he put it. He always finished a good night out by sticking his fingers down his throat.

Chris beckoned to me.

"You and Ed – her hand was soft but icy cold against my cheek – "You're just so . . . *nice*."

"What do you mean?"

"Nice compared to most men." The consternation must have shown in my face. "What's wrong with being nice? Were you trying to be nasty?"

"It makes us sound like we're kittens or babies or something."

"Babies aren't nice." A shudder rippled down her body then back up again. "And I can't stand cats."

THREE

APPROACHING the casino – at ten to two on Monday after-noon – I became aware that a hand was caressing my back. I almost dropped Rhys' football in shock. Why here? Why now? Christine could have done this at any time during the last forty-eight hours. Inexorably, the fingers continued their downward progress until at last they clamped on to my right hip.

Mr Gray, simpering horribly in a mid-blue suit with half-inch chalk-stripes, now emerged from the building. On seeing us he froze: Chris began to nibble my ear and he scuttled back inside.

We hit the swing doors crabwise, setting them into blurring motion. After the fourth revolution, when we reeled out into the foyer, her mouth had glued itself to mine: the tongue, however, remained locked away behind its teeth.

Faces floated out of the shadows: pallid men and women of indeterminate ages. I was pale myself, of course, but in a vampiric or at least an interesting fashion.

Now Gray was advancing again, like James Cagney in leg-irons.

"Where have you been?" He was ignoring me. "Whenever we went to the hotel you were out."

"I was in bed." Chris's voice struck a new note, somehow combining flirtatiousness with deep contempt. "We girls need our beauty sleep."

The women around us had evidently been missing out on their own. Eyes and noses rimmed with red, they were sniffing the air like hounds on a scent. Their back-combed hair looked sugar-frosted: I resisted the temptation to bite off a piece.

Among them was Gigi, sporting a heavily-bandaged right elbow. "Are you OK?"

She smiled wanly but did not answer. A slight inclination of the head revealed that she was not blaming me for her Friday night defenestration: she rolled her eyes – it had all been that Chris's fault.

They pressed closer: some of them were shaking their heads as if in disbelief. The men were all gawping at Chris, poised to flee if she should make an unexpected move. Even Dom, Rhys and Alan, who had evidently followed us in, were acting like they had never seen her before. I returned Rhys' ball: he took it reluctantly, as if it might explode in his hands.

There were no introductions: it was time for us to be uniformed. While Helen led away Chris and Gigi we boys were herded into the locker room.

It is hard to ignore someone in a confined space, but my former friends managed it, despite my jostling, tickling and Arnold-barks. I had developed a raging hard-on: although unreliable in intimate situations, my cock – if it saw a chance to cause mischief – would set like ferrous concrete.

Our new suits were tight and short in the arm and leg. Pocketless jackets and zipless trousers were secured by ragged strips of Velcro: even the smallest waist-size kept sliding off my hips. Helen reappeared and cinched them with three large safety pins: the effect was half-priapic, half-incontinent.

"Better keep that jacket closed," she said.

Our off-cream shirts were almost transparent, with twelve front buttons and three on each cuff. It was an outfit to render impossible the filching of chips or cash. Floppy velvet bow-ties were the finishing touch: they seemed about to squirt water or revolve.

Dark brown, light brown, shit brown: I realized that we had been kitted out as The Luria Boys. Perhaps they were ex-croupiers – driven mad by the glare of the lights, the rattle of the balls and the endless calculations running through their heads?

Chris sashayed over, pretending to fall off her heels. Her dress was ankle-length but dramatically vented and split.

"We DO look terrible" – she batted her extra eyelashes and bumped shoulders – "Don't we?"

The cheap material was shimmering like silk, billowing or clinging quite independently of her movements, its direful shade merely setting off the glowing flesh.

Gigi's bandage had been removed: the elbow had been scraped to the bone so they were trying to conceal it with Polyfilla and Germolene. Her bra had been torqued so that not so much as a farthing could be slipped down her décolletage.

On the casino floor – or The Pit, as we were told to call it – less than half the two dozen tables had been undraped. Gigi and Dom and I were first out, with Helen as inspector.

Apart from us the great room was empty. There was a curious smell of cherry blossom, rancid milk and burning toast. After Gigi sneezed the echoes rolled for fully twenty seconds. The ceiling seemed much higher than I remembered, while the walls were closing in. If this was The Pit then where was the pendulum? Perhaps an enormous blade might scythe silently down while Gray cackled like Vincent Price?

"Keep that wheel spinning," growled Kenny, the pit-boss: he was second only to Gray, third only to God.

"Why? – There's no-one here."

"You're here – and so am I." To demonstrate this, his dark paw put the thing into motion once again.

He was squat and shiny-pated, panting heavily as he tacked back and forth in a sideways stagger, as if The Pit was a ship's deck out in The Roaring Forties. When Chris emerged, he tripped over his own feet. I never did discover whether "Kenny" was his surname, his Christian name or just another Scottish adjective.

Time passed but not a single punter came through the door. At five to four a shadow flickered behind the stippled glass and at five past it opened, just a chink. A chelonian head appeared, blinked twice and then withdrew.

It was casino procedure to blood newcomers when things were nice and quiet but I would rather have been thrown directly to the wolves. The silence was like being inside an anechoic chamber: I was sure that I could hear the beating of our hearts and pulses, the high-pitched humming of our circulating blood.

Chris was at the left-handed table facing me, stacking, proving and cutting with both hands at once, in perfect synchronisation. She appeared to be striking "attitudes" reminiscent of the celebrated Lady Hamilton: Phaedra giving Hippolytus the eye . . . Iphigenia turning into a goat . . . The Penitent Magdalene . . .

❧

On the Saturday morning Ed and I had not discussed the situation: it was tacitly understood that Chris would be staying.

"Just a week or two," she assured me. "Until they say I'm OK and ship me out again."

"What about your hotel?"

"Let's not tell them: it would complicate things. Anyway, I need the wardrobe space."

Ed had already left for Boston Spa.

"What does he do there?"

"It's The British Library's Northern Repository. He's researching post-mediaeval Neo-Latin kiss-poems."

"What?"

"Don't you mean why?"

"Why?"

"Because no-one else is – or would ever want to. He's bought a tiny silver knife to cut the pages: that, I suspect, is the real attraction."

"Well" – Chris growled – "I suppose someone's got to do it. That's what my dad used to say when he went out to see United lose."

"What was your father like?"

69

"He was a bastard" – she shook her head as if in admiration – "To everybody . . . all the time."

At this point she sprang to the sofa, snatched up the sacks of dirty washing, two in each fist, then dashed out of the room. By the time I reached the front door she was already turning the corner of the street.

She had been less than impressed when we explained how we were allergic to soap-powder, flattened by sinusitis if we even passed the laundrette.

"What happens when you've no clean clothes?"

"We buy some more," Ed had replied. Perhaps she was even now fulfilling her subsequent threat to throw the whole lot in the river?

Ten minutes later she returned, empty handed.

"I really *am* allergic." Her eyes were running and her neck was blotched. "They're doing a service wash: you can pick it up in an hour" – she handed me the ticket – "I'm going to the hotel to get some things."

Lugging those bags back up the hill had nearly killed me. How could clean clothes be heavier than dirty ones? Shouldn't the opposite be the case?

I spent the next two hours removing fluff from my black cords and t-shirts. They must have chucked them in with someone else's bedding: that extra weight had been the feathers.

Chris returned that evening with a couple of suitcases – one false zebra-skin, the other shiny and candy-striped.

"Did you bring those on the plane?"

"No" – she gave me a sharp look. "Everything was in storage."

Ed had followed her inside, laden with gilded but dusty tomes. Only he could have extracted loans from a reference-only facility. The librarians either didn't care about their Neo-Latin kiss-poems or he was stealing them – none of these books were ever returned.

Chris's cases disgorged: it was as if they were portals to some mysterious subterranean realm. There were shimmering dresses sheathed in bubble-wrap, shoes in drawstring bags, tiny golden cases that rattled or chimed, diaphanous garments folded in coloured tissue paper: she certainly knew how to pack. There was even a second fur coat identical to the one she was wearing – right down to the silver arrows on its maroon lining – but while the original had been soft to the touch its spare was stiff and sticky like a tomcat's back.

We looked on, fascinated, as a full ordinance of maquillage was arrayed. Soaps in round cases, facial scrubs, night creams, leg gels, body butters . . . Dior, Creed, Chanel, Guerlain – scents so alluring that they were penetrating through their glass . . . Nine lipsticks, three tiny razors and a metal syringe like something from Dr Frankenstein's lab.

Now she had produced a pair of drumsticks. Honey Langtree, Mo Tucker: I had always liked female percussionists.

"Have you got a kit?"

"A what?"

"A drum kit." Twirling the sticks I whacked myself on the nose. She shook her head, pityingly.

"What's that?" Ed pointed to a steel and plastic object. It resembled a chromatic harmonica: I expected her to start blowing 'Genevieve'.

"Victorinox." She tossed it over to me. "Swiss Army issue."

That figured: armed with knives like these – with multiple blades, screwdrivers, bottle openers and even a magnifying glass – you would never need to go to war.

"What does this do?" I thumbed out an evil-looking spike.

"That's the reamer."

"What is it for?"

"Reaming." She took the weapon from my hand and closed it. "In carpentry."

"Does this suit me?" Ed had donned the second coat: it appeared to be a perfect fit.

"No." Ripping it off his back she doused the fur with Givenchy.

Ed stumped off to prepare for the night ahead. This process took half an hour but wrought no discernible change in his appearance.

"Tell me something," said Chris. "Why does he call you Willikins?"

"It's after a character in an old poem. He's a lecherous priest who sleeps with a merchant's wife while the man is away at market. Willikins pays her with gold he has previously borrowed from her husband and then, on meeting him returning, says 'I have just discharged that debt to your wife.'"

She looked me up and down. "And is that what you do?"

"No," I said, "Or at least not yet."

"And why do you call him Eddie Baby?"

"It's from a 'Monty Python' sketch."

"So they're only jokes then? I thought they might be . . . pet names."

"We're not gay," I said. "We used to try it but we couldn't stop giggling."

"Giggling?" Once again she broke a word into its syllables. "What's wrong with gig-ger-ling?"

Out in the clubs she had proved to be a surprisingly energetic performer. I thought she might just revolve, like a statue on a plinth, but instead her body launched itself into a blur of hyperkinetic swoops and swirls. My temples began to throb: it was as if she was generating her own strobe lighting. She kept her arms properly tucked in to her sides except on the faster numbers when she would double clap on every second off-beat.

She did not want to dance with us. Eyes shut, with that half-smile on her face, she remained inviolably alone. Her thoughts were evidently elsewhere, like those dervishes who set their bodies whirling to allow their souls to slip away unnoticed.

"Where did you learn to cut a rug like that?" Ed enquired when she finally joined us at the bar.

"Sunday afternoon TV."

"Fred and Ginger? Ann Miller? Cyd Charisse in *The Band Wagon*?"

She shook her head. "Moira Shearer in *The Red Shoes*."

It was interesting that every pair she had unpacked had been black.

❧

Just when it looked as if we might be languishing in Purgatory forever, Mr Gray descended from the bar to take control. Gigi and Dom were replaced by two cadaverous coves and – after a series of clicks and crackles – the music was turned on. It just had to be Shirley Bassey.

The human tortoise was the first to cross the threshold, indicating that our punters might have if not a hierarchy then at least a rudimentary queuing system.

Anyone less like a 'Big Spender' could scarcely be imagined. Its little head swayed and sniffed: it rejected me, then Rhys, before crawling towards Chris's table.

Everyone else had darted off to the replacement dealers. As the creature drew nearer, Chris's hips began to sway.

The tortoise turned and blindly fled until it hit the rail on the far side of my table. A £20 cash chip dropped from its grasp to hit the baize then roll across to me.

"Thank you, sir." I proved a stack and passed it over then gave my wheel a celebratory flip. "Place your bets please, ladies and gentlemen," I trilled, although neither appeared to be in the vicinity.

Shirley had been turned even further up: that blowtorch voice was already beginning to peel the varnish off the wood.

Soon I had more than my share of punters. They were hard to count for they swarmed like insects, as if about to chew the table to pulp and fashion their nest. None of them would look me in the face but they were fascinated by my hands. Some produced little black notebooks – like Hemingway's – in which they inscribed every number that came up. The bets they placed were the minimum requirement to maintain their presence there.

It was different on Chris's table: her punters were splashing their chips everywhere, anywhere, while pretending not to notice her breasts, even though these kept straining against the fabric of her dress as if about to snap its shoulder-straps. I had never realized that not looking at something could be such an intense activity.

Shirley – having reduced The Talk of The Town to rubble – gave place to Neil Diamond. Every time he scaled the sheer cliff at the chorus of 'I Am (I Said)' my bladder would begin to throb as I fought off an almost irresistible urge to micturate. Evidently 'Piss-Poor' was a specific musical genre. How could the same man have written 'I'm A Believer'?

Bosun Kenny came rolling across his tilting deck: just the sight of him made me feel sea-sick.

"You've just proved two stacks short," he hissed in my ear. "Nineteens not twenties."

He had somehow spotted this from the other side of the room, while facing in the wrong direction. I viewed him with a new respect.

The music got worse. Some bouncy dirges by Lulu were followed by The Carpenters, even creepier. Ed was of the opinion that Karen C's voice was death incarnate. 'Please Mr Postman': you knew that all those letters would be edged in black.

Tony Bennett's '(I Left My Heart In) San Francisco' set off a pronounced betting spike. Everybody in the place must have left their hearts somewhere or other – if only Burmantofts or Wibsey. With horrible inevitability Johnny Cash now made his appearance: not the rockabilly stuff, of course, just the Man in Black tosh The punters were squaring their shoulders and narrowing their eyes to indicate that they had swatted a fly in Seacroft just to watch it die.

I had noticed that the established croupiers were no more dexterous than Dom and I. They had, however, perfected a magnificently blank expression: their lips hardly moved, and they never blinked. I was reminded of priests gathering at an altar or flunkeys dancing attendance on The Queen.

The hardest thing was watching other people smoke while unable to do so myself. They squandered this privilege on filter-tipped Virginia fags that they couldn't even inhale properly.

"Pull on it, man!" I wanted to scream. "Get that smoke down into your lungs! Now hold it, hold it, hold it there!"

For some time, I had been aware of a tallish man standing in the doorway. I had not seen him enter - he appeared to be materializing, gradually coming into focus. Now he advanced, squinting up at the ceiling like a batsman going out to the crease, adjusting to the light. Pale, with receding hair combed back, he could have been any age between thirty and sixty. He wore a suit of fading grey and a ragged blue tie: although his shirt was fraying at the collar his black brogues were polished to a mirror shine. The way he was walking - somehow tense and relaxed at the same time - made me wonder if he might be deaf or dumb or blind.

He stopped at my table but did not take a seat, instead leaning at an unlikely angle against a pillar that only he could see. A cash chip slipped from his grasp then rolled into the centre of the board.

"15/20 split, sir?"

I expected him to withdraw the stake, but he gravely inclined his head and let it lie.

When I pushed over the winnings - "Seventeen pieces, sir" - those dry lips formed the words 'thank you'.

To my disappointment he did not follow up on this stroke of luck, reverting instead to what must have been his habitual method: single chips on odd or even and red or black. When he did win - merely doubling the stake - he would always lay up for the next two spins. Nevertheless, there was something compelling about this glacier-slow progress towards inevitable defeat. He was chain-smoking dark acrid-smelling cheroots: I nearly overbalanced from trying to suck in his fumes.

"Watch that wheel!"

Helen was at my elbow, looking distinctly ruffled, like a thrush whose fledgling is threatened by a hawk.

"34 red to 8 black - you keep hitting the same section."

I had not been paying much attention, idly noticing that 27 had come up twice – or had it been three times? Now I saw that a group of better-dressed punters – small businessman-types – were descending from the bar, followed by the tortoise who had evidently summoned them.

They all bought in at three hundred each and immediately plastered the target area. A mass of cash chips went on 27 and its neighbours. Helen was making little cheeping sounds: perhaps she would feign a broken wing?

I had taken it for granted that the ball fell entirely at random and that no identifiable pattern could ever emerge but if everyone in the business felt otherwise who was I to disagree? I might have been given a wheel with a faulty spindle – like the one spotted by the man from the song, 'The Man Who Broke the Bank at Monte Carlo'.

Helen and Kenny looked almost disappointed when, over the next dozen spins, the ball landed nowhere near those nine numbers. After back-to-back zeroes the medium rollers gave up and returned to the bar and their tortoise seemed to have disappeared.

"Well done," Helen whispered.

"You really stuck it to them," said Kenny.

A shiver ran down my spine and then back up again. Suppose I really *had* caused this to happen?

My thin pale friend, having moved away when the excitement started, now returned to follow his previous strategy. Other punters drifted around the tables dipping in a toe then retreating. Nobody came, nobody went. We had re-entered the Twilight Zone and the music – turned up ever higher – provided the perfect soundtrack.

I had heard that the peerless Frank Sinatra had recently abandoned Cole Porter and Rodgers & Hart to concentrate on more 'contemporary' material. And here it was, an LP entitled *Some Nice Things I'd Missed* – that is, until he'd scraped them off the soles of his shoes.

'Sweet Caroline' – even worse than the Neil Diamond original

- was followed by 'If' and 'Tie A Yellow Ribbon'. Perhaps next up would be Glenn Gould, on the old Joanna, bashing out 'Mouldy Old Dough'?

Finally, we arrived at the centre of Hell: Frank's interpretation of Jim Croce's 'Big Bad Leroy Brown', a choogling paean to a celebrated bar-room brawler. As Satan slowly revolved - upside down, encased in ice - he and all his demons were singing along.

The sound of Sinatra, vomiting over those farting trumpets and belching baritone saxes, was hardly to be borne. I was feeling meaner than Leroy's dog, positively rabid and casting around for a juicy leg to bite - clean off, if I could manage it.

At this point, mercifully, Helen sent me and Chris out for our break. Only now did I register that my shirt was soaked in sweat.

We were directed to the Green Room which turned out to be sludge-grey and fly-blown. I sat on the threadbare sofa, wringing out my shirt, while Chris tried to coax a picture from the TV set. By standing on a rocky table, holding the aerial at full extension, she succeeded in conjuring up the leering features of a popular children's entertainer whose name I could not recall.

"I've met him," she said. "Working at the Playboy Club."

"What was he like?"

"Horrible." She spoke as if the answer was self-evident.

I flicked a cigarette up and out of its soft packet but missed my mouth. I tried and missed again and again until I contrived to spear it up my left nostril.

"So are you enjoying your debut?" For some reason she pronounced this "Dubboo" - the Australian way.

"It's OK. It's just that fucking music I can't stand."

"What music?"

Before I could expound on this the door flew open and Gray entered without knocking. Chris dropped the aerial and turned away, her shoulders hunching, as if she was refastening her dress.

"Well, Christine" - the voice had gone curiously high - "What do you make of our punters?"

She regarded him for a while before answering. Although the words had been perfectly audible, he asked her to repeat them.

"Drippers and pikers" – she had said – "Pushers and pokers, mice in the pipes and rats in the slats."

Now she joined me on the sofa, swinging one bare leg across my lap and nuzzling my neck. Glaring as if I had been working some ventriloquists' trick Gray backed out of the room. He was one of those people who always contrive to present their front: perhaps he did not possess a profile.

The moment the door shut she withdrew her leg. "Aren't you going to smoke that thing?"

"I am savouring the moment." I lit a match then blew it out. "Just tell me . . . why are you suddenly . . . mauling me?"

"Men in here won't hit on me when I'm already... with someone."

"What, with me?"

"Why not?" She shrugged for the thirty-second time since Friday.

"You should have said: would you like me to do anything in particular?"

"Just that little head-shaking thing – it's driving everybody wild."

"What head-shaking thing?"

Her eyes bugged alarmingly, and her mouth split into a jack-o'-lantern grin. The chin rose, the neck stretched and coiled, then the head, in slow rotation, descended once more. Her mime suggested Bengo the Boxer-pup – TV familiar of my infancy – overdosed on Quaaludes.

"What exactly is a dripper?" I enquired.

"A small-time punter who is playing to lose, but does it slowly, drop by drop. A piker is similar but American: he pushes his chips between the columns until they've worn away. They never really lose: the money just disappears."

"What do you make of that grey-haired man at my table? You know, the one with the smile – Yehudi."

"Why do you call him that?"

"He looks like Menuhin, the violinist."

"He looks more like a plumber to me." She had pronounced it 'ploomer' – the first time she had sounded like a Geordie.

I returned the wet and crumpled cigarette to its packet.

"Why didn't you smoke it?"

. "Just to show them."

"Show who? There's only me here and I don't care."

On our way back we held the doors open to allow the new arrivals – three swaddled figures in bath chairs pushed by identical nurses – to precede us on to the floor.

The moment they wheeled in the place..." Miss Bassey was there to greet them.

As I had feared, the casino possessed just the one tape, which would continue on its loop until three a.m. or the end of the world.

❧

Chris and I were given Thursday off and then switched to the weekend late shifts. For her this was to be expected but I had been elevated with indecent haste. It made no sense. Gray drew up the rotas and was obviously stuck on her, so why didn't he keep us apart? He could have put us on different days or different shifts or stuck her on Table One and me on twenty-four, but instead we came and went together – even our breaks were synchronized. Staff relationships were frowned on, but they seemed to be actively encouraging us.

"Perhaps Gray likes me," I suggested.

"Why? Do you like him?"

"No."

"Hasn't it struck you that he might be scared?"

"Scared of me?" Chris shook her head. "Scared of you?"

"Just scared."

I concluded that he must be playing a longer and more subtle game. Perhaps he knew we were faking and was enjoying our simulations? Or was he exploring the possibilities of doubt, jealousy and fear, while knowing that his ultimate victory was assured? Or was it all for the sheer thrill of the chase? I was reminded of one of Ed's favourite ballads in which a Cumbrian staghound pursues its quarry for eighty miles until at last dog and stag return to their starting point and drop down dead together.

On Friday and Saturday nights the casino was transformed. The auxiliary lighting glowed, the music got even louder, and every table was open and in play. The drippers and pikers and the rats and the mice all scurried away as the big beasts came lumbering out to play. Despite the bespoke tailoring and Corona cigars they were sadly no more impressive than their predecessors. They all used the same aftershave, citric with a hint of formaldehyde – PUTREFACTION: FOR MEN. Most were bald or balding, but their ears and nostrils were working to compensate, horribly stuffed with spikes, tufts and curls.

Some would bet in the same patterns while others seemed without strategy. At times they would just stand there, motionless and staring, for spin after spin. We were supposed to banish them from the table after four consecutive passes, but I never saw this rule being enforced. Evidently the true constitution of the place had remained unwritten. After a while they would take a deep breath and once more fling themselves upon the table.

The closest we had to a 'Character' was a shouting used-car dealer who always carried, tucked under his right armpit, a wedge of red fifties the size of a baby's head. A gaggle of caricatural farmers turned out to be chartered accountants, while our solitary agriculturalist – celebrated for his sugar beet – had the fingernails and saurian complexion of a diabolist.

Two-thirds of the croupiers and all the hospitality staff were women but in the ranks of punters they hardly figured at all. Helen's estimate of 92% male had been conservative: there was only the occasional wife or hooker although it was hard to distinguish between them. Sometimes they were even permitted to place a bet – always through the croupier, indicating their number with the little finger of the left hand. Someone had evidently set out the etiquette in such matters. I had been hoping for something a bit more Russian: where were the beautiful and doomed consumptives and the ageless crones who had sold their souls to Satan for the secret of the cards?

The one redeeming feature was Yehudi. Chris had dozens of fans, but people merely drifted on to my table, only staying if they won on the first couple of spins. There was no doubt about it, though, Yehudi always gravitated to me. It had to be admitted that he was no prize catch - making a single stack last all evening, like my grandma sucking on a Glacier Mint - but he was all mine and I loved him.

Chris had been right: rough and swollen, his were not a violinist's hands. The last two fingers on the left were curled uselessly, unable to straighten or bend. His eyes were pale, shifting between green and blue: whenever he smiled, tight-lipped, head tilted back, they would close altogether.

What was his story? I wondered - for a story he must surely have. Were there a wife and children - dead or lost to him? Or perhaps a sainted mother who he was nursing through her final terrible years? I imagined him living in a bed-sit, full of caged budgerigars, with a worktable piled high with manuscript paper - dozens of unperformed symphonies and unreadable prose-poems . . .

I had grown up with that face on dozens of record covers. Menuhin - as a boy with Elgar, resembling a ventriloquist and his dummy; squinting down the violin's bridge as if sighting a rifle; in a horrible paisley shirt, pouring tea for Stephane Grapelli; with Ravi Shankar, struggling to play while in the lotus position. He and his mentor Enescu doing Bach's double violin concerto was my mother's favourite piece of music.

"I was born old, but I have been getting younger ever since." How my parents loved the opening line of his autobiography! I had always feared that they were only kidding themselves . . . Nevertheless, there was indeed something ageless about my Yehudi: it was as if the child and the old man had somehow contrived to meet each other halfway.

Helen told me that she had once seen him away from the casino

– at 6am, walking along Stanningley by-pass. He was carrying a small red metal case and an umbrella – which, even though it wasn't raining, was up. She had not stopped to offer him a lift.

The Sunday shift was shorter and very quiet. Even Yehudi took the day off. Only a few lonely souls came drifting in from The Catholic Cathedral, looking to settle their nerves after confession.

Suddenly, just as the clock was striking nine, the doors flew open, and a dozen short and stocky men came marching in. All were wearing dark mohair suits, each with its own distinctive shimmer and weave, with dazzling white shirts and Cardin knitted ties. The other punters fell back, fearing that St Valentine's Day had come early.

The group paused at Chris's table but then, with evident regret, bowed and moved on to mine.

"Good evening, Young Mr B." The bearded patriarch was extending a hand that I was forbidden to take. "I hope you are on commission because we have come here expressly to lose."

They had lined up opposite me like a soccer team posing for a pre-match photograph: the elders were sitting with the younger, in two rows behind, up on their toes or bending at the knees. I was dazzled by the glare of all the superfluous gold drilled into their perfect teeth.

I should have guessed that The Family would be members here for they would bet on anything. Ed and I – much to our cost – had once been lured into the squash tournament that they ran for their employees and friends, elaborately handicapped and for sky-high stakes.

The youngest grandson leaned across the table.

"I've finished all those . . . books . . . you gave me. Do you have any more?"

"I'm sorry – but after what happened to Ed we've given up . . . reading . . . for a while."

I didn't know why we bothered with such malarkey. Everyone knew what we were talking about.

Although I rolled my eyes and mimed zipping up my mouth, they kept chattering away until – after three spins in which they had kept their promises by leaking over a hundred quid – Gray himself appeared at my side. Grabbing my arm, he virtually frog-marched me from the floor. As we exited, I saw that Chris was floating from her table to mine.

"What's your game?" He spluttered, on regaining his breath. "What are you doing here?"

"They're just some people I know. If it was a scam then why would they be saying hello?"

"How can people like that know someone like you?"

He evidently considered it to be a scientific impossibility that they and I could share the same visual field without the mediation of… trade.

"They're friends of my dad's, importers of mohair and alpaca. I've only met them a couple of times."

In fact, I had been drinking with them since I was fourteen. On long summer evenings my father would drive up Wharfedale until the beginnings of the limestone band where we would join The Family outside The Red Lion at Burnsall Bridge. There they would tell us of the dark and tragic history of the Armenian people, singing and reciting from their national bards – Komitas, Raffi and Frik – who evidently lost a great deal in translation.

"Your father: what does he DO, exactly?"

"How do you mean?"

"What is his job?"

"He works for The Inland Revenue."

Gray's eyes widened and he dropped into a crouch, hands clutching at his hips like a B-Western baddie who has just been informed that the posse is on its way.

"Don't worry," I said. "He only does the Rugby League clubs."

This did not seem to reassure him.

"Does he know that you are working here?"

"I haven't mentioned it – but word seems to have got around."

"Take a break," he said at last. "Christine is accommodating your friends. If this happens again you must leave the pit immediately."

I turned away but he called me back.

"Your tie isn't straight." He tugged the elastic as far as it would stretch and then released it to snap against my neck.

Five minutes later my Adam's apple began to swell and throb. Saliva filled my mouth – unable to swallow, I could only drool. How could these dicky-bows ever be anything but crooked? I would not be falling for that one again.

"I'm beginning to think it isn't me he's interested in," said Chris when she joined me later. Had there been a flash of pique in her eyes? Would we end up fighting like dogs over that shrivelled carcass?

"Well, if he *does* like me" – I croaked – "He's got a funny way of showing it."

⁂

As usual, The Fenton was crowded. Robert Benchley and Dorothy Parker had not yet arrived, but the Luria Boys were on sparkling form. The Littl'un had introduced a pyrotechnical element to his act, breaking wind then applying a lit match to his posterior. Now, having run out of gas, he was experimenting with his ears.

"Why is it always the same in here?" Chris enquired.

"What do you expect? It's the way they like it."

"But it doesn't have to be *exactly* the same" – she sighed – "Does it?"

"Look! Look!" I pointed triumphantly. Ian had changed persona again. The model aeroplane had been replaced by a wig of well-greased curls and the paint-stained dungarees by a black velvet suit with white ruffles at the throat and cuffs. As a final touch he was deftly twirling a silver-topped cane.

He was being Lacenaire! – the murderous playwright from *Les Enfants du Paradis*, our favourite film. At school I had driven him mad by myself impersonating Avril, the killer's Apache sidekick, whose only words – in tones combining adoration and horror – are "Oh! Monsieur Lacenaire!"

Chris merely yawned as if – like Arletty in the movie – she had seen a thousand assassins and not been particularly impressed by the first.

Ed joined us. That fawn corduroy suit indicated that he was meeting Lori and Lorna downtown. Everything was going well, he insisted, although the girls were still pretending that he was a dwarf.

"Stand up," Chris ordered. "Now turn round . . . Yes, you really are a great . . . big . . . midget."

"I prefer dwarf," he said with immense dignity. "Or leprechaun, perchance."

"Have you known any midgets?" I asked her.

"There were two entertainers on the boats. They juggled, sang old jazz songs and did impersonations that no-one could recognize. They said they were brothers, but they looked nothing like each other, except in size."

"What were they like off-stage?"

"They scuttled around like crabs, nipping everyone with their little claws."

"How were they . . . endowed?" Ed enquired.

"About average – but I never saw them getting . . . excited."

She went off to the bar. Simultaneously, as if by some sixth sense, the feminists emerged from the Games Room. They were always trying to draw Chris into their orbit, inviting her to meetings, marches or candlelit vigils but she always declined. Her conscience and consciousness remained unraised.

"She's a woman of the world, all right," said Ed, admiringly.

"Yes, but maybe not of this one."

"You were right, you know." He finished his pint and readied himself to go. "Lori and Lorna are still running their ad."

"They must have paid in advance, for the discount."

He sighed. "I wonder if I'll ever understand women."

"There's nothing to understand." Chris had rejoined us. She was drinking Cinzano - presumably in honour of Joan Collins who she had briefly encountered in Las Vegas.

"We're just like men. Some are good, some bad but most aren't anything at all. There's one thing, though: women whose names begin with L are always trouble."

"Lilith," Ed said dreamily. "Lamia, Lulu, false Lenore."

"Lori and Lorna," she sneered. "They sound like two dolphins at Marine World."

"They do like to swim," Ed conceded.

"You know the score and so do they. They pretend to be in control, and you pretend to be the victim. Next week you'll be swapping places, then back again. Everybody knows the truth about everything, but nobody ever admits it."

"Why is that?"

"Because it's not very nice, is it?"

I saw him wince at these words: he later told me that this was something that Lori often said - and in exactly that tone of voice. Chris, of course, had not yet encountered her.

"They're just playing with him," she said, as we watched him go, "but all you do is laugh."

"He's not really that bothered: he just thinks it's something that he's supposed to do. When Lori stood him up last week he went straight back to the kiss-poems."

Chris glared. "Does he know that there's nothing really going on between you and me?"

"Why should he care?"

"He might be jealous."

"Of me or of you?"

"I don't know, do I?" She was doing Lori's voice again.

We had not been out of each other's company for the last ten days. I had never known anything like this, not even with Ed. It seemed to have little to do with friendship or intimacy - more a matter of proximity, as if we had been manacled together and then - on the way to court for separate trials on different charges – jumped from our prison van.

We had not slept for over forty-eight hours. Chris had told me that once, long before her breakdown, she had not closed her eyes for three months.

"I thought it was like not shitting or not eating – you're supposed to die after eleven days. Perhaps you were just dreaming that you were awake."

"I never dream."

There was no point in worrying about any of it. She would soon be moving on and so, no doubt, would I.

We headed off to Club 'Ush, situated under a railway arch behind the former Corn Exchange. It claimed to be the loudest club on the planet – which, considering the way my trousers were flapping at the sound waves was probably an understatement. No-lighting gave way to low-lighting, to reveal that most of the crowd could barely stand up: they had evidently been exchanging too much corn. The music kept sweeping them like dead leaves across the concrete floor.

Although she remained in the vicinity Chris still would not dance with me. The surprisingly few men who did approach her were moved on in the blink of an eye: some appeared to be wringing their hands.

I watched her twisting and swooping: there was something predatory about it. Sometimes she would stop dead and with the palms of her hands explore an invisible wall that had sprung up between us. It was a standard mime routine: even Bowie looked stupid doing it. When it came to the slower numbers, she would repair to the darkest corner and shuffle around in ever-tightening circles.

Ed thought she was like those scowling Pre-Raphaelite damsels – *Monna Vanna* or *Salome* – but I was reminded of another painting, Delacroix's *The Death of Sardanapalus*.

When my parents and I had visited The Louvre there had been

vast crowds around *La Gioconda* and the other milestones and millstones of Western art but nobody even paused at *Sardanapalus*: if anything, they averted their eyes and quickened their step. We stood before it, as a family, in rapt contemplation, unjostled and undisturbed until my father finally broke the silence.

Well, fancy that!"

This was what he always said when deeply moved or impressed.

The painting was inspired by Lord Byron's play. Besieged by his enemies, the titular despot, fortieth and last King of Assyria, orders his most treasured possessions – jewels, plate, carpets, silks, perfumes, horses, concubines – to be piled up together and then destroyed in front of him, before he draws a dagger and kills himself. Reclining on a low divan, he watches the carnage with a meditative air, as if his thoughts are already turning inwards, without registering that, there in the foreground, a naked woman is being stabbed by his servant. As her jugular vein is severed she twists to reveal the strong line of the jaw while putting her breasts and buttocks on simultaneous display. Chris could have modelled for this figure – right down to the cluster-earrings and silver sandals cinched just above the anklebones.

According to Ed, no such scene appears in either the play or its source, the *Histories* of Diodorus Siculus. At the end of his life, Franz Liszt had been adapting it as an opera, but it remained unfinished. In the Third Act he had been planning – literally or figuratively? – to set the audience on fire.

Now the music had stopped, and Chris was heading towards the lavatory. She always removed her shoes when she left the dance floor, carrying them heel-to-toe in her right hand, as if ready to fight or flee. When she had passed the bar, a familiar figure detached itself from a knot of bouncers and came tripping towards me. Why was it that big men were always so light-footed?

"Well, Christine seems to be getting on all right." Off-duty, my friend the Police Inspector resembled a golfing undertaker.

"Do you know her?"

"I do all the security checks but she and I, once or twice, have met before." He chuckled." I knew you two would pal up: she's always had a taste for strange."

"Purely Platonic," I assured him. "My heart belongs to Ed."

"I've just seen him with a nice little blonde. Tell me, why does he dance on his knees?"

"It's a Russian thing: he's half-Zaphorovsky Cossack . . . "

". . . Half-twat" – he completed my sentence. "How are you getting along with Voragine?"

"Happy St Quentin's Day." I replied.

"Ah, Quentin . . . Stretched on the rack until his veins burst, then whipped by rawhide, with pitch, fat and boiling oil poured all over him . . . Lime, vinegar and mustard into the mouth, two long skewers down the length of his body and, at the last, decapitated. "The Golden Legend" is better than any recipe book."

"I like the way Quent keeps on laughing – even when his head is off."

When Chris returned, he made himself scarce, his feet flickering across the floor like little flames.

"That was that copper, wasn't it?"

"Yes," I said. "I'm beginning to think he might be The Devil."

"Oh well" – a terrible grinding noise started up and she cut a little caper. "Someone has to be."

⁂

On Thursday Rhys and Dom were moved to later shifts with Alan and Gigi following on the Monday after that. I tried to greet them, but they were still ignoring me.

Sometimes, in the quieter periods, I would try to catch their eyes or let a faked cough modulate into a discreet Arnold-bark but if anything, they grew even stiffer. They seemed to be ignoring each other as well: it struck me that it was they who had not been what they had appeared to be.

Alan was still launching his moon-balls, setting the punters reeling and covering their faces, like vampires when silver bullets are ricocheting round the room. Chris was sure that he was doing it on purpose: "They'll sack him: we don't like jokes in this business." She was right: there were plenty of smirks and sniggers, but no-one ever laughed.

Dom and Rhys buttoned their lips and kept their heads down, concentrating fiercely on the job in hand. The former was losing his flashiness while the latter was speeding up. Gigi, however, was everyone's friend. She mothered the women, and they mothered her: it was even worse with the men.

Everything was fine until we showed up and a dead silence fell. A couple of bolder souls might glare but the rest turned their eyes away.

The male dealers played a lot of sport, but they were a sallow crew, exhibiting a variety of skin complaints. When I asked them if they needed a left-back they reacted as if I was propositioning them. As far as I could gather from their mumblings they hated me - firstly, because I was obviously a 'queer' and secondly because I had 'copped off' with Chris. The apparent inconsistency did not appear to bother them. When Chris or I made any sudden movements, they would flinch so we made a lot of sudden movements.

The women, in contrast, were wary but fascinated. As a couple, Chris and I made no sense at all: what could be the secret of my appeal? Sooner or later their gazes would slip from my face, track down my scrawny torso then zoom in on my crotch. I recalled that story about Ava Gardner responding to journalists' questions about why she was marrying "that wop runt" - Frank Sinatra.

"Yeah, he only weighs a hundred and ten pounds" - the most beautiful woman in the world said sweetly - "But a hundred of that is *cock*." Chris tried to get me to stick a half cucumber down my y-fronts but I told her - like Lane the butler in *The Importance of Being Earnest* - that none were available, "not even for ready money." I had been waiting thirteen years for the chance to use that line.

A few of the younger girls were snappy and smart.

"How do you like it here?" I asked the prettiest one.

"It's OK – better than the factory, anyway."

She used to work at Rank Wharfedale – a hi-fi manufacturer in Apperley Bridge.

"What were you doing there?"

"Soldering."

Her ambition was to get down to London and then on to the cruise ships.

"There'll be men" – she winked at me – "Rich men."

When I suggested that she should ask Chris for a few tips she scowled and stomped away.

Anyone who forced a girl like that to "solder" should be hung – first by the thumbs and then by the neck. Ian's quadraphonic speakers were by Wank Rharfedale: I would be having a word with him.

On opening the door to The Green Room, we were hit by a pall of acrid smoke: it was like walking into a crematorium. Naturally, everyone kept complaining about my Caporal tobacco.

"They can talk," said Chris, fishing in her bag, "With their halitosis and BO." She sprayed the can of air-freshener in their faces.

"What's wrong?" She enquired, as they fell back, choking and teary-eyed. "Don't you like Honeysuckle Rose?"

After a while they just left when we entered, preferring to enjoy their sad little ciggies out in the car park, in the rain.

Chris would spend every break reapplying her make-up – expertly and unerringly, without recourse to a pocket mirror. How could she know about that ash-smear on her cheek? How did she sense that a single errant hair was threatening an eyebrow's perfect arch?

"Why do you go to all this trouble?"

"Habit," she replied.

During her time in London and the Americas she had encountered many celebrities. It seemed as if every third person on the TV screen had previously crossed her path. She had generally liked the women but hated virtually all the men. I was delighted to discover that these were often people who my parents and I -sitting on our sofa through those long winter evenings – had, apparently irrationally, taken against. The only one for whom she had a good word was that fair-haired, posh-looking actor, Simon Ward.

"Young Winston – there was a proper gentleman. Now he really knew how to treat a lady."

"Un veritable artiste," I agreed. He had been Stephen Daedalus in the BBC "Ulysses" with the great Milo O'Shea as Bloom. "Did you ever come across Peter Ustinov?"

"I don't know who that is," she said.

At midnight the banqueting suite next door – our sister operation – would wheel across its unwanted food. Sometimes the tables would be piled with smoked salmon, half-plucked pheasants and double-glazed hams but usually there would be merely sausage-rolls and crisps or even – whenever I was feeling particularly peckish – nothing at all.

"Why do you think nobody else would eat it?" Chris watched in disgust as I ripped into a moussaka without picking out the fag-ends and ash. Whether I feasted or starved my weight never varied: ten stone dead. Perhaps I already was?

❧

Ed and I had imagined that, after her flying start, Chris would be working through our library, but she was still on Céline.

"I like it so much I never want it to end."

She carried that book everywhere, using it like a map, a manual, or even a means of divination – her fingers would trace the lines backwards. Sometimes she would ask me to read it aloud.

"There!" Her nail incised the margin, and I would recite.

"'Old mother Vitruve gave off a peppery stink. That's the way with red-heads. They have an animal destiny: it's something brutish, tragic, right there under their skins.'"

"He's certainly down on us copper-nobs," she ducked her head to

92

her armpit, sniffed, then pulled a face. "But I can't say he's wrong."

"What's so bad about pepper?" – I demanded – "All Those lovely gnarly corns rattling and grinding inside a big wooden mill." To invoke this touching scene, I went into a sort of Carmen Miranda routine.

"He didn't have it easy, that Dr Destouches" – although it was a heavy American hardback everything that went into her bag became miraculously weightless – "But at least he wasn't born in West Hartlepool."

Her various costumes, revolving on their hangers like gibbeted bodies, now dominated the flat. We could hear her under-things crisping on the radiators, her tights and stockings whispering to each other along the dado rail.

PLEASE WIPE RIM
PLEASE CLEAR PLUG

She had pinned notices on every available surface. We never saw her putting these up and she never mentioned them. It did seem rather out of character because she appeared to be utterly I-don't-care-ish about everything else.

PLEASE DON'T TOUCH MIRROR

The tip of my nose would always leave a greasy blue mark.

DANGER! – She had labelled all her medication, although it looked like the standard anti-depressants. She had also gaffer-taped her bars of Roger & Gallet soaps – sandalwood and vetiver – in their shiny monogrammed cases.

"I think the whole point of these notices" – Ed was necking her haloperidol – "Is that we should ignore them."

Her handwriting was as illegible as his but in a cruder way. On the fridge door she had taped a memory board across which she would scrawl with square-tipped felt pens. We elected to read

'OPIUM' for 'ONIONS', 'BUGGER' for 'BUTTER' and 'DREAD' for 'BREAD': needless to say, none of these items subsequently appeared. Chris wasn't finicky about her food, except for never frying anything – her eggs were always soft-boiled or poached. She never touched milk or yoghurt but had a serious Jones for strong blue cheeses.

Around the house her hair was tied in a chignon, like Monica Vitti in "Modesty Blaise."

"It looks great," we said. "You should always wear it like that."

Her hands moved to cover her throat like an aristo under the shadow of the guillotine.

"I don't want every Tom, Dick and Harry looking at my neck."

"Not even us?"

The hair stayed as it was: she had evidently concluded that Ed and I were not the decapitating type.

Up on the top floor, she had commandeered the cabinets that everyone had previously ignored. Somehow, she knew that the other tenants – The Hydra – would not be touching her toilet requisites.

"They're harmless," she said, although she had never spoken to any of them. No-one had answered when she knocked on their doors – she left out a cake of vetiver soap for them, but it remained untouched. Whenever one of us was taking a bath, however, they would slip silently from their rooms to press their faces up against the glazed muranese panes. They could not see a thing – not even the faintest blur – while they displayed for us every seam and fold on their thin grey faces.

Ed and I could not recall whether the Hydra that Hercules slew had ever posed any threat to women – or, indeed, to anybody else. The poor beast was probably a harmless herbivore, but its size and all those undulating necks and bobbing heads had rendered it irresistible to any passing hero.

After a month the novelty of the casino had worn thin, but I wasn't feeling any more relaxed. I kept seeing myself as I must appear to the punters: a boy of little faith wearing a shit-brown suit with no pockets, his pants held up by nappy-pins, with a Velcro fly creaking like a parrot on its perch. Chris had observed that whenever I stretched across to clear the table my arse would wiggle in a horribly cheeky fashion. Yes, I could feel it – but no matter how I tried I couldn't make it stop. If this continued, I warned it, there would have to be a parting of the ways. Gurgling noises continually emanated from my stomach and throat: I could see that the punters were hearing them too. I was breathing fast and heavily as if, instead of merely standing there, I was in panic-stricken flight. Gradually, I had slowed it down until it seemed to have stopped altogether. While Chris did not need to sleep, I no longer even needed to breathe.

We five trainees were still on probation. In another month we would sit a second table-test like the one at the interview – but this time under maximum pressure. No matter what you had done over the intervening period, if you messed it up on that morning you were out.

I didn't care whether I stayed or not, of course, but somehow, I couldn't stop thinking about it.

"Gray is just waiting to fail me."

"No," Chris said. "He's strictly business. When you're good they'll keep you, no matter what."

"But am I good?"

"You'll do. At least you stand properly: this lot look like the hangers are still in their shirts."

Something had to be done about that bloody music. I found myself whistling it, walking to its rhythms, even dreaming about Shirley, Frankie and the dogs.

I was not alone: everyone else hated it too.

"I hadn't noticed until you started whinging," said Chris. "Now I can't stop hearing it."

I asked some of the other dealers what they would prefer. Most of the girls went for Stevens – Shakin' or Cat – while the boys, through gritted teeth, all said the same thing.

"The Quo!"

I decided to provide an alternative, so I went round to Ian's to use his decks. I could never remember which house was his: all the hillside terraces were called Brudenell Something-or-other and most of their numbers had been removed. Fortunately, you just had to follow the sound.

He was lying on a chaise-longue, wearing a hairnet – God alone knew what was going on under that – with his face daubed with what appeared to be chocolate milk. I was relieved to see that he had replaced his speakers with Bang & Olufsen. He was full of unhelpful suggestions – Albert Ayler, Wild Man Fischer, Iggy and The Stooges – but I knew that our only chance was to make the tape more subtly subversive.

Sinatra stayed – but it was with 'Only The Lonely', that great heartbreak album made after Ava had left him for the final time. Tony Bennett was also in – but those recent duets with Bill Evans on piano. Shirley Bassey was out, of course, in favour of Ella Fitzgerald's Johnny Mercer songbook. Then we went for 'Diamonds In the Rough' – John Prine for Johnny Cash – and 'Nilsson Schmillson'. Chris insisted on Laura Nyro – at home, her fingers would follow the chord shapes of "Grissom Street" as she played it over and over at 16 rpm.

I persuaded Helen to present the tape to Gray as her own idea. She and Ellen were vice-presidents of the UK Wout Steenhuis Fan Club, which meant that I had to insert three tracks from 'Wipe Out! – With The Wai-Ki-Ki's'.

"The most authentic surf music" – she insisted – "is Danish."

❧

No-one seemed to suspect that Chris and I weren't really an item. Surely it was obvious that I was a front, a shield, a decoy, a block,

96

a merkin or a beard, part-chaperone, part-eunuch. Even Gray had fallen for it: he watched our every move, as if deliberating whether to kill us or himself. His authority lay in possessing – or appearing to possess – the best-looking woman in the place. It was probably in his job description.

After our initial show, Chris had toned down her displays of passion until she hardly bothered at all. Sometimes she would make a wild grab for me, as if we were in danger of being swept away. One night, in the pub, when I had thoughtlessly draped an arm around her shoulders, she drove her stiff fingers deep between my ribs. For the next ten minutes I was paralysed – although nobody seemed to notice any difference. By the time we got to work I was breathing again but I felt that I had been granted a foretaste of death.

Her table was, of course, by far the most popular. Since she arrived fifty new members had joined up. Business was so brisk that when the flow of losing chips was becoming a flood, I would be deputed to stand at her side to gather and re-stack them. This enabled me to observe her technique at close quarters. She never looked at her hands and seemed to call the winning numbers without consulting the wheel. Nor did she make eye contact with punters: that gaze was lasering directly into the brain. A red spot would appear over their pineal glands.

There was something archetypal about it all: a beautiful woman relieving a roomful of ugly men of their cash. A few ogled her – one actually drooled! – but the rest seemed, in their turn, to be ignoring her.

"Tits?" – They would be saying as they adjourned to the bar – "What tits?"

"Was that dealer a woman?"

". . . No, I didn't notice either."

Only the Chinese shunned her: they were here to gamble and to win. As they passed, they would flap their hands, while mumbling such spells as might ward off one of the lesser demons.

I was their favourite: they had evidently determined that I was the casino's vulnerable point. Squawking like roosting gulls they mobbed me – whole families of them, bearing portraits of their more auspicious ancestors. Sometimes they tried to smuggle babies in, concealed under their clothes. Whenever I spun the wheel the oldest of the women would wave in my direction something resembling a monstrous chicken's claw.

They cheated all the time: lightning-fast hands slamming down bets long after the numbers had been called. They sprayed me with spittle and grabbed at my fingers: I had to fight them off. They did not merely want to win, they wanted to destroy me utterly, shrieking and pointing and mimicking my arse-waggling ways. They were so deliriously over the top that I began to wonder whether they were not Chinese – or even oriental – at all. Perhaps the Lawnswood Orpheans were staging *Turandot*.

I retaliated by throwing perfectly legitimate bets off the table and – accidentally on purpose – knocking over their stacks. I slowed the game right down and then abruptly cranked it up again. Having thirty people all cheating at once soon becomes counter-productive: they should have drawn up a rota. They squabbled, got in each other's way and then began to push and shove. When I cleared a winning number – purely by mistake – none of them even noticed. I looked across to Kenny, but he just winked at me.

"Céline would have loved them," said Chris. "Did he ever get to China?"

"I don't think he travelled much – except for fleeing to Switzerland to avoid being indicted for war crimes – but he was always banging on about The Asiatic Hordes."

Yehudi's presence was the place's saving grace. Gentle, rueful and wry, he fascinated me. Those calm grey eyes seemed to be answering a question that I did not yet know how to frame. It felt as if I was being weighed in the balance and not found wanting – examined, shriven, judged, forgiven. I had discovered that he had already been given a different nickname – 'Yiddo' or 'The Yid' – not on account of religion or race or even his parsimonious gaming but because he looked as if he might be . . . thinking about something, which they took as an affront. They felt the same way about me: I was a queer, ginger Irish Jew boy.

One evening, as we were approaching the casino, I saw him out on the street, sparking up a Mahawat Special.

"Pardon me, sir," I said, "But where do you get your smokes?"

"Somers of Keighley" – the voice started high then plummeted to bass-baritone – "Opposite the bus station."

All night I kept thinking about this short, seemingly innocuous exchange. Somehow it had seemed freighted with significance – momentous, even miraculous – as if a blind man had been seeing me, a deaf man hearing me, a dumb man speaking.

❧

"Have you noticed anything unusual about Chris?"

Ed paused until I had finished laughing. "No, I don't mean the things she does – I mean the things she doesn't do."

"How do you mean?" I wondered why he was whispering when she wasn't even in the house. She had gone off to the hotel to collect more shoes: those seven pairs were never going to be enough.

"Take a look at this." He handed me one of her written notices.

"I can't even read it. 'Mink' – is it? Or 'Milk'?"

"No – below that – 'I-S-H-I'" – he was tapping each letter – "'N-G-E-R-S'."

"Is that Swedish?"

"I have concluded that it can only mean . . . *fish fingers*."

"And do we have any of these items?"

"Not yet – but I fear that it's only a matter of time. The fishfingers, however, are beside the point."

"Which is?"

"That Christine never, ever uses the letter 'F'. Not only does she not write it, but she also avoids speaking any word in which it appears. Look at these other notices: 'TOOTHPASTE IS SQUEEZED

OUT' – not 'finished' – 'BINS READY TO BE EMPTIED' – not 'full'. But I suppose there's no way round it with "ISH 'INGERS.'"

"Just now, when I asked if she was off to get her stuff, she replied, 'No, I'm going to get my things.'"

"I bet she winced when you said that."

"Do you know, I rather think she did."

We looked at each other in wild surmise.

"When I asked her about dwarfs she talked about midgets – and about their little pinching hands, not fingers."

"Wonderful!" I cried. "She liked Dom fine until he told her she was 'wonderful' and then she glared as if about to throttle him. And at work she mangles certain numbers – 'or' for 'four', 'ive' for 'five' and so on."

"How does she manage with fifteen?"

"She sort of lisps it – 'ithteen'."

"Doesn't it get mixed up with sixteen?"

"No – because it's 'fifteen black' and 'sixteen red'."

"'Ur coat – she told me take off her 'ur coat. Do you think she knows she's doing it?"

"Perhaps it's become second nature and she's long since forgotten the original reason?"

"That's if she ever knew it."

"Are we supposed to say something? Is it a cry for help?"

"I can't imagine her needing help, let alone crying."

"Maybe it's a superstition – like not stepping on the cracks of a pavement?"

"I've never understood that," I said.

"What do you mean? You do it as well: it was one of the first things I noticed about you."

I stared accusingly at my feet. What else might they not have been telling me about?

"But why 'F'? What has poor old 'F' ever done to her?"

"Perhaps she used to have a cleft palate or a stutter?"

"Some of those avant-garde French guys – OuLiPo – have started doing this sort of thing. Georges Perec wrote a whole novel without using 'e' – the most popular letter in the alphabet."

"How long was it?"

I stretched my forefinger and thumb.

"Wow – cutting out a vowel must take some doing. At least Chris confines herself to a consonant."

"But that's in life – not in art. Anyone can do anything in a book but I bet Perec kept throwing down his pen and yelling, '*Nom de Dieu! Quelle emmerdeuse!*'"

"They call it a lipogram," said Ed, "From the Greek – 'wanting a letter'. Pindar did it in *Ode Minus Sigma*."

"Just imagine how difficult it must be. You can't say 'if' or 'of'. You can't even have feet – you'd have to call them 'plates.'"

"No future – no befores and no afters, only the now. You'd be living in a perpetual present."

"No frankincense, no furbelows. No flash or filigree – all my favourite words would have to go."

"You couldn't even have a favourite."

"You can't be for anything – only not against it."

"You may start something but you can never finish it. Your glass is never full, still less half-full – it can only be empty."

"'The Fair Feld Ful of Folk' – you'll never read *Piers Plowman*."

"Or listen to 'Fulfillingness' First Finale'."

"That's a blessing." He and I had never seen eye to eye regarding Stevie Wonder.

"There's no more fantasy. No fear and no fate. You can't faint, you can't feel, you'll never have any friends. You can't even eat food – unless you call it nosh or scran."

At this point Chris returned, laden down with bags: she had evidently not confined herself to shoes.

"Well," Ed greeted her, "You really are a dedicated follower of fashion."

"Not really." She was suspicious of his emphases. "I'm not trendy:

when I like something I stick with it. Good clothes are always in style."

She brushed off a kitchen chair and sat down.

"Uh, Chris" - my voice was far too casual - "Do you mind if I ask you something?"

She did not reply, just smoothed her skirt, planted her feet and folded her arms across her chest.

"Why do you never use the letter 'F'?"

She visibly relaxed, as if she had been expecting a different question.

"I'm not educated like you boys" - she crossed her legs - "I never think about such things."

"But it is a bit . . . funny, isn't it?"

"Yes, I suppose it is . . . unusual. Anyway" - she sprang to her feet - "I'm going to unpack . . . and then I've got another date with Dr Céline."

Ed shook his head sadly: "She'll never get to call him Louis-Ferdinand."

Later, prior to heading out to clubland, we were consuming a newly purchased pack of delicious 'ish 'ingers when she exacted her revenge.

"Willikins . . . can I ask *you* something?"

"Perhaps."

"That's just it: why do you always say 'perhaps? What's wrong with 'yes' or 'no'?

"I wasn't aware that I did."

"You do, you know," Ed chimed in. "There's no 'perhaps' about it."

"Perhaps I'd better watch it, then."

"It reminds me of Sir Philip Sidney's *Defence of Poetry*. He used the adverb 'truly' as an emphatic affirmative whenever he felt that his argument was running into trouble. 'Truly' merely betrays his own uncertainty: he doesn't even believe it himself. I reckon that your 'perhaps' indicates certainty -that there's no perhaps about anything at all."

He turned to Chris. "So what he's really saying is that this is how things were, are and evermore will be . . . and you'd better get used to it" - he punched his right fist into his left palm - "or else."

"He's right." - she was nodding, enthusiastically - "That Philip Sidney." Fearing a trap, she had hesitated before saying 'Philip'.

I was still wondering about this while we were each dancing in our own separate dark corners. Perhaps "perhaps" was indeed my equivalent of her extirpation of 'F' - a way of controlling things, of secretly imposing my own rhythms on life's alternations of turgidity and flux. All I knew was that whenever I spoke the word my heart would flutter and I would feel a giddy surge of triumph, as if - for five or six seconds - I was floating clear of the earth.

It came as no surprise when, next day, Gray hooked me off my table an hour before the end of the shift. He led me upstairs to the far side of the now deserted bar: man to man, we were going to have things out. The liquid in our glasses was the same colour but I knew that while mine was half-brandy, half-soda, his was unadulterated Pepsi. All night the hopeful punters would be buying him drinks: he and the barman were splitting the money.

"You're not a bad-looking lad." He made as if to lay a fatherly hand on my shoulder but then thought better of it. "But Christine is much too old for you. She's a woman, not a girl, and women have very different needs. I'm sure she's trying to teach you, but it takes a man - any man - five years to really get himself up to snuff. Conserve" - he was staring fixedly at my groin - "Do you know how to conserve?"

"I don't think so." Was he talking about making jam?

"I'm sorry to be so direct but when you get to forty" - he must have been at least fifty-five - "You don't have time to fanny about."

"Have you talked to Chris about this?"

"She said she didn't fancy me."

"I find that hard to believe."

"Actually" – he shook his head as if in wonderment – "She told me to go and fuck myself."

"You must have misheard."

"Christine is a complicated woman" – he motioned for refills – "You wouldn't understand."

I decided to just sit there and let him talk. My second drink was straight brandy but that was mother's milk to me.

We were like two football managers but while Gray was Manchester United, I was Hartlepool. He was trying to work a complicated transfer deal involving Chris and Sally the Solderer who he claimed was his current Innamorato.

"I know she likes you. She says she's always wanted to be a hippie chick." He rolled his eyes in what was presumably meant to depict a state of stoned-out abandonment. "She's wearing me out with all that wasted energy: you could learn to conserve together."

When I did not respond he tried another tack.

"What about Helen and Ellen?"

"Which one?"

"Either – both, if you like."

"But they're lesbians, aren't they?"

"Of course not: there's no such thing as lesbians, only women who aren't taken. They'd never touch each other if a proper man came along – unless he asked them to double-team."

"But they're even older than Chris."

"Something happens when a woman hits forty: it's like they've been reborn. All their hopes and dreams come flooding back. They're as horny as hell, they feel like they're sweet sixteen again – the only trouble is that they don't look it."

"What do you think lesbians do, exactly?"

"Knit, bake cakes, enter dogs in shows." He was evidently confusing them with The Women's Institute.

"Do you know a pub called The Newlands? – It's near the park."

His lip curled. "I've driven past it."

"Well, go into the back room some evening and tell the ladies there what you've just told me. They'll be happy to raise your consciousness – The Infirmary is just round the corner."

"I'm not the one who looks unconscious." He was smirking and waggling his fingers. "Can I ask you something?"

"Perhaps."

"What is Christine like at home?"

"She looks after us – she's quite the little mother. Cooks the tea, darns the socks and tucks us in at night. It's like Snow White and the Seven Dwarfs."

"Which are you? Dopey or Grumpy?"

"Sleazy," I said.

"Let's share her," he said decisively. "We can set up a rota. So long as she's nice to me in here I don't care what she does the rest of the time."

"I'll have a word with her," I said, although I wasn't going to.

Sitting on the stairs I watched the last few spins of the night. A very sweaty man was jumping around Chris's table, desperate to rid himself of all his chips before the lights went down. A final spasmodic lunge caused his tow-coloured hairpiece – to unmoor itself and slide down on to the columns.

"No bet," said Chris. With the regulation glide of thumb and forefinger she returned the thing to its master. He gave it a couple of sharp taps before replacing it, as if it had been a naughty dog that had taken an unauthorized dip in a stream.

"Has anything like that ever happened to you before?" I asked as we were getting changed.

"That was the seventh time," she said dully. "I've had six glass eyes, three plastic hands and someone's lower jaw . . . and too many dentures to count."

'OUR

"WEIRD things are happening!"

Helen's chalk-white face went floating past as Christine and I were emerging from the Green Room for our shift.

"What sort of weird?" I enquired but she had already vanished into the ladies' toilets.

Everything in The Pit appeared to be normal. There was the usual Friday night scrimmage: all the tables were in play.

One of our new tapes was running: the Wout Steenhuis selection. Tinny, leaden, multi-echoic, it seemed to have been recorded inside a crash-diving submarine. The punters were jerking to its rhythms, as if presaging a mass epileptic fit. Surf breaking off The Skagerrak! Wipe out on The Kattegat! Perhaps Helen had suddenly been struck by the insanity of her own musical taste?

A very tall man in a very tight blue suit was getting stuck into the Punto Banco table. His head was almost perfectly square, but this was only momentarily unsettling: in a few seconds I had become perfectly accustomed to it. Gray was watching from the top of the stairs: It was too far off to read his expression. His posture suggested that he had just broken off a hyperkinetic dance routine but even that would have been only mildly surprising.

Chris was given Table Eleven with me behind her on Thirteen. Unlike Ed – with his terror of pavement cracks and hats on beds – I never worried about such things. I was superstitious about everything except popular superstitions.

I relieved Alan, tapping him twice on the shoulder, to signify the end of his stint. As he turned, I saw that there were tears in his eyes. He did not pause to display his empty palms in the regulation manner: in three strides of those great scissor-legs he was gone.

At least he had left me a decent crowd. "Good evening, ladies and gentlemen," I said.

They were, of course, all men. A couple did muster up a feeble response, but their main attention was fixed on a figure at the far end of the table.

At first, I did not recognize Yehudi: I had never seen him sitting down before. He appeared to be larger and more substantial, the shoulders broader, the neck shorter and thicker, while those ruined hands were pressing down on the baize as if he was about to launch himself across the table. Before him stood stack after stack of wheel and cash chips: somehow, I knew that he was not minding these for some high roller who had been suddenly taken short. He did not look smug or triumphant but embarrassed, even a little ashamed.

Just before I announced 'No more bets', the hands flashed out to place his stakes. He was no longer dribbling around his even money slots but going heavy on the columns and sections and an elegant but risky-looking cluster of chevals and splits. These did not appear to favour any portion of the wheel but to be confined to those areas that he could reach without leaving his seat. When he won, he showed no reaction, not even looking at me as I paid him out.

He kept on winning, steadily: even when the marquee bets failed, the two-to-ones moved him nicely along. Those clouded eyes had stopped blinking and he seemed to be growing larger still, hardly breathing as his body slowly petrified. He was no longer smoking Mahawats – or anything else: perhaps this was a sacrifice demanded by the Gods of Chance? I could no longer follow the movements of his hands: the ever-expanding stacks seemed to be bursting straight up through the baize. Helen's "weird" had been something of an understatement.

The others at the table were hardly playing at all. These men of distinction had abandoned their cherished strategies and were dribbling and piking to hold ringside seats as the events unfolded.

I guessed that they would have been laughing at the start – a born loser was unexpectedly lucking into a few quid – but now they were watching in silence, mouths agape. Interestingly, they were not shadowing Yehudi's bets: it was as if all the luck in that room belonged to him.

After a while he motioned for me to cash up his chips. The audience protested but in vain: it was five to eleven – he had just enough time to catch the last bus. Much to their relief, however, he limped straight over to Table Nine, bought in and started winning again.

I thought that he might be sparing me further punishment, but the reverse turned out to be the case. In the next nine spins I contrived to hit zero five times: a few stragglers were wiped out, but the biggest, most fabulous bird had flown.

The cheers told me what was happening on Table Nine, but Yehudi did not stay there long, leading the procession on to Table Eighteen and then, after ten minutes of cheering, all the way out to Table Twenty-Four. Each time the crowds would part and the same prime space would open up for him – elevated and dead centre, looking straight down the board.

It was now apparent that he was singling out the five male croupiers in the room. Was he averse to women in general or only to encountering them under such circumstances? Or were they just unlucky, either way?

Kenny and Helen, also realizing this, were pulling Sally off Punto Banco. What had she done with the square-headed man? I had not seen him leave. Licking her lips, she came sashaying over but Yehudi was up and gone before she reached the table.

He paused to watch as Chris, while seeming not to register his presence, hit 29, then 33, then 35. Third section, reds and odds – all were there, waiting for him but he was not to be fooled. Back at my table his familiar place had already opened up.

I expected to be subbed but he began by losing, so they left me there. He was doing it deliberately, it seemed, cutting the stakes that he had been randomly strewing across the midsections. When

Kenny drifted away, he reverted to the usual targets and I hit 33. Abnormality had been restored: having a lucky streak was one thing but being able to turn it on and off at will – well, that just wasn't right.

"Forty-two pieces, sir."

It was becoming physically painful: every time I pushed his stacks across the top joint of my right forefinger shed another layer of skin.

"Eighty-seven pieces, sir."

From the corners of my eyes, I kept catching fast, low movements, as if bats were crossing and re-crossing the pit. I had experienced this occasional phenomenon since early childhood: harmless specks of matter whisping across the vitreous humour, the doctors had said, but I was not so sure.

"Sixty-three pieces, sir."

Some of my Armenian friends had arrived. They were on their way to Chris's table, ostentatiously ignoring me, when they saw that Yehudi was winning – at which they stopped dead, scowled horribly and, turning on their heels, marched out again. They were men who believed – fanatically – in order, caste and status. I wanted to ask them if anything unusual was happening in the world outside: could all this be the beginning of some universal peripeteia by which the last would be first, while the first were presented with reckonings that even they would never be able to pay? Had we arrived at the Day of Judgement? – or would it be nothing but judgements, judgements, judgements from now on?

When I felt a double-tap on my shoulder I almost jumped out of my skin but instead of a cowled figure with a scythe it was just another of those stone-faced bottle-blondes. As I left the pit Gray, still standing on the stair, raised his glass ironically: why had no-one tried to intervene?

The Green Room's clock revealed that only an hour had passed. Helen was telling Chris how the whole thing had started. "Yiddo," as she called him, had been alone on Dominic's table, pushing his paltry bets to and fro, when the lights had flickered, the chandelier chimed, and a deep rumbling issued from under the floor. This had only lasted until the ball rattled down into its slot - 29 red. Yehudi, having won two quid, added it to his original stake and won again. This time he let it ride.

"I knew right away what was going to happen," said Helen but I didn't believe her. Life is full of mysterious portents, but we never acknowledge them unless something momentous immediately ensues.

Yehudi had kept on winning, steadily, for an hour or so before he graduated to the columns and splits. After Dom's he had moved to Rhys' table before really getting stuck into Alan. According to Helen, the wheel had begun to speed up or slow of its own accord. The ball was seen to be perching on one of the studs, delaying its drop until his numbers came round again. It was evident that she did not consider this to be mere luck: Yehudi was somehow controlling the entire pit.

"I hope he breaks the fucking bank," snarled a raw-boned brunette I had never noticed before. To my surprise everyone else agreed. This was the first time I had heard anyone speak of a punter without contempt. If even Yehudi could perform such feats maybe there was hope for us all?

"He might be a pro in disguise." Chris shook the TV aerial. "Just hanging around, watching the wheels, waiting for the rookies to come out together."

A strobing picture had appeared: not a newsflash of apocalyptic events but a comedian dressed as Hitler tipping a bucket of whitewash over a ringleted little girl as she sang 'On the Good Ship Lollipop'.

"Yiddo's been a regular for five years," said Helen, "And he's never done anything like this. He plays until he's cleaned out then he goes."

"So he's just another little man" - Chris dropped her wrist and a static storm filled the screen - "Having his one big night."

"I can see how you might make money out of poker or Punto

Banco," I said, "There's a human element - you against the dealer - but how can anyone do it at roulette?"

"There's a man named Kerslake" - Chris gave a thin smile - "Who's been banned by every London club. They knew that he must be doing something, but no-one could discover what. Later he turned up at my table in Vegas. I didn't say anything but ten minutes later Security came and dragged him out."

"Are there many people who've been banned?

"Lots," said Helen. "There's a thing called The Disassociated Persons List but most have asked to be put on it themselves."

"Why would they do that?"

"They haven't got the willpower to stop. Mind you, if they happen to turn up waving a lot of money and insist, then the management can use its discretion."

"What became of Kerslake?" I asked Chris.

"I heard that he's still playing but only in private games."

"But who would go up against him?"

"I don't know - probably those other people who always win."

"My God," I said, "I'd give anything to watch that game."

"He's still at it." Kenny's shining head poked round the door: we did not need to ask who he was talking about. "On to the splits and corners, then he hit 26 again and, next spin, twenty-fucking-nine."

Yehudi's head did not turn when we returned but I could sense his radar tracking me back to Table Thirteen. Up on the stairs Gray was no longer alone but hemmed in by a group of nondescript but unusually well-dressed men. I was reminded of the Classics Comics *Iliad*, where the Gods - blonds and blondes - are depicted sitting in the clouds, watching Troy burning far below.

After my opening spin - ten black with no winners - Yehudi cashed up and led his acolytes across. With his pockets stuffed with chips that dragged the jacket towards his knees, he was moving even more slowly than usual.

He took up a new position, halfway up the table and arrayed his forces. Although still heavy on the third column and section he had deserted his beloved reds and odds and was unloading on 27, 29 and 33, while plastering all the crevices in between. Before him were stacks of orange and green chips – fifties and hundreds – that I had never seen before. I prayed that there would be no higher denominations: according to Chris a select group of punters – friends of Kerslake, no doubt – only used chips smelted from silver or gold.

The next few spins were sighters, as the ivory ball reconstituted its atoms then moved inexorably towards the killing-zone. He was toying with me, hitting 18, then 7, on either side of his 29. It was almost a relief when the lazily rolling ball abruptly caromed off nothing to lodge itself so deeply into the 27 slot that my thumbnail split in digging it out.

Even when he missed his primary targets, the chevals and columns still drove him merrily along. Then it was 29 again, with the ball once more almost fusing with the socket. He did not follow up, however, just stared at his watch, an ancient Timex with a scratched glass face.

At the far end of the table his acolytes still faffed about: when one of them lucked into a small win he almost shrank from the payout – it was as if in order to keep Yehudi winning everyone else had to lose. Now he was plastering the bottom right corner with those high value chips that had the same colour coding as the uppers and downers on which Ed and I used to feast.

There was a maximum table bet but I could not remember what it was: I looked beseechingly at Helen but – evidently frozen with shock – she made no move to help.

"No more bets."

My voice sounded normal even though I was wondering if I might be working for the rest of my days, on one unbroken shift, to pay the casino off. Yehudi breathed on the face of the watch then polished it on his right sleeve. I did not even glance at the wheel until the ball had finished its death rattle descent.

"Number ten, black."

It was miles away – at the wrong end of the table, on the opposite side of the wheel. There was nothing to pay out: my trembling hands were already tearing down the cathedral that Yehudi had built. Even before I had raked the rubble into the chipping zone, however, he had already replicated at lightning speed his previous bet.

Only now did I register how much I had been willing him to lose. I had no problem with his breaking the bank – I just did not want to be the one who was standing there when he did it. I reassured myself that I would not have cared if it had been my own money but with the casino's it was different – a matter of professional pride.

"No more bets."

I sent the ball on its way then closed my eyes. On the red field of the lids a black circle appeared which, as the rattling echoed in my ears, turned white.

"Zero."

I had stuttered on the word but among the general groaning no one seemed to have noticed. This had been my twenty-ninth zero but the first one that really mattered, that I had asked for, prayed for, aimed for and hit.

Now Chris was at my elbow, gathering and stacking the multi-coloured chips. Although her brows were knitted, as if in anger, the way her hip kept bumping against mine must surely have been indicating approval.

Yehudi was blinking again: he yawned, as if awakening from a long sleep. Chris's presence seemed to bewilder him: he had seen her before, of course, but had always ducked away before she could fully register. Now he was turning to contemplate the considerable riches that still lay before him: a hand reached out but then withdrew, as if he was afraid to touch it.

The lights did not flicker, nor did oracular voices issue from the floor but it was evident that everything had changed. Even his acolytes were urging him to leave while, up on the stairs, the Gods had already turned their backs.

Nonetheless, he stayed and watched the next few spins. None of his big numbers came up but I didn't hit zero either. Leaning forward, he plonked a single wheel-chip on black and another on evens.

"Twenty-three red."

He was reverting to his old habits: it was as if the events of the last eight hours had never happened.

"Seven red."

The last of the Gods had left and Gray was descending to The Pit. Yehudi, after agonising deliberations, finally placed one chip on odds and the other on evens.

"Zero."

It was time to go. Half-joshing, half-threatening, they hoisted him from his seat, gathered up his winnings and marched him to the cashiers' window. Someone had fetched from the cloakroom his fabled red metal case. When opened, it turned out to be empty: for all these years it had been waiting to be filled.

He wanted the full amount in cash, but the casino's policy was that beyond four hundred you had to take a cheque. Did he even have a bank account? Perhaps he would just frame the thing?

The last bus was long gone but tonight he would not be trudging along the hard shoulder of Stanningley by-pass. Gray had ordered a taxi: "On the house," he said, through gritted teeth.

As Yehudi left, he raised one arm to acknowledge a smattering of applause. He was limping even more heavily than before but – curiously – was favouring the other leg. The punters that remained at my table had begun casting about, as if searching for his lost luck. A couple were crawling on all fours in case it had rolled under the table.

Although I had finally broken his winning streak, I received no credit.

"You should have dropped those zeroes when you first came on." Gray did not appear to be joking.

I estimated that Yehudi must be taking home the same amount that Ed and I had made from a year of dope-peddling, which hardly seemed fair.

"What will he do with all that money?" Helen wondered.

"He'll stick it under his mattress," said Chris, "And lock the door."

Although it was a Friday the crowd was already thinning out. We closed two tables, then a third, then the whole outer circle. Breaks became longer and in the Green Room they were setting up their backgammon boards: Chris and I, however, had both opted to stay out on the floor. It was pleasant and relaxing – we were savouring the sense of anticlimax. I was even beginning to warm to Wout: those tinny reverbs were teasing my liver and my lights.

There were less than thirty punters in the place when Yehudi reappeared. He entered walking backwards, talking to two new arrivals presumably unaware of earlier events. I saw that he was smoking again – one of those Cuban cigars that we sold at absurdly marked-up prices.

His friends seated themselves, but he continued his curious progress: it was as if he was trying to reverse time, to return to the moment of his last successful spin. I could not see whether he was blinking or not: as he passed, he had turned his head away.

Ignoring Dom, he approached Chris's table: from under her lashes, she had been watching him. The long neck snaked, the shoulders rolled, she stifled a yawn with the back of her hand: it was hard to tell whether she was trying to be alluring or to put him off.

Once again, Gray, with a Coca-Cola stagger, had appeared on the stairs. The nondescript Gods had presumably all gone home. There was silence – Wout's echoes had faded, and no-one could be bothered to replace the tape.

"He says he's come back for his umbrella," Helen whispered.

"Is it raining?"

"I don't think so."

Where had he been? What had he been doing? What on earth could he have been thinking about? There he stood, at the far end of Chris's table, his right-hand pressed flat upon the baize. I still couldn't make out his expression, but the head was wagging so those yellow-crusted eyelashes must surely have been going at it like a hummingbird's wings. He peeled off half of his first bankroll and bought in at a tenner a chip.

They were alone together: even the Chris-fanciers had decamped to the left-handed table from where they could contemplate her bottom as it eerily replicated the movements of Yehudi's pocked and speckled skull.

Now that I was no longer directly involved, I found myself rooting for him but he just kept losing, of course – losing and losing. We should have erected screens around that table: it was like watching an autopsy being conducted on someone still alive. Gray, sitting on the stair, kept fluttering his hands: it was as if he was hoping that someone might take him to be the fateful puppet-master of it all.

After forty-five minutes, when the cash was gone, Yehudi went back to the office window and reconverted the cheque. I subsequently learned that we imposed a 4.9% toll on all such transactions: this was just the sort of thing that I hated – why hadn't the cheeseparing bastards rounded it up to five?

I was now utterly oblivious of my own table – who was playing, how much they lost or won, which sections of wheel and board I might have hit. Chris had been right: I could switch off and let my body take over. At one point it seemed that I had left it and was floating above the mismatched antagonists. If only I could have swooped down and borne them, separately or together, clean out of this place!

A hand double-tapped my shoulder but it brought no relief: I had been deputed to chip for Chris in my turn. She needed little help – everything was coming in; nothing was going out – but perhaps Gray had wanted to render the scene even more dramatic. It was like one of those lion-hunting reliefs from Ancient Babylon – I was driving the chariot while Chris speared, again and again, our wounded, toothless prey.

Yehudi was back on the Mahawats, getting through them in three or four drags: the smoke that went in never emerged again. He had settled on 26, 28 and 29 – the same three numbers over and over, as if he was inscribing them on to his own tombstone. He was betting on every spin, determined to drive things on to the bitter end.

Chris's tempo had changed. Usually, she would speed up when

punters were losing but now she was slowing right down as if to draw out his agony for as long as possible. Yehudi's only response was to double his stakes. His expression never altered but the rest of his body had begun to jerk and spasm: money had disagreed with him – he was about to vomit it back out again. His left hand clawed at the fraying collar of his shirt: perhaps he would strip himself naked then haul himself onto the table while I passed Chris a scalpel and a bone-saw, watching as she began to peel the skin from his face?

At ten minutes past two he finally hit twenty-nine and then, three spins later, did it again. Chris speeded up but she need not have worried. Yehudi had gone to pieces: there was no pattern anymore – as if of their own volition, chips were flying everywhere. It was fortunate that he was not wearing a wig because now the whole head appeared to be in danger of falling off.

Chris administered the coup de grace with five minutes to spare. He was already walking away when the ball dropped for the last time, its death rattle echoing round the almost deserted room.

"Zero." She had pronounced it the French way with an acute accent over the 'e'.

I saw that Yehudi was no longer limping. He had slunk out after winning but now he was leaving like a king. Those narrow shoulders were thrown back, the chin was raised, the mouth was smiling, and his eyes were closed. He resembled our old tabby cat when my mother was scratching behind its ears: I was sure that I could hear a deep and chesty purr.

Helen's hand was on my arm. "Don't go feeling sorry for him." She had me all wrong: the only folk I ever felt sorry for were in Russian novels.

Everyone in the Green Room was celebrating. They had forgotten about breaking the bank, hating him even more for getting their hopes up.

"Have you ever seen anything like that before?" I asked Chris, who was struggling with her zip.

"It was nothing much" – she pushed my helping hand away – "He came to lose and he did" – she yanked the dress over her head – "It just took longer this time."

Helen re-entered, brandishing a cane-handled umbrella.

"He's forgotten it again," she said, "And it's raining cats and dogs."

Everyone seemed to consider this to be the funniest thing they'd ever heard.

"I suppose that's the last we'll see of Yehudi," I observed.

"Oh, I don't know" – Chris's words were muffled as she shook down her hair – "Where else can he go?"

As if to prolong the agony the two of us were deputed to cash up – emptying the table-safes, double-counting the money, then checking the totals with the cashiers.

I still couldn't work Gray out. If he was so keen on Chris, why had he not taken this opportunity to get me out of the way? With the lights dimmed he could have got in close to brush up against her, comment on her perfume, let the wind and rain set in, then offer to drive her home.

It was hard to credit the volume of cash that had been stuffed inside those tables. Who would have guessed that banknotes held in confined spaces would give off so considerable a heat and such sulphurous aromas? Perhaps we were money-laundering for Hell?

After half an hour two security guards entered with their smoked visors down, tripping over things and cursing. The women at the desk had collated our totals: all three tallied exactly. Everyone was eyeing us suspiciously: apparently such a thing was unprecedented – they were always a few quid long or short.

Without a word Gray turned and headed for the car park: he would not be offering us a lift. Rain was lashing at the window, but I saw that Chris had taken possession of the umbrella.

While she was trying to open it, outside on the steps, I realized that we were not alone. A small group of pale-faced women, swathed in hooded plastic ponchos, were clustered below. They stared at us in silence – no, I could hear them humming a familiar tune that I could not place. They were the cleaners, of course, kept out, waiting in the rain, until all the cash was safely off the premises.

They ignored my greeting, but their expressions softened at the sight of Chris. Some touched her coat as we passed but she seemed to be unaware of them. She was walking splay-footed, like Mary Poppins, holding the umbrella high above her head.

Gray's silver Jag overtook us on the road. His head did not turn but the car swerved towards the kerb, aiming for a deep and greasy puddle which it fortunately missed.

"I'm tired." Chris yawned. "I'm going to the hotel."

"OK," I said, "I'll see you later."

Her fingers gripped my arm. "Aren't you coming?"

"What . . . to a hotel?"

"Don't worry" – my voice had evidently revealed my consternation – "You're with me, so they just might let you in."

My family had always been nervous of hotels. On our holidays in Windermere or Whitby we had gone to B&B's – always the same so that it was more like visiting relatives. My father's aversion was particularly strong: hotels made him think of death. It was the shoes, he said, left out overnight in the corridors to be polished – when he was trying to sleep, he could hear them galloping about on their own. Our Paris adventure had been the final straw: although its windows were facing Notre Dame, my parents' room was painted crimson – 'so as not to show the blood' – while I was in a converted broom cupboard with a narrow mattress tilted to a thirty-degree slant. It was all straight out of Edgar Allen Poe.

There was no one in City Square except the Black Prince – or, at least, his statue, sitting astride an impossibly flat-footed battle-charger, its front leg lifted like a dog presenting a paw. According to Ed, nobody knew how the victor of Poitiers, eldest son of Edward III had acquired his soubriquet, being fair-haired, kind-hearted and loved by everyone – except, presumably, the French. The expression on his face – pop-eyed with indignation – was, however, all too familiar.

"What is *she* doing with *him?*" Not even the Flower of English

Chivalry considered Chris and I to be an acceptable pairing.

I had often passed the Station Hotel without taking it in. That sheer white stone facade with its tiny window-slits reminded me of the American Embassy in London, in the futile besieging of which Ed and I had sometimes joined.

The lights of the foyer had been dimmed but a maroon glow indicated the reception desk. A night-porter was leaning back in his chair, head parallel with the ceiling. Waxy-faced, with deep eye-sockets and hollowed cheeks he was either asleep or – more likely – someone had just plucked a dagger from his pigeon chest. With an audible click the sharp prow of the chin descended then the eyes glittered and the lips parted to reveal a full keyboard of black and yellow teeth: the corpse was smiling.

"Good morning, madam," the mouth said, "how nice to see you again."

Without looking, he plucked a room key from his board. Chris did not move, waiting in silence until he had dropped it on the counter between them. His other hand added a bundle of letters with red and blue airmail edgings.

"Would you like to order" – the sandy eyebrows arched – "A breakfast?"

"Two, please – in the room: at six – no, six-thirty."

His eyes rolled towards the Roman numerals of the huge clock above our heads.

"PM." Chris said in the same voice that she used to call the numbers.

He winked at me, but I stared blankly back. His teeth clamped on to the lower lip to keep himself from sniggering.

Although the carpets were thick the sound of our feet – in lock-step – echoed down the hall. Fortunately, the lift was empty: if there had been an attendant, especially one in a dinky peaked cap, I would have carried on through the fire escape. As the doors were closing, I saw that the clerk, now up on his feet, was doing a little jig. Out of a dark wet night there had emerged a flame-haired woman in an even redder dress who treated him with utter disdain – who could ask for anything more?

"What was his name?"

"Whose name?"

"That desk guy'."

She shrugged: "No idea."

His lapel tag – as well she knew – had read 'MR F. FERGUSSON'.

The lift stopped at every floor, but no-one got in.

"Gray keeps on at me to move back here. He thinks you're putting drugs in my tea."

"The very idea!" Although I tried to look outraged the man had been perfectly correct. Ed liked to cut up our THC-rich cardboard roaches and stew them in the pot along with his Tippy Assam.

Chris's room was on the top floor, at the far end of the corridor. I was relieved to find that no dead men's shoes were hanging around.

She had disappeared into the darkness. By some instinct I knew that Room 632 must be large. A TV screen flickered into life while away to the left a halo of saffron light had begun to drift towards me. Stepping forward, I fell over something soft and shin-high – surely there couldn't be a cat?

More lamps were flaring from the walls and ceiling. I looked around, bedazzled, but Chris was nowhere to be seen.

How could you have a bedroom without a bed? There was plenty of furniture and three more doors leading off: I concluded that this must be what they called a suite. The far side was obscured by floor-length drapes which when drawn back revealed two casemented windows: no-one was lurking on the rain-soaked balcony beyond.

The dark wood and gleaming metal, the oval desk and revolving chair gave the room a chilly, executive feel. It looked as if no-one had ever sat on that green leather sofa. Chris's perfumes had left no impression: there was a hot, sweet smell compounded of wax polish and boiling jam. The paintings on the walls were all hunting scenes: three spaniels chasing a mallard, two rutting stags and a kennel of beagles, captioned 'A Well-Earned Rest'. I did not think that these had come from her own collection.

The object that had tripped me was a shoebox, one of many that were stacked two-deep in a line that ran across the room to reach the central and largest door. I was reminded of Carl Andre's firebricks in the Tate Gallery. I had fallen over those too, after six pints of Double Diamond in The Morpeth Arms.

Size 7, high-heeled, black and glossy with little red bows: I returned the shoes to their tissue-papered bed. The identical pair below was sixes and the adjacent gold sandals eights. Perhaps her feet would expand or contract to fit them: Cinderella had nothing on her. Some of the other boxes were empty, unless you could buy utterly weightless shoes.

Cautiously, I opened the left-hand door. The lights were already on, revealing a smallish kitchen, featuring a row of well-stocked cupboards, a two-ring electric stove, a refrigerator and an ironing board hinged next to yet another low-handled door.

MORE TEABAGS
HARDER BISCUITS

Had these familiar notices been left for the domestic staff or herself?

BLACK PEPPER – NOT WHITE
ENGLISH CHEESE ONLY

The one on the kettle read 'SCALE!!' and on the fire extinguisher 'EMPTY!!' which it still was.

The drawers contained enough tableware to serve a small dinner party, but the fridge provided the real surprise. It was hard to believe that Chris had a secret yen for Carlsberg Export, processed Wensleydale and pickled gherkins. I discovered that the ironing-board doubled as a trouser press and that the adjacent door was firmly locked. I had feared that these might lead on and on forever. The lights cut out just before the kitchen's door clicked shut – evidently some magic eye or sensor was involved.

"Chris?"

There was no reply. Now that I had escorted her here, was I supposed to slip silently away? I would be happy to go but I wasn't sure that I could face corridor, lift and Fergusson on my own.

"Chris?" I had skirted the middle door and was slowly opening the last.

"Chris?"

I had stepped into a cage of merciless luminosity. Through my tears I could see that all the walls were mirrored: reflections multiplied and distorted, moving independently of each other and of myself. The light was so solid that I cast no shadow: when I stretched out a hand the glass rippled, concaved itself and withdrew. A loud hum set my eardrums throbbing: were there bees up here or was it the sound of raw, unmediated heat?

It was, as I had suspected, the bathroom. Above its sink yet another notice had been pinned. 'TEETH!' it read. Just like in the kitchen there were no switches or cords, but the ceiling was dotted with tiny lozenge-shaped flares, replicated by others set inside the stippled glass beneath my feet.

The bath was wide and deep, while the toilet, set unusually high, sported steel rails on either side. In front of the silver-curtained shower was a saddle of grey porcelain that could surely only have been a bidet. Yehudi's dripping umbrella – three of its spokes now broken – had been draped across it: what with this and the boxes it appeared that Chris was dabbling in conceptual art.

To the right was yet another door which, unless I had lost all sense of direction, could only lead away from the suite and back out into the corridor.

I stepped through it into a weaker, kinder light. Away to my left was a second television, tuned to a different channel of static.

"Chris?"

She was lying on the wide bed, naked, with her eyes closed. There were no blankets, just a groundsheet with pillows. The headboard was quilted in white and gold and there was even a canopy, green and purple stripes with matching valences.

Now I saw that the line of boxes had carried on into this room then bifurcated to encircle the bed. I had read of enchanted maidens being guarded by fire, thorn bushes or dragons but never by haute couture.

"You've certainly got lots of shoes." I ventured.

"Most were presents" – the eyes did not open – "Much too good to wear."

"So, what do you do with them?"

"Oh" – she could shrug while in a prone position – "I just keep them around."

What kind of person, I wondered, would tender shoes as a gift? Was this what 'women of the world' expected of their men?

Her arms remained pressed against her sides. The pubic hair was unexpectedly black, short but thick like Velcro mesh.

"Do you ever talk to them?"

"Talk to who?"

"Your shoes."

" Do you think I'm an idiot? Do you talk to your books?"

"Of course," I said. "I'd be an idiot not to.""

Now the eyes were focussing on me. "Why are you laughing?"

"I don't know. It sometimes happens in situations like this."

"Situations like what?"

She had me there. I was not without experience but all this – the hotel, the shoes, her skin – was of quite a different order.

"Would you like me to go?"

She smiled and then, opening her legs, began to masturbate. I had evidently said the right – or perhaps the least wrong – thing.

One by one her fingers slid inside while the thumb kept rotating – slow, then fast, then, somehow, both at once. Her wrists were evidently double-jointed for now her other hand was reaching back to twiddle a row of dials behind her head. The bedside light waxed golden while the bathroom supernova faded out.

"It's called a dimmer-switch" – the eyes rolled back – "Neat, isn't it?"

"Yes," I said but I did not really approve. Electric lights ought to be either on or off: any gradations were best left to the sun, moon, or stars.

I elected to hurdle the boxes rather than kick them out of my way but only succeeded in tripping myself again. Nose first I was toppling towards the bed when Chris caught me between her knees, then twisted, so that she ended up perching on top, legs apart, nonchalantly unbuttoning my shirt with the wet heat of her groin addressing my bladder. Her cheeks kept frogging out like Dizzy Gillespie blowing stratospheric notes that could only be heard by bats. I saw that my boots and socks had somehow contrived to remove themselves.

"Do you want this?" On the palm of her hand was a red and blue capsule.

"I thought you weren't taking your medication."

"It's not me that needs it," she said. "They call them poppers in the states."

Amyl nitrate: I split it open and snarfed it up. Good old C_5HNO_2! I did not like to mention that it had never made me randy although it was great for clearing out my sinuses. I extracted a Fetherlite from the inner pocket of my jeans: it had been there for some time. The foil wrap had split but the rubber felt acceptably slimy and intact.

"Don't worry" – she flicked it out of my fingers – "I can't get pregnant."

I could not imagine her bothering with coils or Dutch Caps: she must have had sound gynaecological, zoological or even thaumaturgical grounds for this statement. The pill was already working for thick mucus was dripping off my nose.

"Salty," she pronounced, like an approving connoisseur.

Without further ado she moved over and began to suck my cock, taking its full length without apparent effort. The head rotated, the throat pulsed, and those shoulder muscles rippled just as they did when she was at the tables. Her eyes were clenched shut and she was emitting curiously watery, whispery sounds, like an antique cistern refilling itself. After a while her angle of address shifted so that it appeared to be no longer going down the throat but instead being driven upwards, through the soft palette, cerebrum and hypothalamus, until it struck the inner dome of the skull.

I felt that I should reciprocate – wasn't that what a man of the world ought to do? – but as I was inching into position, I received a hefty whack across my left ear.

"Where do you think you're going?" The gurgled words were perfectly intelligible: I twisted my neck to kiss the dimpled knee that had temporarily deafened me.

The sluicing sounds grew louder. I had lost all feeling below the waist, as if I was sinking into ferrous concrete. The she regurgitated my cock, shook it a few times and, after forcing my knees behind my head, thrust her tongue a long way up my arse. I could feel that all right.

I was struck how, despite such radical intimacies, she had not yet deigned to kiss me. Most of the girls I had known would be snogging away – long and deep – within minutes of being introduced. It meant nothing to them but for Chris first base was apparently her final and most impregnable redoubt.

The mouth resumed its sucking: it felt as if red ants were crawling over my glans, striking tiny flares of formic acid. Perhaps it was as well to defer the kissing for a while.

All this activity seemed to be intended to keep me from ejaculating. If we had just been lying there, talking, I reckoned that I would have come – profusely – into the empty air.

At length she broke off and contemplated her handiwork. The poor thing appeared to have been cryogenically frozen – its head ludicrously swollen, with a curious crystalline frosting around those pouty lips, while the shaft was bone-white, veined with Eton blue and the scrotal sac had tightened as if its balls were trying to retract into my body.

I realized that she was no longer completely naked: hanging off her right wrist was a tiny gold watch that I had never seen before. Its hexagonal face displayed no hour or minute hands, but the seconds were passing at warp speed. Why would anyone wear a broken watch to bed? After the shoes, I knew better than to ask.

As I watched, the hand grabbed my cock again, twisting hard, and then dragged it towards the parted labia which looked to have been touched up with coral pink lipstick.

"This woman's crazy!" – The thing was flashing SOS messages to my brain – "Just get her the fuck off of me!"

"Oh no, comrade," I told it, "After all the tricks you've played, you're on your own in this one."

The cunt's grip was even tighter than her fist's. With a woman of the world like Chris shouldn't it be feeling . . . not slack, of course, but just a little . . . looser? Perhaps there were exercises, drugs and surgical procedures to ensure that every time would feel like the first?

Her movements were at once robotic and fluid: the cords of her thighs were biting into my hips. Although I was ten years younger and rake-thin she was making me feel flabby and old. Her thumb slid out of my arse to be replaced by something smooth, cylindrical and cold: it was as if she was taking my temperature.

A giant spatula flipped us over, like two rashers of bacon – streaky and smoked – frying in a griddle. Chris's ankles crossed at the base of my spine, and she squeezed – hard – setting me wheezing like a clapped-out concertina. Her own sounds – squeaks, growls, hollow clicks and clacks – seemed to be echoing back from every corner of the room: unless, of course, mice and rats were squabbling in the wainscot. Her toes ranged up and down my kundalini column, as if drawing the natural harmonics from the strings of a guitar. It was worse than being tickled – a mixture of pleasure and pain heightened by the threat of imminent dislocation, with every bone in my body trying to slip out of place. The bed itself felt to be vibrating: perhaps she had tripped another of her switches?

"Slow down," she said, even though I had remained pretty much inert. I saw that a single strappy, silver shoe with a long sharp heel was hanging off the big toe of her right – or, rather, wrong – foot. Its fellow was nowhere to be seen. Could this be one of those fetishes that I had read about or was she sending me up?

I had no idea of what was going on. The light was now too bright for me to focus on anything: I had always reckoned that I knew where I was in the dark. If her hands and feet were fully engaged, then whose were those nails so enthusiastically harrowing my back? The ceiling shone like water or glass but showed no reflections – of us, the bed or anything at all. Despite the heat neither of us was sweating: her skin had a greenish, vegetative look while mine was pale and sticky. Dark feathers from the now-eviscerated pillow had applied themselves to my arms and neck.

. . . And now there were other voices in the room.

"Welcome to Introductory Thermodynamics Module Two: Diffusion and Ionisation." I caught a glimpse of a bearded man in a toggled cardigan, scrawling on a blackboard. The day's television programmes – from the Open University – were starting up.

"Consider" – the voice grated and the chalk squeaked – "A soap film is suspended over a wire-frame five centimetres square. The wire is displaced one centimetre by an applied force while the surface tension of the soap remains constant at 25×105 N/cm." His eyes swam behind the inch-thick lenses. "Now determine the work done in stretching the film – in Joules."

I had always ignored such matters: surely no physical laws would ever apply to me? At school and then at college, the arts and the sciences had no connection at all. They were not even antagonistic, more like two vast planets on opposite ends of the universe, perfectly content in their own slow orbits of self-regard.

"Now consider a shaft" – Chris's limbs were realigning – "Rotating and exerting" – She leaned right back – "a torque" – Ouch! – "On its surroundings." My cock and spine felt like the two halves of a wishbone. This was more like a commentary than ironic juxtaposition: Toggle-Beard was taking the piss.

"Diffusion may be defined as the spontaneous intermingling of fluids by the natural random motion of the particles."

There didn't seem to be much spontaneity or naturalness about our embraces. I was beginning to wonder if there was more to love than D. H. Lawrence and the Metaphysical Poets had led me to believe: perhaps a thorough grounding in Fizz and Chem would have been a better bet.

At last – from the cerebellum and the soles of my feet – two great pulsations converged in my groin and I came. I felt to be ejaculating inwardly, as if trying to impregnate myself. Chris had stopped moving – although she made no sound, I suspected that at the exact same moment she had brought herself to climax.

Her face came into focus: its expression was impassive but two large grey-streaked tears squeezed from the corners of the eyes to roll slowly down the cheeks. With my tongue I caught what was surely the taste of my own semen: perhaps crying was her means of contraception? The left foot stretched up and back to switch the TV to a different, still dormant channel. I checked my cock: it was still there, if only just. I felt exactly like a soap film that had been stretched out by applied force far beyond its wire frame. I wondered if Chris could calculate the work done, in Joules.

Ah, the post-coital smoke: I could handle that all right. In among my Gauloises were four tightly-rolled sticks of Temple Ball cut with Halfsver shag. After a couple of drags, Chris plucked it from my mouth. I thought she was coughing at the taste but then saw that she was slobbering, snorting and smacking her lips in what could only be intended as impersonation. It was true that I always liked to share my pleasure when I smoked.

"That TV guy was like someone I used to know," she said. "He only ate beans and slept in a big metal box."

"Did he wear a toggled cardigan?"

"Not when he was in the box."

The bedside telephone had begun to ring with a low, sarcastic double-purr.

"Don't answer" – her mouth was still working away – "It's the switchboard."

Only now had I started to sweat: my eyes were stinging while my hair was like cold wet string.

"Can I ask you something?" She did not reply. "Was this why you brought me here?"

"Yes" – had she actually blushed? – "I can get a bit noisy at times."

"Ed wouldn't have minded: he'd only have turned the music up."

"No, it's the others" – She pointed at the ceiling – "All those men upstairs."

"Don't worry about the Hydra: it's perfectly harmless."

"I don't want them to think that we're" – she paused – "Taunting them."

How her teeth had clashed together for that triple alveolar stop! I wondered whether, like me, she had once been a stammerer.

"But why here? Why tonight?" What I really meant was 'why me?'

"It's my birthday. You've got to do something, haven't you?"

"You should have said – we'd have got you a present. What would you like?"

"Shoes," she said. "A nice pair of Jesus sandals: I've always wanted to be a hippie chick."

She had spoken in a deadly impersonation of Punto Banco Sally's Seacroft twang.

"How old are you?"

"Twenty-nine," she said, with heavy emphasis.

"Coco Chanel stayed at twenty-nine until she hit eighty."

"That's about it."

"Is that why you've got all those letters?"

"What letters?"

"Those ones the desk clerk gave you."

"Oh yes," she said. "That's right."

This was when I knew that it was not her birthday: perhaps she did not have a birthday at all.

The silence that followed was more awkward than companionable. That perfume of hers had a spike all right – having drilled up through the septum it was now probing my brain. At last, her lips parted and – very slowly – she blew a spit bubble. It grew alarmingly but did not pop, hanging there shimmering until it was sucked back inside.

"Any road" – She was reverting to Sally – "You've got what you wanted."

"How do you mean?" I was pretty sure that whatever this might be it was not what I had wanted at all.

"I saw it in your eyes the moment we met."

"You must have misread them."

"How would you know? You can't see your own eyes."

"I was probably looking interested," I said. "I was wondering who you might be."

"*This* is who I might be." Her nails dug into my cock which still showed no sign of wilting: perhaps I should wear box-pleat trousers?

She turned her back then straddled me once more. Her anus felt more like a second cunt. I had never been here before except briefly with Ed – just beyond the tip, before laughter or shame had overcome us both.

I folded my hands behind my head. In the immortal words of Lady Hillingdon, I was going to lie back and think of England.

Waves of energy were rippling down her spine then she tilted back until her face appeared, upside down. The mouth was watching me, but the eyes had nothing to say. The more abandoned she became the less sound she made – she did not seem to be breathing any more. At last, that mouth opened in a silent scream: perhaps she believed she was being noisy through hearing it in her own head?

Sometimes we felt to be drifting weightlessly, at others to be sinking through the mattress – down and down until we hit something hard – probably millstone grit – and were cannoned back to the surface once again.

Suddenly we were out of the bed, moving across the room until a window catch bit into my spine. I realized that my feet were off the ground: she was taking my full weight on her back. Then she disengaged and gripped my forearm just above the elbow and twisted, just like the murderous attendant in "Sardanapalus." My chin shot up, my right hip turned, and I felt her forefinger drawing - very slowly - across my throat.

Back to the bed once more: my nose kept stabbing into the penumbra of a freshly shaven armpit. I was sneezing uncontrollably: Céline had been right about redheads and pepper. Until now I had felt boneless, bodiless, mercifully anaesthetized but now my tendons and hamstrings were cramping up. The left knee locked, then the right, then back again: I recalled how during his attacks of gout my father would claim that he could literally see the pain jumping from one big toe to the other.

I had the curious feeling that what had happened to Yehudi had somehow been the cause of all this. Did Chris feel good or bad about it? Was she rewarding or punishing herself? All that I could be sure of was that when it came to England, I had not produced a single thought worthy of its name.

Although I had not felt it, I guessed that she must have come again because she abruptly pitched my body aside - like a wrestler who has obtained a submission via a Boston Crab - briskly wiped the sheet between her legs and repaired to the bathroom. My inner thighs were coated with an opalescent substance like dried candle-wax - tasteless and odourless - which flaked away under my nails.

Still naked, I tottered out on to the balcony. The air was surprisingly fresh: the traffic fumes did not reach up here in the troposphere. An unbroken stream of humanity was emerging from the railway station to cross the square, en route to offices and shops, giving the Black Prince the widest possible berth. Leaning on the art nouveau rail I felt as if I should make a speech, some stirring call to arms - but no words came so I confined myself to a clenched fist salute.

Down below everyone continued to ignore me: the stone horse, growing tired, had switched its leading leg.

A metal chair and table were chained to the floor: maybe they'd had The Who or The Faces staying here? The bundle of letters was lying on the seat: the topmost envelope had been washed clean by the rain but the handwriting on the others looked oddly familiar. Surely that was Chris's very own unmistakably looped 'C': could she have written them to herself?

Back inside the phone rang twice with a louder, sharper tone. I saw that Chris, having plucked it off the hook, was cradling in her hands that king-sized Swiss army knife. I thought she was about to cut the wire but instead she extracted, with a musketeer's flourish, a white plastic spike and then commenced to pick her teeth.

All the televisions had now come to life. As well as those in the living room and bedroom there was a third set up on an adjustable arm on the kitchen wall. Half a dozen racehorses, their numbers and colours obscured, were ploughing through the Uttoxeter mud.

"Why do you always put the TV on?"

"Habit," she replied. "In the States there's always something to watch."

"Perhaps we should get one."

"You'd only break it." She gestured. "There are beers in the mini bar."

"Do you mean the fridge?"

She winced. "Don't you want one?"

"Not from a mini-bar I don't."

"There's Carlsberg Export."

"Go on then."

She opened its door very gingerly, holding a tray in front of her, as if she feared that gamma rays might enter through her navel.

I was struck by the way that Chris paid no attention to subsequent programmes – not even when Perry Mason embarked on one of his climactic cross-examinations. She only looked up when the adverts came on.

Clement Freud appeared on every single commercial break, always accompanied by Henry, a patient but ever-hungry bloodhound. Chris had been right about his eyes. "Empty," she had said, "not even mean like my dad's – just empty, like a shark's."

By some weird synaesthesia I could even smell him, a mixture of gardenias and rotting teeth. Every time he spoke the words "meaty morsels" his eyelids would flutter. I wondered if he might be thinking of Chris.

"He was always taking his thing out, right there in the club," she said, "And his pet name for it was . . ."

"Henry," I said.

"That isn't even his dog: he rents it by the hour. They only pair up in the studio – he said he was allergic to the thing. We could never work out just why he was a celebrity."

"He's a Liberal MP," I said, "Who appears on comedy quiz shows. His brother's an artist in Soho and his granddad invented psychoanalysis . . . No, I don't get it either."

She told me how he would always arrive at midnight, accompanied by that fat actor who although well into middle age was still playing the Greyfriars schoolboy Billy Bunter.

"Yarooh! Leggo, you beasts!" I squeaked. "Did he wear the chequered trousers and the tiny little cap?"

She nodded, covering her eyes as if to blot out the memory.

To propitiate the Gods of chance the pair would lick their chips then rub them against their groins. Tipping was still permitted in the Playboy Club: they would strew money over the floor and then kick the girls' bob-tailed bottoms as they went crawling after it.

"They used to pinch my nipples then make a honking noise . . . I was a blonde at that time," she added as if that explained it.

"Why didn't the management stop them?"

"They knew Mr Lownes, and they lost a lot of money. Victor used to say that it was harmless banter, but he didn't know how to read people's eyes."

"What can you read from my eyes?"

She examined the left then, more closely, the right.

"Sensitive," she announced at last.

"How about Ed?"

"Lonely . . . but lovely."

"The Luria Boys?"

"Mad."

"What about your own eyes?"

"I don't know" – she gave a thin smile – "I've never seen them."

"What about in mirrors?"

Her smile vanished: "Mirrors always lie."

Perhaps she was right: when she had returned from the bathroom, I had observed that all the figures moving along with her had resembled quite different women. Seated in the single blind spot in the suite I did not even have a reflection. Perhaps some of these mirrors might even be two-way: they had not been hung but were instead bolted into the walls.

'Sensitive': many people had told me this, but I had never taken it as a compliment. I knew that what they really meant was 'weak'.

I had always wondered if I would one day meet a woman who would change my life – the Eternal Feminine in person. I did not know whether, like Dante's Beatrice, she would lead me by the hand to hazy supra-liminal realms or instead – like Joyce's Nora, with her easy peasant sensuality – burn away all my awkwardness and doubt . . . But did you have to plump for one or the other? Would it be possible to combine the two?

I did not think that Chris was this woman: redemption was evidently not what she had in mind. Was I perhaps required to redeem her first so that she could then return the favour? Or were we supposed to do this mutual redeeming together – simultaneously or even in shifts? And how would we know when the moment had come when we could leave off and just begin to live?

Now she was advancing once more with her feet splaying out at unnatural angles, lifting her knees in a curious slow-motion dance.

A half-forgotten snatch of music came into my head. As a child

I was taken as a seasonal treat to a matinee of *The Nutcracker*. In Act II, when the three Arab dancers, heavily veiled but surely naked beneath, had begun swaying to their sneaky, smoky tune I had been overwhelmed by an ecstasy of terror that went far beyond Christmas, scary mice and sweeties.

When Chris came within range, she lowered her head and butted me just above the heart. When I took a step back, she repeated the manoeuvre –then again and again until we hit the far wall. Then the legs parted, and the feet braced as she impaled herself once more. I did not seem to be bearing her weight: either she was wearing suction pads, or her arms had somehow morphed into the plaster.

Were all Women of the World like this? I wondered how Gray could handle such an onslaught when he could hardly bend his knees. I suspected that his vaunted "conserving" techniques might entail locking himself in the wardrobe or tying the sheets together to abseil down to the street.

Chris was no longer silent: clucking, chuckling sounds issued from the back of the throat, while the neck pulsed, and the face twisted and writhed. Ed and I had giggled all the way through *The Exorcist* but perhaps demonic possession wasn't funny after all.

After a while she peeled me off the wall and we toppled back on to the sofa. Her trailing heel had stabbed deep into the sea-green leather: the wounded thing bucked and thrashed around until it threw us off. I wondered whether it would deflate or form a scab.

We rolled around on the carpet for a while – up, down and across until the shoeboxes had been shifted to the corners of the room. Then an invisible hand pulled us back to our feet again and, as if we were pieces in a board-game, moved us on. I recalled how, playing Monopoly as a child, I had insisted on soldering together the top-hat and the iron.

Passing through the bathroom I saw that I had become visible once again. All my reflections were mouthing "Help!" Although I appeared to be carrying Chris it felt more as if I was hanging on.

Her free hand plucked Yehudi's umbrella from the bidet to spear it unerringly into the plughole of the bath.

At last, we had regained the bedroom: I had no idea how much time had passed. When I finally ejaculated the seminal fluid seemed to be drawn from the very bowels of the earth: it felt more like going than coming.

"Suck it out" – Chris ordered – "Then kiss it into my mouth."

When I tried to put this into effect, however, her stiffened tongue began driving it back down my throat. After a long contention I had swallowed half the ichor while she turned her head to spit out the rest. I realized that this had been a hugely significant moment: together we had rolled back time to insert – admittedly under the disguise of felching – that vital romantic requirement: Our First Kiss.

I fell asleep and dreamed of prehistoric monsters. They were pursuing me down endless tunnels of light, while I kept stumbling over what could only have been more boxes of shoes. Chris was running backwards at my side: much to my embarrassment I saw that she was wearing a fur bikini, just like Raquel Welch in *One Million Years BC*. Then the shadow of a pterodactyl fell across us, and I awoke with a cry, but the creature continued its roaring: vacuum cleaners were evidently stalking the corridors. My breathing was shallow, and I could feel the saliva dripping from my lips, like Henry waiting for his meaty morsels.

Chris was sitting bolt upright in the white cane chair, legs apart, hands clutching the armrests, as if awaiting electrocution. She wore a short purple bathrobe, its paler upper half well-bleached by foreign suns. Her eyes were closed but I knew that she was not asleep. As I watched, the left arm rose to press a forefinger to the side of her head and her tongue clicked like a cylinder hitting an empty chamber.

She had taken an evident pleasure in dirtying the bed. Patches of semen and cunt-juice, drool, urine and shit were overlaid by a curious gritty substance like ground-glass or sand. There was also a surprising amount of blood – from pale pink through scarlet to black. Most of it must have issued from my nose and back but those menstrual-looking clots must surely have been hers.

Another double-knock sounded from the door, but it was different from before – softer, interrogative, a servant's knock. The clock said six-thirty: I had never considered the possibility that the breakfast Chris had ordered might appear.

Throwing off the robe she sprang back on to the bed.

"Put these on." She handed me a pair of round-framed dark glasses – the projecting comedy nose had presumably broken off.

"Come in." She partially preserved my modesty with her left knee while utterly sacrificing her own.

A tow-haired youth in a stripy waistcoat entered, balancing a tray on either hand. He resembled a traumatized Harpo Marx. Although he seemed to be fighting off a violent attack of hiccups, his hands remained rock steady as he positioned the plates and dribbled brackish tea into the bone china cups. Chris tipped him with a tightly rolled pound note which, like a magician, she had produced from behind her left ear. Blushing scarlet and jack-knifing at the waist he backed out of the room.

I had always wondered what kedgeree might be – perhaps something Aboriginal, like witchetty-grubs? – but it was only smoked haddock, bafflingly cut with sultanas, curry powder and rice.

There was enough food for five or six: dishes of eggs – scrambled, poached or fried – Cumberland sausages, crispy bacon and extravagantly curling brown or white toast. Chris confined herself to one slice which she did not eat but slowly crumbled into nothingness.

Each tray boasted a small, scented candle. After lighting them she held her left palm above the flame for a full twenty seconds before licking her fingers and snuffing it out. I followed suit but only lasted for five or six, giving my thumb a nasty scorch. With her knife she applied a twist of butter to the burn.

Soon all the plates were clean: even the crumbs had gone. Chris was looking at me in horror but even though I must have snaffled the lot I did not feel in the least replete.

"We can't just leave these sheets," I said. "Shouldn't we hide them somewhere?"

"No-one cares" – she blew her nose on the pillow case – "They'll pick them up with tongs and chuck them in the machines. It's what they're paid to do – it's just hotels."

I was not convinced. I could imagine how Harpo and Fergusson would gloat over our stains – sniffing them, lapping at them, subjecting them to forensic analysis – before adding their fluids to our own. Would they be dreaming that one day they might be able to act just like us? Or of a yet more glorious day when we might be cleaning up after them?

Chris was opening the largest of the wardrobes. Her clothes were so tightly packed that not even a Man of the World could have wedged himself inside. After much struggling, she extracted one of three identical dresses swathed in polythene. I was pretty sure that I had glimpsed – lurking at opposite ends – a third and a fourth fur coat.

Once dressed, she dropped to her knees and with unerring precision rebuilt those walls of boxes. I could tell that she was not placing them at random but following a strict order of colour, chronology or style.

When it was time to go to work, I had to force myself out of the chair. It wasn't that I did not want to leave the room, more that I feared that it would prove physically impossible for us to do so.

Chris had put a 'DO NOT DISTURB' sign on the doorknob: I hung it around my neck. A couple of wide-hipped chambermaids were pushing the linen trolley down the corridor towards us. They were blushing and tittering, but they hadn't seen the sheets yet . . . And tonight, there was an actual lift-boy – or rather a lift-man.

"Ground," said Chris.

He stood between us, legs braced, with an expression of extreme effort on his well-lined face, as if he was personally generating the motor force that drove the contraption up and down its shaft. On the third floor it stopped: an elderly couple made as if to enter but then decided to take the stairs. Lift-man winked at us both, simultaneously.

It was the same when we wafted through the foyer. Fergusson was beaming and waving, while the guests whispered and pointed, their fingers shaking with righteous indignation or the palsy.

"Hotels" – Chris sighed – "It's just hotels."

Outside it was raining again but Yehudi's umbrella was still in the bath. We approached the Casino from a different direction – passing silently through the dank and dripping railway arches with the sixteen coaches of the London train rattling above our heads,

When we arrived, it was without any of our usual displays of affection. We were not even looking at each other: all that had quite slipped our minds. The expression on Helen's face was the same as when she had greeted us twenty-four hours previously. This time, however, the "weird things" were evidently Chris and me.

It was as if we had walked in naked, as if they could read from our faces every detail of what had taken place. This struck me as being against all logic: now that we really *were*, shouldn't they be thinking that we weren't? Gigi turned her head away; Dom's jaw was clicking like a broken doll's; even Rhys and Al had forgotten that they were supposed to be ignoring us.

How could they tell? Chris had been careful not to leave any visible marks on our skin. Did we appear transfigured – like immortal Gods or ageless demons? Or did we just look shagged-out? Unfortunately, there was no-one in the place capable of telling us just what they could or couldn't see.

"You've been pissing us about," – Gray was shouldering his way through – "You think you're better than anyone, don't you?"

Evidently Dom had been talking.

"I don't know," I said, "I haven't met everyone yet."

Rhys and Al were pushing in tight behind him, trying to give the impression that they were holding each other back.

"I can't think why I hired you" – Gray's spittle was spraying my face – "You're just a ginger nutter."

"You didn't hire me," I said, mildly enough, "You offered me a job."

"And he took it," Chris sneered, "And we're lucky that he did."

'IVE

FOR the next week Ed was either absent or unreachably asleep: on his table the markers in the books never moved. When he finally did resurface, all he could talk about was L&L. They were driving him crazy by alternately ignoring him then pretend-fighting each other - "Like kittens up on their hind legs" - above his unresisting form: he could not speak or move without permission. Sometimes they allowed him to sleep in the bath only to steal in and turn the water on - Lori the hot tap, Lorna the cold.

"How I wish I was in a proper relationship" - he whispered in the hall - "like you and Chris."

I did not like to tell him that there was little to be jealous of.

Since Yehudi's exit, we had not returned to the Station Hotel. On Sunday morning, when I went to kiss her, she had ducked away, the flesh of her forearm petrifying under my touch.

"What about last night?"

"It was my birthday . . . It was raining."

"It's raining now," I told her although it was more like mist.

"Maybe next year," she said.

At home we had undressed in silence with our backs to each other. She made no move to join me on the sofa nor did I approach that bed which I no longer thought of as my own. She raised her book to hide her face: grabbing another at random I did the same.

After a while she began to laugh.

"It's Céline," she explained, "He's up in his bloody balloon again."

I had tried to discuss what was happening. Chris had heard

my speculations without responding, looking bemused. Wasn't it obvious that if she had been interested in me then we would never have gone to bed?

How could I have failed to grasp this basic rule of human relationships – that what my mother would call "intimacies" were neither a first step towards a deeper union nor a bit of fun but instead a quick and efficient ejector seat? I might have taken that night to have been a dream if it had not been for the bruises and cuts. My lips throbbed and burned until blisters had arisen at the corners of my mouth – fortunately undetectable, unless I forgot not to smile.

The book I had taken was Voragine's *The Golden Legend*, a calendary history of the Christian martyrs – the Police Inspector's recommendation.

Tonight's Saint was Ursula who, to avoid a forced marriage to a heathen prince, had recruited eleven thousand virginal maidens to make a pilgrimage to Rome. After adding the Pope and his bishops to their ranks they marched on to Cologne which was under siege from the Huns.

"The moment the Barbarians saw them they fell on them like wolves on a flock of sheep and put them to the sword. They slaughtered everyone until they reached Blessed Ursula. Their chief was so captivated by her beauty that he sought to console her, offering to make her his wife. When Ursula spurned him, he let fly an arrow, transfixing her and thus accomplishing the martyrdom."

Evidently her intention had not been to convert the Heathen or to relieve the good citizens of Cologne but to contrive that her own death was staged in the most spectacular fashion possible.

Now that I was laughing Chris had stopped. She was eyeing my cover dubiously – of St Clement, smirking despite the anchor round his neck, being pitched into the ocean.

"You're not going religious, are you?"

"Don't worry," I spluttered, "I am not a boy of faith."

Back at the casino things were changing. The other dealers still cut me but as their heads turned away the eyes would flicker to register if not quite acknowledge my presence. Some people were even talking to Chris - hellos and goodbyes - but only Dominic would venture a smile.

We still arrived and left together but on our breaks we often sat apart. I didn't mind - just as long as she was in my sight everything was fine but when she went my chest would tighten, and I'd begin to sweat. As for her, she seemed mildly surprised to find me still there.

One evening in the Green Room she had marched straight into the ladies' toilet. Just as I was starting to twitch Dom approached and spoke.

"Christine is looking happier."

I could not think of any reply to this.

"Tell me, how's your friend getting on?"

"What friend?"

"You know - that biker who was in the pub."

"What pub?" I finally said. "What biker?"

"That one with a moustache."

"What moustache?"

I was quite prepared to keep this up all night - until we got to "What world? What solar system? . . . What universe?" - but Chris mercifully reappeared, looking neither happy nor unhappy, and Dom slowly backed away.

For some unaccountable reason we found ourselves stuck on a midweek early shift. It was purgatorial: no-one appeared until five o'clock and the seventeen who finally obliged might as well not have bothered.

I kept thinking about Yehudi - of how I was missing him in all his manifestations. Dripping and poking, victorious then vanquished, humiliated yet weirdly triumphant: I felt that I had not yet seen the whole of him, as if he had left us with his secrets unrevealed.

"You know," I said to Chris in the Green Room, "It's really not the same without Yehudi."

She did not reply so I repeated my words. Another silence ensued then - just as I was about to try again - she spoke.

"Who?" She had been muttering so perhaps that wasn't quite it. There had been no interrogative inflection: could she have said 'Huh' instead? Either way I was not going to pursue the matter.

When we at last got outside she turned left instead of right. Although it still wasn't raining, we were evidently returning to the hotel.

As we crossed the square the feet of the equestrian prince were kicking up and out of their stirrups: how had I missed this the last time we passed?

At the entrance she placed her palm against my chest.

"I want to be alone tonight."

"OK," I turned away. "I'll see you later."

I was surprised by the wave of relief that had passed through me. I didn't love her – I didn't even like her – how much better things would be if I were never to see her again!

There was no-one else on the streets: it was as if I was the last man on earth. Even the hospital was quiet, with not a single ambulance heading in to or out of A&E. All that moved were the glowing eyes of the cats in the bushes which didn't blink even when I called 'puss – puss – puss?'

Along Clarendon Road the wind got up: I stopped and stood for some time listening to the trees soughing back and forth.

Although I had heard no music on the street Ed was home. He looked guilty at being discovered sitting at his desk once more. It was piled with new books with yet more propped open against every available surface.

"I have just learned something of importance," he said calmly. "Out in Indonesia there developed a remarkable strain of dwarfism: Homo Floresiensis. They were merely hominids of average size until the ocean levels rose, cutting them off on the new and tiny island of Flores. With resources drastically reduced, survival of the fittest became survival of the smallest: they shrank until they settled at about three feet and four stone, hunting the population of dwarf elephants that that obligingly dwindled in proportion."

"When was this?"

"They vanished twelve thousand years ago but I like to think that we'll be seeing them again, if only through a microscope."

I examined his new texts – on genetics, anthropology, heraldry, animal husbandry: what did all this have to do with Layamon and Brut?

"Don't worry" – it was as if he had read my mind – "Everything will come together in the end."

I went into the front room to contemplate Chris's shoes. Three pairs had been laid out on an altar of nine stacked boxes. I tossed a pale blue sling-back up towards the ceiling then watched it float back down, light as a feather. Although she sprayed their inners with lilac atomiser it did not smell of flowers but – even nicer – of burning toast.

Why had she returned to the hotel? What if she had an assignation with Fergusson, Harpo or the lift-man – or even all three? I closed my eyes and there they were, desperately ploughing away at her, trying but failing to conserve. This vision did not make me jealous: I only hoped that she wouldn't be hurting them too much . . .

. . . Nevertheless, my fingers had begun lacing up my boots: I had to go back even though I guessed that the hotel would not be letting me in. Perhaps I could scramble up on to the stone horse's back to watch and wait for a shadow to pass a window far above? There seemed to be no other cure for my restlessness, this unaccountable feeling of severance and loss.

Carefully, I tiptoed out. I did not want Ed to know that I had gone. In the unlikely event of his quitting his chair he would put me down as having been just another hallucination. After silently closing the front door, I became aware of a dark figure, motionless at the gate.

"A spider," said Chris. "There was a spider in my room."

This seemed odd because she had never shown the least aversion to the cardinals, wolves and pirates that emerged from the floorboards to swagger round our flat. I saw that she had retained enough presence of mind to scoop up more shoeboxes before taking flight.

"We're not going clubbing, are we?" Ed dolefully enquired.

"No," Chris smiled sweetly. "Let's have a quiet night in."

Filing through to the kitchen we scraped out the last of the coffee and sat down. It was quiet. It was night. We were in. The university clock struck midnight, augmented by Holy Trinity and Christ Scientist's coming in on the seventh stroke.

"How nice it is," said Chris as the echoes died, "to be sitting here with my two little priests."

"*Priests of Love*," I said, "Like D. H. Lawrence."

"Muserum sacerdos" - Ed's hands traced a hieratical pass - "High votaries of the Muses."

"Two . . . little . . . priests" - She was really spitting out those t's - "Two . . . Itsy . . . bitsy . . . priests!"

We looked at each other. "Let's go out," we said together.

Twenty minutes later, on the sticky dance floor of Club 'Ush, I discovered that I had now attained the status of Chris's dance partner - for all except the slowest numbers when I had stay six feet away, facing in the opposite direction. I noticed that when I danced with anyone else her eyes would swivel: why hadn't I understood that her prohibition extended to the whole female sex?

Halfway through 10cc's 'I'm Not in Love' I realized to my horror that the head that had burrowed into my armpit was Lorna's, as were the squared-off toes that were hacking at my shins. Squinting through the gloom I recognized Lori and Ed hanging off each other in what looked like terminal exhaustion.

This was just the first of a series of awkward encounters. For the next week whenever we went out Lori and Lorna appeared.

"They think you're following them," Ed told us.

"How can that be, when we're already here?"

"They think you're lying in wait."

"We didn't know that this place existed," I said, "And neither did you."

"Must be telluric force," Ed concluded, "Some of these clubs were built on ley lines."

It was curious how the three of them contrived to be simultaneously in flight from each other and in pursuit. Lorna buzzed around like a trapped bluebottle while Lori's languid carriage and drooping eyelids gave her a narcoleptic air.

"That's not a proper yawn" – Chris demonstrated – "it's to show what a sexy little mouth she's got . . . and she isn't being modest when she pulls down her hem, it's to draw your attention to her bum."

"You're not seeing them at their best," Ed confided at the bar," They get self-conscious."

"Why?"

"They don't know why someone like you is bothering with her."

Whatever I might have responded was drowned out by Hawkwind's "Silver Machine." As we watched, Chris grabbed Lori by the belt and dragged her back out to dance. Their heads were bowed then they doubled over as if fighting their way towards some deadly centrifuge at the disappointing climax of a science fiction film. The lights were on the blink but the couple seemed to be generating their own strobe effects. Chris was alternately spearing her partner's head into the ceiling and jack-hammering her feet through the floor. I thought they were kissing but her mouth was against Lori's ear: what could she be saying? I feared that a forked tongue might come flickering out of the poor girl's other ear.

"Hello" – a heavy elbow dug into my ribs – "We've been hearing things about you."

"What sort of things?"

"You and her" – Lorna pointed at Chris who was now shaking Lori like a carpet – "You're croupiers, aren't you?"

"She is," I said, "I'm only pretending."

"Does it take long to learn?"

"Two weeks training but it's not enough."

"What were the other trainees like?"

"OK – with working shifts I hardly see them now."

Chris and Lori had just contrived to pass clean through each other's bodies, with their atoms recombining on the other side. Ed was hovering but wisely did not try to intervene.

"Lori thinks we know one of them."

"Which one?"

"What are they called?"

"Dominic, Rhys, Alan and Gigi – she's a girl."

"What are they like?"

"Gigi's a gypsy, Rhys is Welsh, Dom's got religion and Alan's got long rubbery arms. Do any of them sound like your friend?"

"No" – she gulped – "It must have been someone else."

The ladies had finally left the dance floor. Lori's hair had spiked up and her mascara had run. She looked terrific.

"Are you OK?"

"Oh yes" – she took the glass from my hand then drained it – "That was fun."

"She's not a bad dancer," Chris conceded as we watched Lori tugging at her skirt once more – "Considering she's only six years old."

"I don't know why the girls always have to leave so early," Ed complained.

"Because they've got proper jobs": Chris made this sound like a disease – serious, perhaps even fatal.

It was fortunate that we did not have a phone. Ed spent hours illuminated in the call box opposite, knee-deep in chip-wrappings and empty cans. Most of the time he was silent – the girls' line was usually engaged – but sometimes he would start yelling and waving his arms, drawing a small but appreciative crowd.

One night, however, we watched him walking back with his arms aloft.

"I'm seeing Lori tomorrow," he said, "And it'll be just the two of us."

"Does that mean she's made her choice?"

"She said I was through to the semi-finals."

"Tell me something," said Chris. "Have you ever met any of these other men?"

"No – but if the phone rang, they'd always take it in their rooms. When I asked who it was, they'd just say 'Wong numbah' in a silly voice. I wondered if it might not have been some Chinese dwarf."

It was hard to keep a straight face to this stuff but in the light of my 'proper relationship' with Chris what right had I to laugh?

At least now it would be just the three of us, back in our old nocturnal regime. Chris and I were about to enjoy our first weekend off – so we decided to do something special.

Ed had heard some exotic tales about the clubs of Batley, a small town fifteen miles to the south.

"All the mills are gone," he told us, "And now everyone's running their own clubs – they've nothing else to do."

"It sounds like Soho," said Chris. I had thought she would cry off but even when it came to sorting out the drugs, she remained surprisingly keen.

"This . . . 'tripping'," she asked, "It won't be like in *Easy Rider*, will it?"

"Not so long as we keep away from graveyards."

"Most acid is cut with speed or strychnine or God knows what," Ed explained, "but this is pure mescaline – a safer, shorter, smoother ride. It takes you up nice and slow, lets you mooch around the clouds for a while then brings you back down without a bump."

"I nearly drank some once," said Chris, "but there was a worm at the bottom of the bottle."

"No, that's mescal – alcoholic, like Tequila, from the sap of an aloe tree – but mescaline's a hallucinogen used in Pueblo Indian rites: the buttons of desert cacti – Lophophora Williamsii – that grow along the Tex-Mex border."

When Ed's fist slowly opened Chris burst out laughing. "I thought they'd be all prickly not just little white pills."

"It's synthetic, of course," he sighed, "Out of a West German lab – the Mexican deserts are a long way off."

We took the pills before getting on the train: just as Ed had promised they had no effect until the journey was over.

Batley Station did not promise well. No-one else had alighted, its other platforms were deserted and the guard at the exit silently declined to punch our tickets.

The road twisted then began to climb. My vision tunnelled while my chest grew tighter. There was nothing to our left or right but up ahead everything vibrated then sharpened in definition as if the grey buildings were enveloped in some locust swarm. Far above, two figures had turned to watch: perhaps they were Dante and Virgil, waiting to induct us into the eternity of clubs?

On reaching the top, however, all that greeted us was the wind. Ed was struggling with a paper scroll: evidently Bilbo Baggins had drawn him a map of the area.

"This must be Bradford Road: now look out for side-streets."

I tried to oblige but my neck stayed locked until Chris's head came floating into view and I found myself counting the pores on her nose.

"Are you getting anything yet?"

"You asked me that already," she replied without moving her lips.

"And what did you say?"

"You asked me that as well."

"Look – teddy-boys!"

Ed was pointing triumphantly, like Professor Challenger identifying flora and fauna in *The Lost World*. A group of men with duck-arse haircuts, in brothel creepers, bootlace ties and drapes, were standing outside a long, low structure resembling an abattoir.

Drawing nearer we could see yet more of them, queuing in the cold. I realized that they were not boys at all but – with their seamed faces, sunken cheeks and paunches – teddy-men or even teddy-granddads. Wasn't it only twenty years since *The Blackboard Jungle*? At least their teddy-women had moved on, now favouring bright headscarves, shortie-coats of white or black plastic, ribbed tights or fishnets and precipitous heels – stilettos only, no stacks.

"A Neolithic burial mound!" Ed indicated a mini-alp rearing up behind the building.

"More like a dunghill." I hated how my voice sounded when tripping: 'snide' was the only word for it.

"What is this place?"

"Do you really not know?" The pupils of Chris's eyes were like pinpricks and sweat glistened on the downy hairs that fringed her upper lip. "It's Yorkshire's answer to Las Vegas – Batley Variety Club!"

There was indeed an illuminated sign to this effect, but half its bulbs were dead and both the 'Y's had disappeared.

"What's she doing with *him*?" The teddy-folk's heads had turned towards us. "No – what's he doing with *her*?"

I knew what would happen next. An arm coiled around my waist, and I felt a sharp pain as Chris – like an unweaned kitten – started suckling my left earlobe.

The men were cracking their knuckles. Although the mills and mines were gone, they had evidently kept in shape: I wouldn't have lasted twenty seconds with any of them.

"No need to queue," said Chris, "We can use our licences."

"You're joking," I protested, "They'll kill us – well, Ed and I, at any rate."

"Don't be silly: they're scared to death because they don't know what you are."

"I don't know what I am either," said Ed.

"That's what I mean. That lot over there" – her fingers snapped in their direction – "know exactly what they are – and what they aren't."

The crowds parted and we followed her. I'd forgotten my temporary pass and Ed had produced a comedy visiting card – 'Sebastian Melmoth' – but the doormen waved us through. I wondered if Chris had given some secret sign.

"How did you hear of this place?" I asked her.

"It's on the club circuit – *real* clubs, not like the ones you go to."

My face must have fallen because she gripped my arm. "No – I mean clubs that aren't about anything except money."

The foyer was lined with signed photos of artistes who had appeared here. Marlene Dietrich, emerging from a gorilla suit; The Bachelors, smiling like an Irish dentifrice advert; Louis Armstrong, sitting on a toilet; Jayne Mansfield, holding a couple of milk bottles next to her breasts . . . There was no indication who would be headlining tonight: I was hoping for The Big 'O' or Jerry Lee Lewis.

The place was huge, cavernous and echoing. Up on stage a grinning pianist was playing high-speed Chopin on a gleaming Bechstein Grand. A teenage waitress in a tiny red dress with matching shoes and knickers took us to a table at the front, just left of centre and then removed with a flourish its 'Reserved' sign.

"Colours," said Chris, "I'm seeing colours I've never seen." She picked up a plastic fork as if about to stab. "And I hope I'll never be seeing them again."

Ed and I went to the bar.

"I'm not drinking Tetley's," I said, "Or John Smith's."

"I wonder if they've got any . . . Red-Eye?"

It was time for our 'Sperry & M'Gurk' routine. We had lifted it from the Hope & Crosby film, *Road to Utopia* in which the pair became gold prospectors, assuming the identities of two notorious killers. Everyone ducks for cover as they stamp into the saloon . . .

"Gimme a shot of Red-Eye," snarled Ed-as-Bing-as Sperry.

"And I'll have a lemonade," I fluted, as-Bob-as-M'Gurk, "In a dirty glass!!"

"Oh no" – the barmaid rolled her weary eyes – "It's that Sperry and M'Gurk again." And there we, thinking we were the only ones.

Returning with our lemonades we saw that a thick-set man in a dinner suit was seated next to Chris. On seeing us he kissed her lightly on the cheek and moved away. His expression had indicated that he knew exactly what we were and was not impressed.

"Who was that?"

"Mr Corrigan: he owns this place."

Corrigan was evidently a popular figure: people were standing to applaud him as he crossed the floor.

"Is he a friend of yours?"

"I've met him once or twice."

"In London?"

"No – in Vegas. When he started this club, his biggest ambition was to sign up Dean Martin, so he came across to meet his agent. When he offered £35,000 for a week – twice what he'd paid Louis Armstrong – the man just laughed. 'That money," he said, "wouldn't even get Dino to wake up and piss." While Mr Corrigan told us this, he was looking pleased as punch – it was like he'd travelled all that way just to be humiliated."

"Why did he open his club in Batley?"

Chris shrugged: "He says he was born here."

The menu was basic: a choice of chicken or scampi, basket served. Chris put down her plastic knife and fork.

"Can I have proper cutlery, please?"

"Sorry, love," was the reply. "It's to keep the noise down for the turns."

It was hard to imagine anything cutting through the pandemonium of five hundred sets of false teeth clacking together.

My trip was proving uneventful with no hallucinations apart from that dorsal fin poking through Corrigan's dinner-jacket but now I was aware that the teeth were trying to communicate some message that I was just on the point of understanding. I clapped my hands over my ears: I did not want to hear any tales that they might have to tell.

The pianist had bowed and left the stage. The curtains – pink and blue and weirdly diaphanous – swished silently across only to re-open, vanishing upwards this time, as a squeaky voice – surely not Corrigan's? – came over the PA.

"Ladies and gentlemen: please give a big Batley welcome to your friend and mine – back by popular demand – all the way from

Kingston, Jamaica . . . Mister Desmond Dekker and his Aces!"

Everyone went crazy when the band burst on to the stage as if the hounds of hell were at their heels. They were dressed in billowing black silk jumpsuits with matching pink belts and boxing boots. Although DD and his two harmony vocalists were smiling broadly the rhythm section looked distinctly underwhelmed. They went straight into "007 Shanty Town," a song that had felicitous associations for me.

"*Dem a loot, dem a shoot, dem a wail – Shanty Town.*"

The teddy-folk had thrown back their heads and in perfect patois were singing along. This explained a lot: I had always wondered how there could have been enough skinheads and rude boys in the country to elevate music like this – with almost no radio-plays – to number one in the singles chart. I'd have liked to get a look at the teds' record collections: where did they stand on Sinatra or Glenn Gould?

The drummer was playing a stripped-down kit – bass drum, snare and hi-hat – but with gigantic sticks that threatened to flatten this flimsy edifice. The neck and body of the bass player's battered Fender were joined together by duct-tape: his fingers were so long they appeared to be drawing notes out of the air. The organist abandoned his buzzing Farfisa and began comping gleefully on the Bechstein – it sounded just the same.

There wasn't a single black face in the audience. Perhaps there was some exchange deal going on – so that, at this very moment, five thousand miles away, a twinned Trench Town Variety Club was skanking to the Brighouse & Rastrick Brass Band.

The musicians appeared to be shrinking before my eyes, growing ever more skeletal, as if they might be blowing away like dust at the end of their set. Why were there no fat Rastafarians? Even the fabled King Tubby had turned out to be as thin as a rake. It struck me that theirs was a religion that would bear further examination.

"Let's go." Chris was on her feet, putting a right hand on Ed's shoulder and the left on mine. Although we hated to leave before hearing "Israelites" we meekly followed her out.

Suddenly there was a huge man – bigger even than Corrigan – blocking our way.

"A . . . lovely . . . tea," he enunciated, slowly.

I tried to sidestep but he was enveloping me.

"Her" – he pointed at Chris who was trying to look 'don't-careish' – "Bet she . . . makes . . . a . . . lovely . . . tea."

"Yes, she does." I wondered if he might be about to eat her.

"Is there . . . cakes?" – I nodded – "Is there . . . jellies?" – I nodded more vigorously – "Do she . . . cut . . . them crusts . . . off the sand . . . wiches?"

"No," I said, "Them crusts are the very best bit."

This was evidently a satisfactory answer because he beamed and hopped aside. There had been no hidden meanings in his words or tone. For this one blessed soul a lovely tea was just . . . a lovely tea.

On the Bradford Road the wind had relented, and the rain had stopped.

"I don't like reggae," said Chris.

"Strictly speaking, it was ska" – Ed always chose the onomatopoeic option – "The offbeat's the same but reggae's slower."

"Whatever it's called it makes me think of insects" – she waved a hand as if warding them off – "Big insects buzzing round hospitals at night."

Although there was no moon the darkness above us was riddled with glittering points of light.

"That sky . . ." – Ed had laid down on his back for a better view – "I don't recognize any of it."

"We are all in the gutter" – I joined him on the ground – "but some of us are looking at the stars." How good it felt to be quoting Oscar Wilde!

"What stars?" By the look on Chris's face, she suspected that they might be insects too.

The rest of the night was a blur. We found plenty of clubs but none of them were on that map. Nobody had even heard of ours: "The names get changed" – someone explained – "to protect the innocent."

The Viaduct was the first we entered: it was halfway down a semi-derelict terrace with nary a viaduct in sight. The music was early Motown but most of the crowd looked about twelve. Perhaps it was the lighting that gave everyone except Chris that sickly, greenish pallor? Only the boys were dancing while the few girls stood by the exit in case the ceiling came down. Most of the dancers were barefoot with some even stripped to the waist. Despite the heat, they shivered while they sweated, snorting and tossing their heads like horses in the ring, and the air was thick with soured amphetamine breath.

"They're like . . . they're like" – Ed was obviously taken by them – "they're almost like they're . . ."

" Midgets?" I suggested.

"No" – he beamed seraphically – "Elves."

We moved on to The Bear's Claw where there were no bears to be seen, only one very stoned girl dancing with a large, headless Victorian porcelain doll . . . Then there was a nameless place at Soothill that did not even have a dance floor just old mattresses lying around. It was more like an air-raid shelter than a club.

The Hook – a disused wool-combing shed, still reeking of suint – turned out to be the biggest, darkest and loudest and there we stayed until the bitter end.

It was like being on some military night exercise, with everyone moving fast and low, weaving in and out of each other without losing speed or stumbling. We had never seen this dance before: Ed reckoned that it must be called The Hook.

Most of the kids in the city clubs had ignored Chris but out here they were outraged by her very presence. Ed and I were the objects of a different sort of hostility: why had we brought our mum along?

As I was leaping up in anticipation of the final chord of 'My Generation', something struck my temple, hard. When I came to, I was flat on my back once more: far above I could see, still swinging from the impact, the dangling hook of a rusted winch and beyond that, through a hole in the roof, Ed's unfamiliar stars, evidently much amused.

"Don't worry" – Chris's face interposed itself – just let it clot." – She licked her fingers – "Did you know your blood tastes like tomato juice?"

I sprang to my feet and rejoined the dance but now in a low-shouldered, hunchbacked crouch. It was curiously satisfying – I was doing The Hook! A few minutes later Ed – accidentally on purpose – contrived to head the winch himself. A deep red furrow ran just below his hairline, but no blood flowed. Ed never bled: if he did then surely its colour would be blue or even gold, like that monk in *A Touch of Zen*.

We looked at Chris. We looked at the hook. We looked at Chris again.

"I'm not doing that!" – yes, she was really laughing! – "Not even with you two!"

We were not surprised to discover that no-one else was leaving Batley on the early morning train. This was, quite inexplicably, sixteen coaches long – re-commissioned dog-box carriages from between the wars. There was no driver in the cab, nor did the engine have a jolly human face like Reverend Awdry's anthropomorphized rolling stock.

Every seat in our carriage had long since shed its springs. The sticky floor clamped my boots, while the ceiling was tobacco-cured to a lovely golden brown. Safe from observation, I took out our stash and rolled an eight-skin of temple ball and sinsemilla which Chris refused to touch.

"You look ridiculous sucking on that thing." She closed her eyes and pretended to be asleep.

It had been an interesting night: I had forgotten most of it already. We sank deeper into our seats: outside a dawn chorus seemed to think it was spring. At length the train jerked, groaned and then set off in what was surely the wrong direction.

After only a few minutes we stopped. Ed was sneezing uncontrollably: Chris's eyes remained shut but the corners of her mouth were twitching. Leaning across, I forced the window to relieve the fug.

I was confronted by a scene of utter desolation. Overspill from a scrap yard had slipped down the cutting to threaten the track itself. Smashed glass, crushed neon, part-melted plastic, rusting harrows of what had once been a Waltzer, jagged fragments of a Ferris wheel: at the top of the pile a gutted ice cream van completed the composition. It was odd how frequently we encountered a funfair while tripping – it was even more bathetic than the cemetery.

All this stuff must have been here for some time, but it was still shifting, settling even more comfortably into itself. Brought together in the press two merry-go-round rides – a lion and a unicorn – were merging into a single creature.

Next to the points was a small metal sign: 'LADY ANNE'S CROSSING'.

"Why have we stopped?" Chris enquired.

"The Lady Anne is crossing," I replied.

This notion enchanted me. One Sunday morning, bored or mad or jilted, Lady Anne had cast herself beneath the flashing wheels of the London express. Now every train running at this hour would pause to allow her silent spectre to cross. She would be beautiful, of course, but only just visible, spookily veiled in a bloody wedding-dress, strewing flowers like Ophelia, attended by a small white doe that wore about its neck a silver bell that sounded 'Ting-a-ling, ting-a-ling'.

"Ting-a-ling," said Chris. Evidently, I had been speaking out loud.

Now figures were indeed moving up the line. There were two of them – big and blue, unmistakably policemen. A third man joined them by falling miraculously out of the sky: a tubby driver had jumped down from his cab.

I slammed the window shut. Fortunately, our carriage door was well above their heads but even if they didn't see us they would smell us all right. I crushed the joint and tossed it from the far window.

Then I dropped to my knees to ram the rest of the stash down the side of the corner seat.

Ed and Chris were staring at me.

"Coppers," I said.

They hit the floor and together we crawled back to the window.

When we had screwed up our courage to peep the trio were standing with their heads bowed only five yards away. The policemen's helmets – for vertical use only – were slowly sliding forward. The object of their contemplation was a grey bin-bag split open to reveal a bundle of newspapers and rags.

Then I saw the feet. The left one was bright scarlet and bunioned, with raised blue veins: it looked like a foot that had seen some drinking in its time. The other, also sockless, was encased in a large surgical boot. This was not The Lady Anne: only a man could have chosen such feet. They did not appear to have been severed, nor was there any gore: perhaps the victim's head was rolling back to Batley?

The men had stepped away and were looking up the line. Capping their view against a watery sunrise, they were evidently expecting someone. Two hundred yards away, beyond another set of points, the track curved into a dark, mossy tunnel from which, on cue, a curious contraption was emerging.

I would have taken it to be the culminating hallucination of my night if I had not heard Ed and Chris also catching their breath. Small and silent and evidently mechanical it was rapidly approaching on the other line.

As it drew closer it resolved itself into a blue-clad railwayman pedalling on a manual pump-powered handcar. Buster Keaton had employed one in *The Railrodder* but I hadn't realized that we used them over here. The driver kept looking over his shoulder as if expecting a black-moustached villain to appear on a similar machine.

The coppers waved enthusiastically, causing him to redouble his efforts. His jaunty railway cap flew off, but he did not stop to retrieve it. The slipstream sent the wings of his comb-over lashing across his face.

Only now did I recognize him. Who else was it ever going to be? Why would we have taken that mescaline if we had not been wanting him to appear?

"Oh my God" – my voice still sounded snide – "It's Yehudi."

Chris and I ducked out of sight, but Ed reopened the window and stuck his head right out. Chris was shielding her mouth with the back of her hand – just like Lori did but I assumed that she was not being flirtatious.

Now voices were being raised in greeting: Yehudi had reached the others. After much chaff and raillery someone started laughing like a donkey: I hoped that this might not be him. To laugh in the face of death is a fine thing but only if that death is your own: surely another's corpse should be treated with respect?

I was shocked at his unexpected resurrection. I had not thought of him as being dead exactly but somehow elsewhere, in an intermediate state – a marginal presence, like Lady Anne, faintly visible both here and in eternity.

"That dead man has just stood up," Ed announced, "And he's bumming a fag off your friend."

The driver's door slammed and the train, smoothly and silently this time, began to move.

"The dead man is dancing," said Ed.

I rejoined Chris but Ed stayed at the window, waving farewell.

"What are you doing? You don't even know Yehudi."

"He started waving first."

I was still groping for the stash when we were plunged into darkness. Last night the passage through Morley Tunnel had gone unremarked but now, even though the train was picking up speed, it seemed as if we might never re-emerge.

"Was that really him?" I asked Chris.

"I didn't see anything." The whites of her eyes were flickering in the darkness.

"He doesn't look much like Menuhin," came Ed's voice, "More like Stephane Grappelli."

A whistle blew and once more the carriage was flooded with light. I tore out the cushion and the last of the wadding but there was no sign of our drugs, only the wood and metal of rails and sleepers rushing past below.

"Ting-a-ling," said Chris.

⚜

"Dwang-dwang-dwang-da-dwang!" – Kenny's round head was filling my vision – "Da-dwang-da-dwang-dwang-dwang-dwang! Sorry, old son!"

Looking down I saw that he was handing back our tapes.

"We've had complaints: no-one round here wants that miserable stuff. This isn't London or the Big Apple or Gay Paree – things are bad enough already."

His face split into a huge smile: "We're keeping those surfing ones though." He took up his air-guitar again: "Da-dwang-da-dwang-dwang-dwang!"

"Never mind" – Helen was taking her victory with good grace – "You'll never guess who's in tonight."

"Lord Lucan," I suggested, "Riding Shergar."

"No, it's your pal Mr Ratledge."

"Who?"

"I think you call him Yehudi" – she smiled thinly – "He hasn't started playing yet, he's up in the bar with Mr Gray."

"What did you say was his proper name?"

"Ratledge: that's a rat" – she pulled a mean and toothy face – "and a ledge" – she backed up against an invisible wall, like a suicide preparing to jump.

"He's back," I said to Chris, "and it's all Ed's fault."

"That wasn't him yesterday" – she was applying the final layer of fixative to her hair – "and anyway he couldn't have seen us in that carriage."

"Perhaps he smelt us."

Out in the pit the echoes of Wout Steenhuis' Jutland Wipe-Out had faded, only to be succeeded by something even worse: Sinatra's version of Roger Miller's "Ing-er-lund Swings"

Help me! Help me! You could hear the desperation in Frank's voice but Ing-er-lund just kept on swinging like a hanged man at the end of his rope.

On my opening spin an elderly man slapped a chip down well after the ball was in its slot. Everyone just laughed but then with no attempt at concealment he did it again on the next, with two other punters joining in. My own calls of 'No bet!' were being echoed by Chris and the others round the room. After the third spin they all desisted. The pit-bosses had not intervened: this had not been a serious attempt to cheat, just another joke that I did not get.

I had not seen Yehudi descending from the bar: he just materialized at a table on the far side of the pit. He was dressed as usual, with his head cocked at its customary angle but there was something different about him. It was a while before I realized that he was now wearing glasses: perhaps yesterday's ride on the handcart had jarred his optic nerves? Thick-lensed, heavy-framed and almost square, they resembled those X-Ray Spex advertised in Marvel Comics. For just a few dollars you could see women naked without them suspecting a thing!

In the next few hours, he visited every table except for Chris's and mine but whenever I looked across his eyes were flicking between us. When he saw me, his right hand rose and, like a glove-puppet, gave a little wave. Other punters were wary of him. One of the Chinese touched his shoulder – so lightly that he did not notice – then ushered his own party to a distant table.

Although he had reverted to dribbling and piking, I saw that he now used £5 chips instead of the minimum stake. Perhaps he had been pulling heavy overtime out on the tracks? During our break Helen told us that on every fourth spin he would switch from red to black and from odds to evens every eighth. If he doubled up and won, he would immediately decamp to the next table. During the night his chips grew to a full stack then two. Previously he had been playing merely to remain . . . then we had watched him win big and fast . . . only to lose it all even more quickly . . . but now he was different, shrewdly accumulating through some cockeyed system all his own.

I did not see him leave but at ten past two he wasn't there. I had been so focussed on his presence that I could not recall what had happened at my own table except that there had been a high incidence of zeroes: could that have been what was keeping him away?

"I'm tired." Chris was struggling with her knee-boots. She could never quite cinch the topmost buckles but would never let me help.

When we stepped outside, she checked both ways before descending the steps. After we had turned the corner, she stopped and put her finger to her lips. There we stood for fully two minutes as the silence grew deeper: evidently no-one was following.

"I'm going to the hotel" - she took my arm - "I need to check something."

I had expected to be left at the door, but her grip tightened, and she drew me inside. As before, the clerk was asleep but now his cheek was resting on the desk: tonight, the knife must be sticking in his back. His head came up in jerks, as if a fishing-line had snagged his upper lip, to reveal not F Frederickson but a cove with an even deathlier pallor and a sharper widow's peak. I could not read his name - the tag was upside down - but it contained at least three F's.

"Will it be the usual" - his throat cleared - "breakfast . . . for madam and sir?"

"No," said Chris, "Kippers at six-thirty." She made these sound like her weapons of choice for a duel. Personally, I would rather have been shot than see that kedgeree again.

The lift was empty, and our ascent was fast and smooth, depositing us almost opposite Chris's door. The corridor seemed shorter and the ceiling lower: it was as if the place was shrinking. Inside the room there were fewer lights and mirrors. One of the three TVs had gone. The furniture was dingier and worn, and after I'd jumped to touch the mini chandelier a thick dark dust coated my fingertips.

I followed her into the bedroom: she was wiping off her lipstick with the back of her hand. There was no trace of the spider that had terminated her last visit, nor did she seem worried that it might return.

The bathroom's floor and ceiling lights were dimmed. To engage with the washbasin, I now had to bend my knees. Looming out of the mirror was something resembling the missing link.

Chris had already undressed and was lying on the bed. With her right leg bent and the foot folded into the opposite thigh she resembled one of those mimsy modernist sculptures that you trip over in London parks.

"Do you remember that photo in Batley – the blonde who died in a car crash?"

"Jayne Mansfield," I said.

"Well" – she thumped the mattress twice – "This is where she slept when she played the club."

"Jayne Mansfield slept in this very bed?"

"Not exactly – she had these lapdogs that weren't house-trained, so everything had to be burned."

"We always liked her," I said, "My dad said she had the sweetest eyes he'd ever seen."

"She came on stage and recited Shakespeare then played a violin: everyone jeered and threw things. So, she took her hair down and undid some buttons then went back out and wiggled around, sitting on laps, nibbling ears and talking dirty. When she crushed an old man's head between her tits the whole place went wild."

"What Shakespeare did she do?"

"Hamlet and that."

"Did Mr Corrigan tell you this?"

"No" – she smiled – "Someone else. She'd gone on a European tour to escape from a Satanist group in LA: she hadn't known that Jim and Betty Corrigan were devil worshippers too."

I thought of Jayne in *The Sheriff of Fractured Jaw* – majestic in gingham, driving a buckboard, while serenading Kenneth More – Douglas Bader with legs! – with the sweetest, soppiest song you'd ever hear.

"Most blondes come to a bad end," Chris continued. "And brunettes get sadder and sadder, but we redheads just keep rolling along."

"Stinking of pepper" – I sniffed but I had lost all sense of smell. She switched off the bedside lamp: all the others, circuited together, went out in sympathy.

My hands moved through the darkness towards her.

"Not tonight," she said.

"How can you see without lights?"

"I don't need light to see . . . obvious things."

"What's wrong with obvious? Do you want me to be sneaky?"

"Once, at the Playboy Club, Mr Lownes got me dealing in the dark – just to see whether I could do it."

"And could you?"

"Of course not!" – She chortled, as a flying elbow struck the side of my head.

"Not tonight," I said.

Shutting my eyes, I listened to that slow but regular breathing. The tide came in, paused, then went out again, came in and went out.

For the last month she had hardly left my sight, but I was wondering about that training week. Perhaps she had spent those nights fucking everyone that she was required to fuck – just to get it out of the way?

Now I could not hear her breathing anymore. As I was turning over, something hit me hard in the face: maybe it was that pesky hook again? My mouth was filling with blood, I was choking . . . Then the lights came on to reveal that Chris, her left fist still raised, was sitting on my chest.

"You punched me!"

"No, I pushed you" – her fist opened, then closed again – "There's no knuckles in a push."

"Punch," I insisted.

"Push: you were snoring."

"I wasn't even asleep."

"Your eyes were shut."

"I was . . . resting."

"Shamming: you were watching through your lashes."

She rolled off and I spat on the pillow. There was no blood, only yellow-brown froth. All teeth were present and correct, but my tongue felt to have been pebble dashed.

"I don't sleep much," said Chris, "But when I do I do it properly – like a log, like a baby, like a corpse."

"If it's snoring you want you should try my dad."

"I don't want to try anybody's dad" – she feigned a second, mortal blow – "Thank you very much."

Lightly, I ran my fingers across her inner thighs, but she did not react. The left felt different to the right – sticky, with a slight abrasive cling. Dark grains, glistening like mica, seemed to be moving under the skin.

"What's this?"

"It was when my clothes caught alight" – she smiled – "In a toilet on a train."

"How did that happen?"

"Someone put a match to them."

"Why?"

"I can't remember – it's just what kids do."

A silence fell. The pain was now retreating behind my left ear.

"Can I ask you something?"

"More questions?" She thought about it. "OK – just one."

"What is it about you and 'F'?"

"Me and who?"

"The letter 'F'." My forefinger traced it in the air.

"It looks so ugly," she said, "Nasty, not right, like it's been . . . amputated or something. At school they made us draw it like a money sign: the way you did it just then was better."

"As a capital?"

She nodded. "I don't like how it sounds. When people say it they show their teeth like rats" - she demonstrated, silently but convincingly enough - "and then their breath hits you - hot, wet and crawling with germs . . . It smells even worse than it looks."

"How old were you when you stopped using it?"

"Very young."

"Did you tell anyone?"

"No."

"What did your teachers say?"

"Them?" - she made the rat face - "They never notice anything."

"Did anyone else ever notice?"

She shook her head. "You've had six questions."

"One question and five supplementaries," I said.

"Now I really AM tired" - she lay back. "I'm going to sleep like a log, like a baby, like a corpse."

She had counted these off - 1-2-3 - on her fingers.

I followed her but she did not figure in my dreams. Strong hands were dragging my broken body across cobblestones towards a fridge that was the size of a cathedral . . . but fortunately my feet would not fit through its door.

When I awoke my mouth was full of biscuit crumbs and I could hear a faint rustling sound. It was light enough to be able to see the obvious things: Chris was no longer beside me but crouching by the window, holding up a black kitten-heel as if it were a phone. I could not tell what she was saying for I did not speak the language of shoes.

I slept until all the lights went on together, revealing that the room had reverted to the dimensions of our previous visit: it was as if our breathing had somehow re-inflated it. Chris was busy tuning in the televisions: the third set had reappeared.

When breakfast appeared - at six thirty on the dot - it was just the same as last time.

"Where are my kippers?" I demanded but I had evidently used

up all my supplementaries. Céline was propped against Chris's tray, so I opened my Voragine and got stuck into the kedgeree. Perhaps "kippers" had been some sort of code?

"So who's the Saint today?" Chris asked when we had finished eating.

"Elizabeth of Hungary - she's one of the longest entries."

"But I KNOW her!" - she was clapping her hands - "I know all about her!"

Springing to her feet she struck an oratorical pose.

"She healed the sick and helped the poor and let the lepers into her castle." Her voice rose way above alto, steady and pure as she began to sing.

"She is a saint, and she is a *Queen/ May she rule over us in joy/ There never was a better seen/ 'Twixt Paris and old Cathay!*"

She had snapped her fingers to emphasize 'Twixt and changed Cathay's second A to an O to make it rhyme. Arms stretched wide, eyes round, cheeks aglow she looked about five years old.

"Did Lownes or Corrigan tell you about her?"

"She was in *Girl Annual, Number 7*" - the eyes grew even rounder - "And there was Helen Keller - she was blind - and Lottie Haas the explorer - she was a blonde - and Mrs Pankhurst."

"What did she do?"

"She scowled until she got a vote."

"The Blessed Elizabeth," I mused. ". . . Tell me, what did you make of Master Konrad?"

"Who?"

"The monk who was appointed as her spiritual adviser: the more she prayed and fasted the more he punished her. After all the miracles she wrought and privations she endured he whipped her even harder to drive out the sin of pride. He sacked her faithful maids and replaced them with bitter nuns who hated her. Does your Annual relate the story of Radegund?"

Chris shook her head.

"She was a local girl who loved dancing, famous for her beautiful hair. When she came to visit her sister in the newly built hospital she was seized and dragged before Elizabeth who personally shaved her head and told her that she would never dance again."

"What did Radegund do?"

"Thanked Elizabeth, praised God and joined the nuns."

"What colour was her hair?"

"Voragine never distinguishes between blondes, redheads or brunettes. All his women are beautiful at the beginning and saints at the end."

"Perhaps there's another Elizabeth - it's a common name."

"I fear not: the earlier parts broadly tally with *Girl Number 7's* account."

"Let me see that." Her face fell as she read. She tugged at the pages then held them up to the light as if I might have forged a Penguin Classic ready for a moment such as this.

"Did you know that she died at twenty-four?" I enquired. "In agonies of the body but ecstasies of the soul - apparently you can't have one without the other."

"That Master Konrad" - Chris frowned like Mrs Pankhurst - "I suppose he lived happily ever after."

"No - a month later he was hacked to death in a forest."

"Serves him right!" She clapped her hands again.

"It wasn't to do with Elizabeth, I'm afraid - merely part of the struggle for power in the intestines of the Catholic church. Ask Ed about it: they were all as bad - or as holy - as each other."

Chris stormed into the bathroom and locked the door. She did not emerge until it was time to leave thus ensuring that while she was immaculate, I looked more dishevelled than ever.

"That was nice, wasn't it?" She said as we waltzed through the foyer.

"What was?"

"Being back here."

The other guests had evidently held a meeting to decide on their position regarding our presence . . . but how can you ignore people when they are already ignoring you? And what is the point of turning your heads away if you're leaving your eyes behind?

That evening Yehudi continued to pursue his new strategy with some success. He even chanced the Punto Banco table, sitting with his hands extended as if anticipating a manicure. According to Sally he had little idea of the game: when she paid out, he'd look surprised, and if she didn't, he'd curse under his breath. "Even my granny can count up to ten," she sneered.

He had moved to stand opposite me for a few spins, avoiding my eyes: all he wanted was for me to watch him watching Chris.

The other croupiers no longer made faces at him or guyed his plunging walk: he scared them now. "I don't like the way he looks at me" was the common complaint even though he only had eyes for us. These were growing ever larger behind their thick lenses until he resembled an enormous fish glaring out of its silted-up riverbed.

I had once known someone who had bought a pair of X-Ray Spex: he informed me that they had been a con.

"You amaze me," I said.

"No, no. You can look through women's clothes all right but then you go straight through the flesh right down to their bones so all you can see is lots of skeletons walking around."

Yehudi continued his stately crawl until one-thirty when he doubled up and won, then doubled up the double-up and won again at which point he left as if the Hound of Heaven was at his heels.

"I think he's still mad at you," I said.

"Why?" Chris did not need to ask who I meant.

"Because of the money he lost at your table."

She reached over to the TV aerial. "How could he lose anything when he had nothing to begin with?" At last, the test card came into perfect focus.

I thought back to Yehudi's Big Night. It was surely significant that although all his winnings had come from men he had switched to her table after his first serious reverse. Perhaps when a man fears that things are going wrong, he needs to find a woman to blame. I wondered whether Master Konrad – while they were disembowelling him under the elms – was consoling himself that it had all been that Elizabeth's fault.

On leaving the casino Chris made for the taxi rank.

"Aren't we going to the hotel?"

She shook her head in evident disbelief: did I really want a second push in the face?

Every club I suggested elicited no response: the driver was taking us straight home.

Our windows were dark, and no music was playing but there was Ed, sitting on the doorstep. He had evidently been waiting for us.

"Look at this! Look at this!"

He was brandishing a large white invitation card. At the top right corner, a fat-cheeked angel was sounding a trumpet while sitting bottom left was a monocled Dachshund in a top hat.

"It was there on the mat when I got in: no stamp, hand delivered."

Under the street lamp I traced the silvery letters:

LORI AND LORNA

REQUEST THE PLEASURE OF YOUR COMPANY

AT THEIR GREAT

D-DAY PARTY

—— "THE BIG REVEAL" ——

SUNDAY 27th NOVEMBER

EIGHT UNTIL LATE

DRINKS AND NIBBLES

RSVP

In the margin someone had scrawled "To Ed and pals!" with a smeary felt-tip pen.

"When I was on the phone to Lori today, she never said a thing."

"Have they really got a dog that wears a hat?"

"I can't remember. What do you reckon that D stands for?"

"Defenestration?" I suggested.

"Death," said Chris, "Or the Devil."

"I think it must be *decision* – that they're finally going to announce their choices. In last night's paper their ad was no longer there. Lori's mind was made up long since, of course, but she's been waiting for Lorna."

"Yes, I can see how Lorna might be a bit" – Chris paused, lethally – "Choosy."

"Do you know how many responses they got?"

"Quite a lot, I think."

"Hundreds?"

"Thousands?"

"Every lonely man in the world?"

We looked up the darkened stairwell towards the shadows of The Hydra, silent on its landing.

"Well," I said, "I hope it all goes off OK."

"Aren't you coming? You're invited too."

"Are we supposed to be these . . . pals?"

"Why not?" – Chris sucked in her cheeks – "Can't I be somebody's pal?"

"We're working on Sunday," I said.

"No, we're not: they've changed the rota."

"Do you want to go?"

"Drinks and nibbles" – she flexed her taloned fingers – "Too good to miss."

We each took an arm and carried Ed off to clubland where Chris danced with him for hours. She even went in close for the slow numbers. Although she kept kissing him her eyes were always on me: I grinned maniacally and gave the thumbs-up.

"There's just one thing," said Ed as we crossed the park. "You don't think that Lori and Lorna might have invited all the . . . failed applicants, do you?"

"Of course not" – Chris laid a reassuring hand across his forearm – "Why would anyone want to do that?"

When we got to work Gray took me on one side.

"So" – his manner was grotesquely avuncular – "How's it going then?"

"OK": without meaning to I had yawned in his face.

"I'm sorry you find us boring."

"That's OK."

This really set him off: "You think you're hard, don't you? Well, you should have seen the boys that used to come in here – they'd have parted your hair for you."

"I'm not hard" – I was resisting a second yawn – "I'm plasticine . . . putty . . . a real pussycat."

He flinched and moved away. Perhaps this had been the sort of thing that really hard boys would say.

In the Green Room I discovered Chris talking with Dom and Rhys who left even before I went into my broken-stringed puppet routine.

"What was all that about?"

"All what?"

"Nattering away to those two."

"I don't . . . natter."

"OK – chattering, yacking, yarning, chin-wagging, shooting the breeze, slinging the goss . . ."

"I don't do them neither." She stalked out: if she had possessed a tail, she would have been swishing it. When I turned, I found myself sinking into the fathomless depths of Gigi's dark brown gaze.

"So, how's it going, then?"

Overtures were certainly being made. I danced like the puppet until she went away.

Yehudi was already out on the floor, poised at the far end of Chris's table. I expected him to retreat but he didn't: every time I looked, he had edged a little closer. It was amazing how much older he was looking: a shadow of the man who had burst from the tunnel a few days ago.

After a while he had worked his way up to the top of the table, but he was still looking at everything except her. The left eye was sweeping low, while the right kept checking that the ceiling was still in place. Then I twigged that her image must be reflected in the curving upper and lower rims of his lenses, allowing him to focus with microscopic clarity on every pore and follicle, every tiny freckle or scar.

Now Helen was whispering in my ear. "You're getting pretty good." Once again, I had been paying no attention to events on my own table.

"I like how you slow it down every fifth spin, so they start over-betting then crank it up again . . . but don't let on that you know you've got them . . . and try to smile a bit more."

My face twisted into a horrible leer.

"Perfect": she leered back.

Although I had not been aware of new arrivals the floor was now packed. Chris was no longer visible, but cheers and groans were sounding from that direction: someone was either riding a rail of freakish luck or committing hari-kari in slow motion. Every table was open so there was no slack to take up: we worked flat out for five hours with a single ten-minute break on which Chris and I did not coincide.

"Hotel tonight," she said as we passed each other. Her tone indicated that we might be dynamiting it rather than sleeping there.

"So how did it go?" I was buckling her left boot at the end of our shift.

"He was up thirty-two quid," she said grimly. I did not need to ask who she meant. While great waves of cash had been breaking over her table, she had been focussed on Yehudi's pickings and pokings . . . from black to red, from evens to odds and back again.

There was very little conversation during this, our third night in the hotel. When I spoke, she ignored me and, if I persisted, clapped a hand over my mouth. From the moment we entered the room she had made it clear that we were reverting to sex.

The same things happened in roughly the same order. The strappy shoe and the broken watch were much in evidence: on subsequent nights I never caught her putting these on or taking them off. Sometimes the dangling shoe would cross from one big toe to the other and once I thought that the hand on the watch had moved from ten past to twenty to, but it was merely upside down.

At first, we confined ourselves to the bed. Whenever Chris tried to pitch me off the mattress would tilt and stretch itself to hold us. For reasons that surely went beyond exercise or pleasure she was changing positions even more frequently than before. I suspected that there might be thirty-six of them: some red, some black, some odd and some even – whatever would happen when she finally called 'Zero'?

She was making a lot of noise, but I was sure that whenever she *did* come she still fell silent, biting her lips and turning her head away. She must have learnt how to render herself weightless for sometimes her body would flow over me like water . . . but mostly it was all bone, as if she had now clenched herself into a single fist.

"Did you come?" I enquired.

"I don't like that word."

"Climax? . . . Orgasm? . . . What do you want me to say?"

"Ask me whether I popped my cork."

"Well, did you?"

"Did I what?"

"Pop your cork?"

She blew out her cheeks and then, after licking her forefinger, popped first the left and then the right.

Something about all this had reminded me of a light-engineering factory where I had once worked. It had been full of bustle and heat and noise but not even the foreman had known what it was that we were making. I had the feeling that at the end of each shift a procession of small metal spheres was silently following me home.

As dawn broke the bed finally capitulated and Chris began to ride me round the carpet. Sometimes we would half rise to negotiate table or chair but only after we hit the wall did we return to the vertical.

At the end of each subsequent bout – taking in bathroom, kitchen and hall – I would find myself lying at her feet as if to acknowledge just who had won. All I could see of her face was that line of jaw and chin: she never looked down until my head was back between her legs.

Finally, without a word, she walked into the bathroom, slamming then locking the door. I decided that it was now time to take stock of the situation.

"Well, is this what you were expecting?" I asked myself.

"I wasn't expecting anything."

"What do you think is really going on?"

"I don't know." Through the door there came an indistinct murmur: Chris and the shoe were also in conference.

"What's going to happen next?"

"Search me," I said.

These were the only answers I had ever come up with. It did seem likely, however, that visits to the hotel had all depended on Yehudi – whether he had been absent or present, whether he had won or lost. Was I here as a protection or a consolation? Was I her punishment or reward? What I did not like to contemplate was the possibility that I might be standing in for him.

All three TVs had been turned back on at even higher volumes. From the Open University I learned more about thermodynamics, Cromwell's Long Parliament and upland irrigation: their Russian course was teaching a wildly different language to the one I had failed at 'O'-level. During the afternoon's advertising breaks we would look up to see Clement Freud eyeing us with evident distaste while Henry's paws came poking through the screen.

In the early evening we found ourselves athwart the WELCOME mat, tonguing each other's anuses. While I puffed away like a tuba-player her embouchure flickered round my ring like Clifford Brown playing 'Cherokee'. Without knocking, a wan chambermaid entered, carrying our breakfast: she casually stepped over us as if we were playing Ludo. Although I had not smelt them there turned out to be nothing but kippers on the plates.

That night Yehudi finally broke his silence. For hours he had been neither winning nor losing with each bet cancelling out the previous one: even when he uncharacteristically ramped up his stakes stalemate immediately restored itself.

At eleven thirty those dry lips cracked open and began to whisper. Although he was still not looking at Chris, he could only have been speaking to her. Through a gap in his teeth, I could see a yellow tongue tapping at the soft palate.

There was a good crowd in – many were celebrating some anniversary – but the rhythm of his words if not their sense was audible across the room. Soft but insistent, as if the speaker had no need to pause for breath, there was something familiar about it: Yehudi also spoke the language of shoes.

"What's he been saying to you?" I asked Chris on our break.

"Who?" Her head lolled as if I'd asked her to name the lost tribes of Israel in alphabetical order.

"Yehudi, of course."

"Nattering, chuntering" – she had not forgotten yesterday's exchanges – "I just ignore it."

Opening her book, she stabbed a forefinger into the page. Leering out from his back cover, Céline was about to say something but then decided against it. Just like Christians with their bibles and Muslims the Koran, she appeared to use it as a means of random divination: after tracing a few lines she snapped it shut, frowning as if her worst fears had been confirmed.

When I tried it with Voragine I got St Mary of Egypt. She was a reformed prostitute who followed an eremitic regime, surviving in the desert for forty-seven years on just three loaves of bread. She did not just survive, she thrived, levitating at will to cross and re-cross Sinai at twice the speed of sound. When I tried to share this with Chris, however, she did not find any relevance to our present situation, and she did not find it funny at all.

On our way back to the Pit we passed Yehudi standing at the cash desk. He was silent and looking more relaxed: I guessed that he had started losing again. The cashier was presenting him with a fresh stack, but no money seemed to be changing hands. According to Helen only thirteen punters had been granted a credit account and four of these seldom came in. It was curious that this privilege had been extended to a railway worker who carried his thermos in a red tin box.

For the rest of the night, I was out of whispering range but from the angle of Yehudi's head I guessed that the chuntering had not stopped. The other punters seemed unconcerned: they were too busy losing while his new stack had been joined by a second then a third.

As he was leaving – later than usual, well after two – I saw that his eyes were no longer swimming about but had settled and focussed at the dead centre of those lenses. He was not looking at Chris, however, but at me. Slowly, unmistakably – I could have sworn I heard a click like a camera's shutter – the right eye winked.

It was our cashing-up night, so we did not reach the hotel until after four. I was delighted to find that F. Ferguson had returned but he ignored my smile: Chris shook her head just as she did when I talked to cats and birds. He did not mention breakfast – evidently that routine had worn thin – but silently handed her a brown paper parcel too small to be shoes. When she tossed it to me it rattled.

"It won't explode," she said up in the room. "Open it."

I handed it back: a bomb was unlikely, but I feared a boxing glove or a scary jumping snake. Her nails slowly picked away the tapes: well before she uncovered the white rectangular case, I knew what it would be.

"Not from the suppliers" – she mused – "Local postcode . . . No message" – she shook it – "Batteries already in."

I had glimpsed vibrators among the drugs paraphernalia advertised in the Underground Press, but this was the first I had seen in the flesh – or plastic. The length was not intimidating but the width most certainly was. At least its colour was neither ebony nor pink but dark orange, like over-baked clay. I did not trust standalone electrical devices: if there was a flex for you to trip over then you knew where you stood – if you put a battery into something you're giving it a soul.

Chris had upended the base which began to hum. The shaft pulsed then inclined itself towards me in grudging acknowledgement.

"I wish you could see your expression," she said.

"Did you order it?"

"It's not my colour."

"So, who sent it?"

"It could have been anyone." She was staying casual, not even trying to laugh it off.

"What are you going to do with it?"

She winked. "Put it with the others."

"What is it called?"

"It's a . . ." – she consulted the box – "Squirmy Rooter."

On hearing its name, the thing jerked and reversed its flow.

"It can't have been christened that – let's call it . . . Winston."

"Why?"

"After Churchill: there's this play – *What the Butler Saw* – where his severed cock gets pickled in formaldehyde."

She looked genuinely outraged. "Nothing's sacred to you, is it?" I suspected that she was not being patriotic but remembering Simon Ward.

I saw that the vibrator's shaft was not perfectly smooth but dotted with indentations like the fading characters of some dead language: perhaps Ed's pygmies had worshipped it as a god?

There was no slit in its glans: no matter how much it rooted and squirmed the poor thing could never pop its cork – Winston would have to fake it, in his turn.

Already Chris was naked, but I could tell that she was not in the mood. I wasn't either: a throbbing plastic shadow had fallen across our sequestered romantic idyll. She had produced her Swiss Army knife and with its tiny scissors began trimming her pubic hair.

"Live from Rome Colosseum!" I boomed. "Victorinox Champion versus the Squirmy Rooter! Who do you think will win?"

"No contest." She kissed the knife's scarlet casing.

The only thing that troubled me about Chris's games with 'F' was that although she would never speak or write the letter, she had no qualms about using things that contained it. Forks, fur-coats, fags, flip-flops . . . I had even seen her munching falafel and sipping Liebfraumilch. I could accept a little blurring – as when she called the numbers at work – but carrying a knife was her own free choice.

"What do you call this?" I plucked it from her hand.

"The Champion!"

"No – it's a knife. That's K-N-I-F-E, isn't it?"

She did not look in the least put out. "No, it's not."

"So, what would you call it? How would you spell it?"

"I'd call it . . . a blade. B-L-A-D-E." Her Geordie accent was at its most pronounced – as if this object was something you might take to the fabled Blaydon Races.

Thumbing out the fish-scaler I prodded at the Rooter.

"No, you don't" – she snatched back her knife – "How would you like having that done to you?"

I wouldn't, of course, – but my cock appeared to disagree. One thing led to another until I ended up on top of her – but only so that she could pick out targets for the scaler.

"What's 'blade' in Russian?" The three TVs had come on.

"Nozh," I said.

"What about 'book'?"

"Khnigi."

"Khnigi . . . Nozh." She was savouring the words – I had to admit that they sounded good. "Perhaps I should have been Russian."

"There's not many 'Fs in their language and the letter in Cyrillic looks nothing like our own." I took up pen and pad and drew.

"It's like a one inside a zero – or maybe a ten. I wouldn't mind saying it when it looks like that."

"How does 'fran-t'e-cha 'sound to you?" – I had deliberately 'v'-ed up that 'f'.

"OK" – she said warily – "What does it mean?"

"Smart woman."

"Is that clever or . . . well turned-out?"

"Both." Leaning forward I kissed between her brows.

"What's paper? What's pen?"

"Razeta . . . pykya."

"What are Russian writers like?"

"They make ours look like shit – except for Lord Byron and Henry James."

"Are they better than . . . Céline?" She whispered so that he would not hear.

"No – but all good French and German writers get honorary Russian citizenship."

I could have sworn that Chris had turned Winston off and returned him to the box but within the hour he had squirmed back to the bed. Rather than hurt his feelings we let him do whatever he wanted until the humming rose to a shrill unbroken blare and his batteries finally cut out.

❧

Chris had ordered a car to take us to Lori and Lorna's D-Day Party. This turned out to be the black Daimler from her training week but with a different driver.

Nobody said anything, although Ed's mouth kept clicking open only to close again. He was dressed as he had been in court – tweed suit, cream shirt, old school tie and brogues – personally I would have given him ten years for the tie alone. At least the bowl of a briar pipe was no longer projecting from his top pocket. Chris had applied so much make-up that I hardly recognized her. She wore a long silk dress, punctuated by slashes and slits, as if bound for Mayfair not Alwoodley.

"What colour is that?"

"Misty blue," she said.

The girls were living halfway up a steep hill. The street was wide and well-lit, but cars were parked nose-to-tail with yet more clinging to the verge.

"Drop us here," Chris commanded. "Come back in three hours."

"I'll wait" – the man's voice was reedy yet resolute – "Round the back of the church."

Now I saw that it was the same driver, after all. After half an hour of squinnying at Chris in the mirror his eyes were about to merge above the pineal gland. He reminded me of Death's chauffeur in Cocteau's *Orphée* whose name I could never remember.

"Heurtebise," said Ed. Had I spoken aloud or was he reading my mind? Had I really heard him at all? Now Heurtebise's cyclopean eye was burning into mine: I opened the door and got out.

It was a strangely quiet party: you could only have found it by the lights. There had been an intercom at the building's entrance, another by the lift and a third on the top floor outside the flat itself. The corridor was even better carpeted than our hotel and the soundproofing was such that when the door slid back the volume of sound almost knocked us over.

They were playing "Bohemian Rhapsody," of course. That song was ubiquitous – on TVs and radios, blaring out of jukeboxes and shops. The only safe places were the clubs because no-one could dance to it: the hospitals were full of people who had tried. You couldn't get high to it, fuck to it, get born or live or die to it but you could *spend* to it all right. It was acquisition music, tinny as a million cash registers opening and closing together.

The living room was huge and well-furnished: I could see why Ed had been impressed. With those double steps leading up to the bedroom/bathroom area it resembled a stage set from some dire Whitehall 'farce'. There appeared to be no access to the fabled kitchen with its saucepans and spoons – or perhaps I was too unenlightened to see it.

"There's thirty-nine people here," said Chris.

"Forty-two" – Ed corrected her – "counting us."

Chris was the solitary woman: Lori and Lorna were evidently still in make-up, preparing for their grand entrance. After a stunned silence – as everyone stared at Chris – the music recommenced, more softly. Unlike Queen it was just possible to dance to Cat Stevens and seven of we forty-two had elected to try.

"We should have brought some sounds," said Ed but I reckoned that whatever had been playing the result would have been the same.

Everyone was drinking orange juice: there appeared to be no alcohol except perhaps for a huge silver punchbowl, brimming with a maroon liquid. It smelt of cloves and Brasso with just a hint of garlic and dung. Black bubbles kept breaking on the surface as if something was stirring in its depths.

"There was a ladle," said a gangling man with a tiny head, "But it seems to have melted."

There were no ashtrays, and nobody was smoking: Chris lit up and surveyed the scene, her expression conveying that she was simultaneously shocked to the core but had just had all her worst suspicions confirmed.

"So where are all the dwarves then?" She enquired, loudly.

I knew that Ed was worrying about the competition but as I looked around it was apparent that Pinhead was by no means the biggest man here. Two coves in wheelchairs parked by the food tables might have posed a threat but only if having no legs could confer midget status. One was asleep or dead while the other was stabbing his own nose with a cocktail stick.

"Those guys in the corner look familiar" – Ed was pointing – "But I can't place them."

"Oh fuck," I said. Seeing that they had been recognized, Rhys and Dominic were turning their backs.

"Who are they?"

"Those croupiers I trained with. They were with me and Chris that first night in the 'Newlands'."

"Did you tell them about Lori and Lorna?"

"Of course not: it was you that was talking about it. They must have bought the paper then responded themselves."

"Now I remember" - Ed frowned - "They didn't *look* as if they were listening."

"Things take a while to sink in - but they get there in the end."

"Have they said anything to you?"

"We've not spoken from that day to this."

"You boys are lovely" - Chris tapped her ash into the punch - "But you talk too much."

At this the music ceased and all the lights - except those along the balcony - were extinguished. A smattering of applause soon petered out. I saw that the three white doors were each tagged by a large baby-blue letter: the 'B' presumably stood for Bathroom whilst the two 'L's were self-explanatory.

When all coughing and shuffling had ceased the 'L' doors swung slowly open and Lori and Lorna came bounding out. They were dressed identically, in short white flouncy dresses with knee-socks and pink satin sashes from shoulder to hip. The effect was way beyond any scale of wholesomeness: at least neither was carrying a milking-stool. I could hear Chris, behind me, hissing like a snake.

The music - 'Cinderella Rockefeller' - began again, even louder.

The girls were miming - no, they were really singing along. Lori carried the tune with Lorna rumbling beneath. A curious dance accompanied it: the arms dog-paddled frantically while the legs were lazily goose-stepping below. At the end of each chorus, they bumped bottoms, bouncing off as if moulded from rubber. On the last chord they leapt high then landed in the silence with a double thud.

Without using the stairs Dom and Rhys had somehow contrived to appear at their side. For a moment I thought that they were haloed but it was only someone messing with the lights. Joining hands, they came right up to the balcony rail then raised their arms in a victory salute. Rhys, his feet well off the ground, was dangling between them like a chimp.

"So here we are" – Lori was tapping an invisible microphone – "and here it is! I can't begin to tell you how hard it has been to make our selection from all you wonderful people. You are all just so special – more special than you will ever know. We're giving this party to thank you for all the hours of joy . . . for all the hugs and laughter but also . . . the tears. We went looking for love and romance and we've found it" – here both girls stooped to rest their heads on the shoulders of their new partners – "But on the way we discovered other things that were just as important – the life-lessons that we learned from all our great new friends."

Around us, the white faces of the great new friends were turning grey. They were like character actors in some well-made play, chewing on cordite before the elegiac final act, 'twenty years later' . . .

"What do you make of all this?" Ed asked.

"I think it's what 120 *Days of Sodom* would have been like if De Sade had possessed a sense of humour."

"Or if he'd been a proper sadist."

Above us the four principals were raising their voices in song.

"We're getting married in the morning –

Ding-dong the bells are going to chime . . ."

"Did they ever say anything about marriage?" I enquired.

"The advert read 'For fun and good times."

"Does that sound like marriage to you?"

"You boys make me laugh" – Chris was not laughing – "What else were you expecting?"

"I wonder what will happen to them now."

"They'll all live happily ever after," I said. "And it serves them" – Chris was laughing now – "bloody well right."

Any hopes that the Great New Friends might be setting fire to the place – or at least storming off in a huff – were soon dashed. They were numbly surveying the empty tables where the wheelchair duo – having snarfed up all the nibbles – had assumed an all too innocent air. Everyone was still giving that punchbowl the widest possible berth, but Ed had begun to lap up the liquid from his own cupped hands. I saw that Lorna – as if anticipating the firstborn – was now cradling Rhys' rugby ball: it was certainly taking after its mother.

A somewhat older man came shouldering through. In his loafers, slacks and Intarsia sweater, the Inspector looked more like a copper than ever.

"What brings you here?" I asked.

He punched himself over the heart: "You're looking at one very proud dad."

"Lori and Lorna! So, which one's yours?"

Those thunderous brows descended. "Isn't it obvious?"

"Ah yes" – neither of them looked in the least bit like him – "Of course."

"Don't worry" – his eyes were twinkling, horribly – "They're both of them mine."

"I didn't even know they were sisters."

"They don't either: they're half-sisters, of a sort" – a huge hand flapped – "These things are always . . . complicated."

It had to be admitted that Lori and Dom made a handsome couple – like Fred and Daphne in *Scooby-Doo*. They were seated a little apart, surrounded by a heart-shaped nimbus, heads bowed, and fingers intertwined, exchanging shy glances from under lowered eyelids. Behind them Rhys had wrestled the child from its mother and was now spinning it on the tip of his right forefinger.

They'll be giving in their notices at the Casino," said the Inspector. "It's time to start a proper life."

"The Force?"

"You must be joking." He moved away but then turned and made a throat-cutting gesture. "It'll be banking or accountancy or even . . . quantity surveying."

Chris had returned to the dancing area where various items of furniture were stealthily inching their way back to their customary positions. With her hands at her sides and her head thrown back she began turning in slow circles, loudly clicking her fingers. I joined her, hoping that I could pass off my cursing and kicking of occasional tables as a new dance craze. Then 'Bridge Over Troubled Waters' came on and I felt strong fingers clamping on to my shoulders, while Chris's nose slid along my jaw. For a while we moved together, incontrovertibly dancing to a slow one . . .

"The good thing about you," she said at last, "Is that you're not bothered about looking stupid. You really don't care what other people think, do you?" Before I could answer she walked off to help Ed finish off the punch.

It was true that I did not care but it had never crossed my mind that I could ever – to anyone, under any circumstances – be looking stupid.

The rejected suitors were still hanging around: they gave the impression that they would never leave but slowly fade away. With a loud and blinding flashbulb, the Inspector was photographing the happy four – full front then from both sides, for identification purposes. Now that the bowl was empty Ed had evidently filched a bottle of rice wine from the invisible kitchen. Normally he could drink any amount to no ill effect but sometimes, in direful circumstances, he would decide to let himself go. I could see by the angle of his right elbow that –quite understandably – this was to be one of those nights.

"Please tell Ed that he was my first reserve," Lori was saying. "He might even have won if you'd not been already spoken for. As Lorna and I were looking as a couple we thought it would be nicer if we took another pair as well."

"I'd do anything for Ed," I said, "Except that."

"I hope you'll see that Christine is all right," said Dominic, "She looks a bit upset to me."

"She's broken hearted," I told him. "You were always the one for her but you know how shy and sensitive she is. Now all her dreams are shattered: we'll be on suicide watch tonight."

Even after the wine Ed appeared perfectly sober until we hit the fresh air when he took off like a rocket: even running backwards he easily outpaced us. Heurtebise finally cornered him in the graveyard where he was clinging to a stone angel: unlike Peter Fonda in "Easy Rider," he wasn't crying or calling for his mum - Ed's drunken laughter was expressing an anguish that was way too deep for tears.

He was perfectly coherent on the drive home but - as none of us knew much about Caedmon - he had largely wasted his breath. On alighting, however, he crumpled, in stages, like a dynamited tower block until at last he lay flat on his back in the moonlight. When I offered my hand, he did not seem to see it.

"We are all lying in the gutter," he enunciated carefully, "But some of us are looking at the kerb." On which perfect note he passed out.

I carried him inside and laid him on the mattress where the books rearranged themselves around his boneless form. He was the only man I had ever met who - heartbroken and off his face - was capable of improving on Oscar Wilde.

Chris had remained in the doorway. "I'm off to the hotel."

I saw that once again Heurtebise had waited.

"I can't leave Ed," I told her, "He might try to choke on his own vomit."

She got into the back seat then wound the window down.

"You're just so special" - she was lisping horribly - "More special than you will ever know."

"I know," I said - but the car was already almost out of sight.

I was not going to tell Ed that he would have won if I had not been "spoken for." For one thing, I had no idea whether Chris might speak for me or not.

On her reappearance, an hour later, she walked straight past me and sat cross-legged by his side. Thereafter she never took her eyes off him - not even when talking into her shoe. I did not tell her that she was looking stupid because it would not have been true.

"Don't let him sleep on his back," I said but she did not respond.

When Ed drank, he really drank and when I slept I slept - far too deeply for dreams. When I awoke it was still dark: the light of another day had been successfully blotted out.

There was no-one in the front room, but it had been tidied:

I wondered how Ed felt about his carefully arranged dust being disturbed.

Chris was sitting alone in the kitchen, dressed and made-up ready for work.

"Where's Ed?"

"Gone – he got up at midday, vomited for twenty minutes then jumped on his bike and went to college."

"How did he seem?"

"Like always: we didn't talk about last night."

"So – where's our kippers?"

She did not smile at this. "There's nothing here to eat."

Ed had wolfed down everything: even that mouldy loaf had gone. I spooned so much coffee into my cup that I was chewing it. Now Chris had finally produced those drumsticks that I had seen when she first moved in. After twirling them impressively she began – with a penholder grip – to play fast paradiddles across my knees. I hardly felt a thing but whenever she pinged my nose a cymbal crash would echo round my head. Ed had evidently thrown up outside the back door but now a near-apocalyptic storm was sluicing the vomit away.

"Don't worry, we'll take the cab." She waved a stick and through the deluge the faithful Heurtebise began to sound his horn.

"Yum . . . Yum . . . Yum."

From three tables away I could hear Yehudi's voice ringing out like a cracked bell.

"Yum . . . Yum . . . Yum . . . Yum . . . Oh, what a lovely pair!"

Through the crowd I caught a glimpse: his expression was anything but lascivious – with those round eyes and gaping mouth he resembled a toddler apostrophizing the fruit in a greengrocer's window. That voice had risen since he left off smoking and he was lighter by at least a stone: every single penny was earmarked for the tables. Chris's right shoulder was dipping as she paid out on yet another pike-poked bet.

Now there was no holding him. Whenever she called a number he would gurgle it back at her, like a demonic Tweetie-Pie. He pounced upon those 'ours and 'ives, dramatically stuttering the missing 'f's. When Sinatra came on, he would harmonize erratically but otherwise impersonated the cries of the curlew, blackbird or thrush. When Chris finally went on her break, he serenaded her retreating form with the 'Match of the Day' theme – *Bum-bum-bum-bum-bu-bum-bum-bum-bum'* – and much hilarity ensued.

"Is that clown bothering you?" I asked her in the Green Room.

"About" – she drew thumb and forefinger together until they almost touched – "*that* much."

As we were returning to The Pit Yehudi started whistling again. *The Bridge over the River Kwai*: even I laughed at this because Chris could not keep herself from falling into step.

Other patrons who had ignored him were now egging him on. A party of large men in club blazers were pressing in closer: their skins glowed with rude health and their necks were even wider than the shaven heads they bore. There were eight of them – like a rugby scrum waiting for someone to feed them a ball. Unfortunately, Rhys was on compassionate leave. Whenever Chris leaned forward, they dowsed towards the deepening declivity between her breasts.

A dapper old gentleman with a walking cane kept skimming a cash chip across her table. "Numero soixante-neuf" – he would trill – "Twenty pounds on sixty-nine."

"No bet": again, and yet again Chris politely returned his stake.

I could see that Helen was not happy. She stepped forward then back, her mouth opening and closing, but did not intervene. Her expression said that Chris had brought it all on herself.

Suddenly there was an explosion of noise, and a blast of hot air struck my face. Without looking up I knew that the largest of the Chinese families was moving towards my table: a score of people sounding like two hundred. As they passed Yehudi the older women fluttered their hands as if warding off the evil eye. They gambled for the sake of gambling, wildly celebrating every penny they won while also – if in a more minor key – enjoying losing just as much. I had never been so pleased to see anyone: for the next two hours I could lose myself in their stamping and screaming, in their rhapsodic cheating, in the tears and smiles of their blithe and innocent madness.

Yehudi finally left just before two. His stealthy accumulations had left him £100 up until with a sudden spasmodic movement he lumped the lot on evens. When 14 Red came up, he did not even correct Chris's pronunciation but grabbed his chips and ran. Helen told me that he had sat out the six previous spins without betting, staring silently at the ceiling as if waiting for a sign.

If you concentrated long and hard, to the exclusion of all else, could it be possible to penetrate the atoms of ball and wheel and – if not on every spin but often enough to matter – direct their motions to your will? If so, it would surely be necessary to neutralize any similar capacities possessed by others in the room: perhaps Yehudi was not merely trying to put Chris off but to psychologically – or even psychically – destroy her.

❧

After all this time she was still surprising me. Not content with crossing her legs behind her head she was now nibbling at her own toenails.

When work finished, I no longer asked, and she no longer told me: we made straight for the hotel. When we tried to see Ed, he was never in: we left him a note telling him to ask for us at reception, but he did not appear. The Casino and hotel were enough for me now – I no longer even registered the faces on the street.

Chris had peeled off her false nails only to apply a new set – shorter but even sharper – which turned out to be her scratching-nails.

Now I was trying to distract her with tales of St Benedict – of his celebrated but incomparably feeble miracles: The finding of the

192

lost billhook . . . the inexhaustible wine-jar . . . the mending of the broken sieve . . . the spurning of the seven naked girls.

"What's spurning?" Chris asked.

"Knocking them back, giving them the brush-off, resisting their . . . blandishments."

"Blandishments?"

"Charms, wiles, temptations – they were coming on to him."

"I bet it was them spurning him and his" – She gave my cock three detumescent flicks – "Blan-dish-ments."

I had started asking questions – "Where were you born? What star sign are you?" – to which I did not want to know the answers, reckoning that she might, if only out of weariness, let slip something important.

"Did you have any pets?"

"Any what?"

"Pets."

She thought about it. "Three dogs and an armadildo." Her expression warned me not to pursue this line.

"What was the cause of your breakdown?" Taking a direct approach had never worked so I was surprised when she did respond.

"Everything, I suppose."

"But what actually set it off?"

Wincing at that double F she lit the last of my Gitanes.

"Well," – she leaned back and blew a smoke ring – "There was this house on my street that I liked to walk past. It had wooden shutters and an English-looking garden. A white cat was always in the window – its mouth kept opening but the glass was too thick to hear it mew. When it put its paws against the pane, I saw that it had only three legs. One night it wasn't there: I waited but it didn't come so I sat on the ground until they took me away. It was odd because I've never liked cats – I suppose I'd just got used to this one."

I was preparing to be deeply moved when her eyes flickered, and that little smile twitched the corners of her mouth: I believed in three-legged Puss about as much as the Armadildo.

Getting to her feet she bobbed a curtsey to her reflection then reached down to crank up my cock again: at least she had handed me the remains of the cigarette. She had evidently led a curious and eventful life, but I found it impossible to imagine her being anything other than she was right now.

After a while I registered that the sheet beneath us was sopping wet. Were we bleeding or had we pissed ourselves?

"Don't worry," said Chris, "It's only spray."

"Does that mean you've come?"

"Of course not – it's just something women get."

When I did withdraw and ejaculate, she aimed my cock at the pillow as if we were icing a cake. Then she produced her knife and made a series of tiny incisions – which did not bleed but rose as throbbing purple studs – before extracting a white plastic spike – maybe a toothpick? – which she unerringly thrust down my urethra.

"How do YOU like it?" she enquired. Evidently, I was being punished for something that I was yet to do. Perhaps we were about to re-enact a puppet version of St Benedict's martyrdom with my cock standing in for that unfortunate saint.

"Well, clever-clogs," – she withdrew the spike then licked it – "What would you call that?"

"Algolagnia – it's when you derive sexual pleasure from pain."

"It's nothing to do with pleasure."

"What is it then?"

"'Un" – two of the new nails were nipping at my rectum – "'Un."

Had she really said "Fun"? Had there been just a touch of a fricative there? Her face was utterly impassive: this was going to be fun without laughing.

"Al Golagnia" – she mused – "Didn't I meet him once in Vegas?"

Later, after burning off my scanty pubic hair – which frizzled away to nothing before the flame could reach it – Chris was lighting her seventh Kool of the night. I had failed to convince her that these were the absolute acme of uncoolness.

"That Yehudi" – she sighed – "He's The Devil."

"That's what you said about Gray and the Inspector and Billy Bunter and Freud: they can't all be, you know."

She shook her head then nodded.

"Do you mean that *all* men are devils?"

"No – all men are *The Devil*." Her fingers had traced those capitals in the air.

"What – Satan in person?"

She nodded again.

"Did Mr Corrigan tell you that?"

"He didn't need to."

"And am I The Devil too?"

Cupping a hand under my chin she turned my head this way and that, peering intently into my ears.

"Not yet," she concluded. "But you're getting there."

"I'm not like the others," I insisted. "All your so-called Devils are scared shitless – you can see it in their eyes."

"You're just too stupid to be scared" – she was twiddling the earlobes as if trying to retune me – "So you'll end up worse than them."

"Say that again."

"No." She stubbed out the cigarette on the sole of her left foot: as usual there was a faint smell of burning rubber not of flesh.

To be even worse than The Devil: now that really was something to aspire to! Why had Career Advisers and Labour Exchanges never once mentioned this option to me?

As we dressed, I observed that her skin was unmarked whereas the shirt was already sticking to my back which was itching and burning as if scratched by the three-legged cat's missing paw. Who knew what germs might have been incubating under its claws?

By the time we reached the Casino, however, all my aches and pains had somehow cancelled each other out. I was up on my toes, dancing rather than walking, my breathing soundless but regular and deep. My eyes were back in focus, registering once again every detail of each face that passed. When we finally entered the Pit, I could clearly see my own features peering back from the rims of Yehudi's Specs.

Three hours later when my euphoria had worn off Chris was still sailing blithely through the waves of insult and innuendo that were breaking over her table. Only my hearing remained heightened: I could catch every single word.

"What wouldn't you give to chew those cunty lips?"

"What wouldn't you give to bite those tits?"

"What wouldn't you give to fuck her? All three of us together!"

The rugby boys kept droning on about "back-scuttling": if it ever came to it Chris would give them a good scuttling all right – leaving them to rust and rot at the bottom of the deepest oceanic trench, chuntering away for all eternity.

"Aren't you going to do something about him?"

Yehudi was the only one keeping his mouth shut but Helen knew exactly who I meant.

"Why? He's only just breaking even, and all the rest are losing. No-one wins when their minds aren't on the game."

"What if his luck changes?"

"It won't. He's a Jonah – Gray says it's like having three zeros on the board."

"Don't you hear what they're saying?"

"It's only banter" – her upper lip curled – "Isn't that what you men like – bantering with your mates?"

"Not this man" – I had so nearly said 'boy' – "Banter's what you do when you're too scared to hit someone in case they hit you back."

"Look at her" – Helen had flinched as if she had seen in my eyes a blow beginning to formulate itself – "Can't you see how much she's enjoying herself?"

At this, Chris glanced in our direction. "No, she's not," I said.

"That pouty look was just for you," Helen sneered, "To show how lonely and sensitive she is . . . underneath it all."

I determined to take this up with Chris but when I followed on my break, I found her lying on her stomach with her nose almost touching the TV screen. Two other croupiers were cowering in the far corner of the room.

"You've just missed a new 'Chunky Minced Morsels'," she said. "Clement's dog was wearing a hat."

The commercials had ended but now Oscar Peterson was ripping into 'Tea for Two': this was not the right time to speak.

Yehudi was nowhere to be seen when we went back out. I assumed that he had hit his nightly target and left until we heard the same pitiless laughter that had sounded across the railway tracks.

Standing together at the top of the stairs, with brandy schooners in their hands, Gray and Yehudi were looking straight at us. Chris had stopped: her chin slowly rose as she held their gaze until they fell silent. Only then, rolling her hips in leisurely fashion, did she take her place at the table.

After his descent Yehudi remained subdued as a third stack of chips arose before him. The rugger-buggers were still getting slaughtered but – panting with their tongues out while regularly adjusting their trousers – they did not seem to mind.

For a while the focus of excitement shifted to my table. A party of guest-members came trooping across, laid down maximum stakes, lost a great deal very quickly then marched away again. All I had been thinking about was how I could be experiencing such aches and pains in those parts of my body to which Chris had not yet turned her attentions.

Now that all the casuals had returned to her the noise levels were rising once again.

"Twenty on soixante-neuf," called the twinkly old gent. The rolling maul's anal symposium had now reconvened itself. In among the gurning throng a row of calm and serious faces caught my attention.

It was the Armenians! Still obliged to ignore my existence they had now stumbled into this bewildering new world. I closed my eyes in pleasurable anticipation: this was going to be . . . interesting. They were ruthless capitalists, of course, and fanatical Catholics but above all they were gentlemen – more English than the English – and therefore doughty protectors of the fairer sex.

I recalled how the patriarch had once taken me on one side.

"There is something every man should know," he said, "and it is just six . . . simple . . . words."

Looking up into his dark and liquid eye I realized that my will was no longer my own.

"Nothing . . . is . . . ever . . . a . . . lady's . . . fault."

"Is that a quotation from somewhere?"

He had beamed at me. "It is . . . Milord Edward Fox in . . . *The Go-Between*."

If anyone even swore in front of a woman, The Family would intervene. In their factories it was a sackable offence. One night outside the 'Red Lion' a middle-aged couple were conducting a loud argument until the four brothers each took a limb and then threw the man into the middle of the River Wharfe. After struggling out he came round apologizing to everyone. Although the Armenians had no idea who he was he had addressed them all by name.

And now here they were, with a canal and the River Aire and an Emergency Hospital conveniently to hand. They looked from the crowd to Chris and back again and then they looked at each other. The youngest brother had begun to crack his knuckles.

The ball rattled down to its slot. "Twenty-'ive red," Chris announced.

"Twenty-fuh-fuh-five," Yehudi echoed.

This sparked off a terrace chant – "Twenty-'ive / Twenty-'ive / Twenty twenty / Fucking 'ive!" that just swelled and swelled. I watched as my Armenians softly stole away: they seemed to vanish long before they reached the exit . . . Nothing was ever a lady's fault – except when that lady was Chris.

Chris's silver syringe had finally reappeared, but it proved to be for extraction purposes only.

"Is that thing sterilized?" She was drawing 20cc from the crook of her left elbow.

"Of course it isn't," she said even though I had seen the kettle boiling in the kitchen.

She called this 'giving blood' but no accident victims would be offering grateful prayers to her name.

"Why do you do it?"

"It's healthy – it gives you energy, it puts you to sleep."

"How can it be doing both?"

"It depends on when you take it."

This made little sense because for her there were surely no times of day.

Although I had always preferred darkness to daylight, I no longer felt that I had much choice. There were no mornings, evenings or afternoons in our hotel – only nights and, in endless recession, the ever-darkening nights of those nights. The door to the balcony had been locked but I did not ask after the key, while the heavy curtains remained closed as if to keep something in or out. Although the traffic and rain remained audible, they now seemed like sympathetic companions in the room.

Sex had become incidental to pain. We fucked clutching plastic-headed pins ready for their cue. I kept on dropping mine so that when Chris shouted "Now!" my empty hands could only twist or nip which – as she made clear – was worse than doing nothing at all. Those lost pins, however, continued to abrade and stab – randomly and annoyingly, to no erotic or aesthetic effect.

In the mirrors she would proudly reveal her handiwork. My shoulders were studded with alternating red and black pinheads, perfectly aligned.

"Let's try again."

"It's useless," I said, "I don't have your . . . precision."

"You'll never learn anything that way." She began to retrieve the bloody things.

She approached her own body like a surgeon, extracting from its white leather case a second, smaller knife - a scalpel-bladed X-Acto - to cut away at the insides of her mouth. Now I knew what gave her lips that bruised and labial swell.

Cigarettes had to be stubbed out in the hollows behind our knees, as if these had evolved solely to be used in such a way. I had known some bikers - Satan's Slaves from Buttershaw - who would do the same, but their skins had resembled wormwood-riddled teak. Perhaps Chris would start opening beer bottles with her teeth or igniting her own farts.

There was something hectic about it all - as if she had made a list and was now rushing to get through it. Sometimes she consulted the broken watch to check that we were still on schedule.

My foreskin, red and sticky, had now glued itself behind the glans.

"Have you ever thought about circumspection?" she asked.

"No - I always try to throw myself into things."

Only later did I realize that I had misheard.

Her skin would heal up as I watched while mine retained traces of every blow and blight: even adolescent acne that had bedded down with the freckles. This was all too apparent in those clubs with mirrored walls and ultra-violet lights: I looked like I'd been holidaying in Hell while next to me Chris's face shone as pure and untroubled as the moon. She would stare in fascination at my reflection, as if she might be looking at my soul.

Not only was it healthy to let blood it was even more so to drink it.

"Who told you all this?"

"No-one: you can know things without any telling."

Nevertheless, I did tell her what Montaigne had written about the Mayas who - as a penance for gossip and lies - would draw blood from their ears and tongues as offerings to their Gods.

"Ear blood" – she winced – "I wouldn't like that. Anyway, I always tell the truth."

After sliding the knife between her teeth, she spat out a ball of pinkish foam.

"They didn't merely prick their tongues," I said, "They used to pierce them then pull thorn-studded ropes through the holes."

"You've made that up."

"When you're in London go to the British Museum. On the first-floor landing – opposite the sarcophagi – are the lintels of Yaxchi'lan where you'll see the Mayan royal family doing just that – and a good deal worse."

Chris seemed miffed that someone had got there before her, as if she had been hoping to patent these procedures. Even less did she appreciate my evincing neither excitement nor disgust.

Blood itself had never bothered me, except when it was up on a big screen in Technicolor. What did disturb was watching Chris removing or inserting her contact lenses: my gorge rose when her fingers started dabbling in her eyes. Blindness was the thing that scared me: I wouldn't care if my body was being slowly hacked apart so long as I could watch or – when I grew bored – open Voragine again.

"They weren't all like St Elizabeth" – Chris had been enquiring after other female saints – "Some of them could get pretty nasty. St Juliana used to catch devils by their tails, whirl them round her head then toss them into the privy."

"The – what?"

"The toilet . . . the shithouse . . . the bogs."

"But wouldn't those devils have liked that? I bet they were begging her to do it."

Rising from the pillow she surveyed the awful carnage of the sheets. "These will have to be burnt as well."

"Let's blame it on the ghosts of Jayne Mansfield's dogs," I said.

Her legs scissored and once again she was on her feet, stretching her arms above her head.

"Hit me."

"I beg your pardon?"

"Stand up and hit me: I owe you one punch."

I had not realized that she had been keeping accounts: perhaps we would be going Dutch on all those breakfasts?

"Is this negotiable?"

"No." She took two steps forward then – as if recalculating angle and distance – one step back.

I scanned her face, wondering how I could inflict minimal damage. If I turned my wrist then the fist would slide up her jaw, burning and numbing the ear without threatening its drum, before smashing into the bedroom wall.

"Not up there" – she was rubbing her stomach as if miming extreme hunger – "Down here." If she was seeking parity how was this supposed to match my loosened teeth and locking jaw?

I dropped into a crouch which I knew must be looking ridiculous. The fingers of my right hand had curled back but not into the palm. If I was to fake it, Chris would be insisting on retakes so that we'd be arguing over the difference between a push and a punch until we had to go.

After a melodramatic wind-up, just as I was swinging across and down there came a loud hydraulic hiss as the breath drove itself out of her body. Before my blow could land it encountered something harder coming in the opposite direction: there was no doubting it – her tightly-clenched abdomen was out-punching my fist.

The impact had jarred up my arm to lodge like a bullet somewhere in my back-brain while my mouth tasted of sea-salt and a third tooth, a back molar, was drilling deeper into its gum. Before my eyes my hand was trying to shake off its own fingers.

Chris was still standing motionless, her feet planted well apart. Without a word she began to back away. When she had reached the bathroom, the door slowly closed itself behind her. Although she had not locked it, I knew better than to follow.

She was gone for some time. Taking up Voragine I worked through a few more saints – Cecilia, beheaded in her bath . . . Clement, thrown overboard with an anchor round his neck . . . and Catherine, who had not died on her torture-wheel but instead smashed it with such force that four thousand watching pagans were killed. The noises from the bathroom might have been sobs or groans but they sounded more like gig-ger-ling to me.

When she finally emerged it was with the same decisive stride with which she would approach the Pit. Her skin looked darker, but it glowed and gave off a scent like a grouse-moor in August: evidently some special lotion had been applied.

"Why do I always have to tell you what to do?"

"Because I don't know what you want."

"Why not just do something and see what happens?"

"Because I don't want to make the wrong move . . . Maybe you should write some instructions."

She picked up my T-shirt and scrawled on it in lipstick then tossed it back to me.

"BLOW YOUR NOSE."

As I obliged, she took off her shoe and laid it across my lap, then stuck her bottom in the air and wiggled it about. Her face, looking back over the right shoulder, wore an expression of simpering terror.

"Now say 'I'm going to beat that sexy bum with this nasty big shoe'."

I had got as far as 'sexy' before laughter overcame me. When I finally regained control, I saw that she had held the position.

"Not with the sole," she said after the first blow, "Use the heel."

The thing kept flying out of my hand so that I was scrabbling to retrieve it.

"That was nice," she said after a while, "But it's not really a bum shoe, is it?" Rolling on to her back she raised her legs. "Hit my soles with its sole – but stay away from the toes."

During the subsequent bastinado she appeared to have fallen asleep.

My arm was getting tired. "Would you like to do the same to me?"

"Don't be stupid" – one eye opened – "It's a ladies' shoe."

I did not press the matter: a single swipe from my black suede stacks might put me in the mortuary.

"I think I've finally got it," I said. "With you, every move will always be the wrong move."

She winked and gave a thumbs-up. "That's right."

Breakfast proved to be a disappointment. The coffee was weak, the toast dry and my kedgeree's usual sultanas had been replaced by raisins, to catastrophic effect. Then the candles guttered out: we couldn't even burn ourselves properly.

"Never mind," Chris produced a small cut-glass object like an antique salt cellar. "Try some of this."

On holding it up to the lamp I saw that it was half-full of a dark, viscous liquid. After shaking it, I unscrewed the silver stopper and held it under my nose.

"What is it?" I could smell nothing at all.

"It's me – or rather it's mine . . . my blood."

On further examination it seemed to be coagulating.

"It's not ear-blood, is it?"

"Tongue" – she said – "To show that I wasn't lying to you."

She poured half into a teaspoon and passed it over to me, then did the same for herself.

"Cheers." She had frowned when the spoons clinked together.

I didn't know what I was expecting – maybe Imperial Tokay? – but it was merely salty-sweet and metallic, just like mine had been in 'The Hook'. Either everyone's blood looked, smelled and tasted the same or hers and mine were the one and only perfect match. Perhaps I would have to spend the rest of my life biting people in order to resolve this question?

"Did you ever try to kill yourself?" I enquired. "I mean, really try?"

"What good would *that* do?" She looked at me as if it should have been self-evident that she could never die.

❦

On Friday the Casino, although packed as usual, was oddly quiet: even the music had been turned down. The densest area was around Table 8 where Yehudi and his acolytes were already in place: one of the inspectors had evidently leaked the secrets of the rota. On sighting Chris and I they started to whistle – loudly and derisively – 'Dance of the Cuckoos', Laurel and Hardy's signature tune. I did not find this funny and, going by their expressions, they had not intended it to be.

I was on Table 12 where the curvature of the Pit would give me a perfect view of the main event: I would rather have been out on one of the unpopulated boundary tables with a plastic bag over my head.

Chris was in half-profile while Yehudi, directly opposite, was crouched behind a great wall of chips – surely far more than he had won in the last fortnight. Perhaps he had set up a tollbooth at Lady Anne's Crossing or started selling off the rolling stock?

"F-f-f-f-fourteen/f-f-f-f-fifteen split" – he smeared a fistful of chips across the baize, forcing Chris to re-stack them before placing his stake. She did this with a celerity that nearly took his fingers off. As usual, no-one else moved to shadow his bet.

My opening spin came up zero: nobody was on it, of course. I could have sworn that the number's round green eye was winking at me.

"You're on the wrong table," I muttered, retrieving the ball. "Get yourself over to Eight."

"Seventeen black," Chris announced. Yehudi had also plastered reds, evens and the third column but despite this setback had begun to replicate the spread.

Just before I spun the wheel a skinny hand shot out to cover zero and its trios. I had not seen the Chinese approaching my table.

"Zero," I said again, to wild applause.

"I'teen black." Despite the jeers and groping hands Chris remained impassive as she paid Yehudi out.

For a while the Chinese kept me fully occupied but I was not in the mood. One myopic nonagenarian was following a mad zig-zag pattern through the numbers 1–34.

"It's called a snake bet" – Helen whispered in my ear – "You don't see them very often."

"36 red," I called.

"That's why you don't."

I couldn't see how Chris was getting on, but feared that the cheering was not a good sign. It was shaping up to be a reprise of last month but this time we had seen it coming and, in the interval, Yehudi had learned how to ride his luck without falling off.

By the tilt of her head, I guessed that she was looking down her nose: not even Yehudi would meet that gaze. All the rest were hypnotized by her breasts. The folds of the dress kept shifting: the shoulder blades rolled and flexed while a succession of ripples ascended the spine but never came down again.

When she finally went off for her break everyone was chanting – "Twenty-'ive/ Twenty-'ive/ Twenty/ Twenty/ 'ucking-'ive!"

"You'll be chipping on Eight when you come back," said Helen when I followed a few minutes later, "Things are hotting up."

Many of the punters were heading for the bar: they looked remarkably cheerful considering how much they had lost. Yehudi alone remained at the table: his left hand was pushing two chips towards evens while the right poked two more on black.

In the Green Room Chris was in her usual place, staring at a screen of static.

"The aerial's bust," she explained. Someone had snapped it in two and thrown it into the corner of the room.

I lay down next to her. Those teeming black and grey flecks looked ominous – like the opening credits of *Twilight Zone* – but their hiss and fizz had settled into a soothing tidal rhythm.

"Have you ever wondered," I said at last, "How those creeps are getting away with it?"

She yawned even more widely than usual: "With what?"

"All the chuntering and the insults - all that stuttering shit."

"Oh, that" - her mouth had stayed open - "I never bother with such things."

"That sixty-nine clown hasn't placed a single proper bet."

"He's playing on Table Seven: he just pops over as a laugh."

"Ha, ha," I said. "Where do you think Yehudi's stake has come from? They dole out chips but no money ever changes hands. How can he suddenly have an account when he's only a poor sap who's been losing for years? Hasn't it struck you that Gray is using him against you?"

"Why would he do that?"

"As a test, maybe, or a trial - or to punish the two of us for getting together?"

At last, she finished off her yawn. "You and your fantasies," she sighed.

"Chris," I said, "Fantasy has got an 'F' in it."

"Oh no it hasn't" - she was levering herself to her feet - "There's no 'F' in fantasy."

Off she marched to the ladies', this time bolting it behind her.

"Phantasy" instead of fantasy: if this had been a trap I had well and truly fallen into it. What was surprising was that she had been aware of this older spelling with its roots in Latin and Greek: perhaps she had picked it up from some admirer with a classical education - hadn't Billy Bunter been a public-school man? I switched the TV to another channel where the black flecks were slaughtering the grey.

When Chris finally emerged, I saw that she had reapplied her make-up. Without looking at me she walked straight out.

It wasn't until we were halfway down the corridor that I fully registered just what she had said. If there was indeed no 'F' in phantasy there was definitely a bloody big one in 'F'. I decided not to pursue this further: she already had enough on her plate - even higher and shriller, the whistling was starting up again.

Perhaps my chipping was meant to break Yehudi's luck, but I suspected that it was to increase my own mortification. I had begun to suspect that side-bets were being placed as to when and how I would finally lose my rag.

The faces around us twisted and snarled: when they stopped yelling you could hear their teeth grinding. In contrast, Yehudi was perfectly calm: his blissed-out smile had reappeared, but I was not to be fooled. He had finally discarded his comedy glasses and, without blinking, never took his eyes off Chris.

After the first five spins he was seven hundred up but for the next five none of his bigger blows landed. He showed no sign of discouragement: although the luck had slipped its leash, he knew that it would soon come bounding back to him: in the meantime, the outside bets kept things ticking over.

I was bombarded with chips for everyone else was still losing. Instead of depositing these at the mouth of the clearance area Chris would flick them up to strike my chest and face. When her body brushed against mine it felt rigid as if anticipating another punch. I could hear her exhaling but never breathing in.

Yehudi was soon back on track. 33–16–24–5–10–23–8–30: that was his favoured section of the wheel. The straights and splits of 23 were his linchpin but he also loved the 'ours and 'ives, as if their 'f's were working like garlic on a vampire.

The other punters' gambling grew desultory, as if they were only staying to watch, until – without any signal or cue – they launched a sudden blitz on the columns, the dozens and the numbers low and high. Only when Chris called "No more bets" did I register that, for the first time, Yehudi had not ventured one single chip.

"Zero," she announced. Even while she was sweeping the table clear I saw him leaning forward with two full stacks ready in his hands. He evidently felt that once this number had been drawn out – like the Joker in a pack of cards – it would be unable to reappear.

"Speed it up," Helen growled, then "Slow it down" but neither was going to work. With every spin the momentum grew: 24-15-5-8 - then 24 again.

Although the fateful zero had utterly cleaned them out the crowd were still making their presence felt. Their comments were not directly addressed to Chris but were in the non-specific and deniable third person.

"I'm going to fuck her in all her holes" - declared the man who I thought of as the Blind-Side Prop - "All three at once." I wanted to ask how he would be managing this when - judging by the hang of his Farah slacks - he was at least two and a half cocks short.

"Her arse is like my youngest girl's," said a head that appeared to have been grafted onto someone else's shoulders, "Nice and tight and juicy." You could tell by his eyes that wife and children - if these had ever existed - no longer figured in his life.

Chris was now doing the hoppy-swoopy move that she favoured in the clubs. A shock wave passed up her body, setting the breasts jiggling alarmingly, and then, more slowly, worked its way back down into the earth. Her groin was pressing hard against the table's edge while her teeth had clamped on to her swelling lower lip. The left leg rose behind her to kick at me but missed. I stood there helplessly, my arms dangling - everything was going out, nothing was coming in.

"'Ourteen red." Her smile was now mirroring Yehudi's.

"I'd give every penny on this table to have her reaming my arsehole for an hour." Mr Soixante-Neuf tapped his watch face for emphasis. "She'd need to make some noise, mind - to show how much she's liking it."

He was not playing on Table Seven or on Table Nine. He was inescapably here, with that single slimy cash chip continually slipping from his grasp. This was no gambler but a local revenant who had sneaked inside for some warmth before returning to an unconsecrated grave.

"Me, I'd make her hum while she's doing it."

"What tune?"

"*Bum-bum-bum-bum-bu-bum*

Bum-bum-bum-bum-bu-bum
Bum-bum-bum-bum."

It was the National Anthem: the whole table was patriotically joining in.

I became aware that Chris had gone with Helen taking her place. Even she had realized the need to intervene.

A relieving hand was now pressing my own shoulder. It was Dominic, his eyes full of tears, muttering something that I could not catch. He seemed shorter and wider than before: Lori had been adjusting him to fit.

As I moved away, I saw that Yehudi had left his seat to follow Chris. Like a swimming dog his arms were paddling the air while his mouth gaped wider and wider.

"Isn't she f-f-f-fantastic?" Despite the stutter it was an actor's – no, an orator's – voice, originating not in the chest or throat or head but bubbling up from the guts and bowels. It was a voice you could smell.

"Isn't she f-f-f-fabulous?"

Chris did not seem to have heard him. Head high, back straight, she moved imperiously through the crowd then floated up the stairs: when she raised her hem her feet seemed to be not quite touching the ground. Yehudi's third shout was choked off as he stumbled over the second riser.

I was gaining on him at the same rate that he was gaining on her. I had assumed that he would stop at the 'STAFF ONLY' sign but instead he pursued her along the corridor. As she neared the sanctuary of the Green Room her knees began to pump but Yehudi was already slowing down, planting his feet, clearing his throat.

"Isn't she wonder-f-f-f-ful?"

Chris staggered and almost fell.

"Isn't she wonder-f-f-f-f-f-f-ful?"

Her hands groped behind her as if an arrow was lodged between her shoulder blades. Then, with a final effort, she threw herself at the door which, after swallowing her, snapped shut like a mousetrap.

Yehudi was advancing yet further, his flattened palms ready to push on over the threshold, past the broken TV and into the ladies' toilet and beyond. There was only one thing to do.

"Excuse me, sir," I said, "I'm afraid there's a little problem with your car."

"I don't have a c-c-car" – he smiled up into my face – "I c-c-came on the bus."

"That was it," I nudged him towards the foyer, "Problems with your bus."

My arm snaked around his waist and squeezed. He was chronically ticklish, giggling and wriggling as I waltzed him through the revolving doors. It must have looked ridiculous, but the stony-faced bouncers and the cloakroom girl did not seem to register us.

Where had this stutter come from? He was trying to say something else beginning with 'C'. I wanted to throw him into deep water, to see if he sank or swam, but the river and canal were ten minutes away. Even in the town centre someone might have tried to intervene, so I led him round the back of the building. His body went slack, and he dug in his heels, so I took him by the scruff and dragged him through to the car park.

Punters preferred the well-lit multi-storey opposite the brewery – ours was only used by staff. Apart from Gray's Jag there were only a few old bangers and something resembling a joy-driven hearse. Who the hell was driving a white Heinkel bubble-car?

I saw that their windscreens were glistening with the first frost of winter. Yehudi's breath was condensing alarmingly, as if he was wreathing himself in ectoplasm. There was no lighting or security camera, but a full moon was augmented by a scattering of stars.

When a white fist flashed out I half-turned to see who might have thrown it. Although it had missed, Yehudi was reeling back as if buffeted by displaced air. My second shot hit him clean, but he was already going down. While the body crumpled his still-beaming face was floating like an unmoored balloon. It seemed about to ascend into the night but then thought better of it, plummeting down to reconnect at a curious angle with the neck.

It felt as if my anger had broken free to incorporeally work him over: he was thrashing around, being dribbled by large but invisible feet. When I prodded his ribs with an exploratory toe he giggled once again. My presence seemed redundant: I might as well have gone for a piss and left them to it. Now the stars themselves were winking at me, as if they were in on the joke.

I had been expecting a proper fight. He was short but stocky and those hands revealed years of hard physical work. "Watch out for the little'uns – my father liked to say – "especially the Scots." Perhaps Yehudi was drawing me in before launching some irresistible riposte.

Around his body broken glass was glittering in the moonlight so I grabbed his lapels and restored him to the vertical. The face seemed unmarked, but his palms were raw, and his trousers ripped, with one skeletal kneecap poking through. The eyes were unfocussed while the lips moved but made no sound: I realized that I was patting his back as if to reassure him.

This curious tableau – we two clasping each other, faces close – felt curiously familiar: perhaps it had been one of those dreams that I had contrived to forget?

Then I saw that he was on his toes: the body tensed, and the head reared up while the eyes betrayed a nasty glitter. I flashed back to when an over-enthusiastic skinhead at an Enoch Powell rally had essayed a headbutt only for me to get there first: tonight, the tables had been turned, for Yehudi – legs locked around my waist, hands pressing down on my shoulders – had me on toast.

At this moment an arm as thick as a python coiled round my neck to pull me away. Yehudi was flat on his back again, pecking like a chicken at the empty air as a second bouncer stepped in between. When the third and fattest came puffing up I guessed that they had been holding off, laughing too much to intervene. Pouring through the fire exits the chorus were making their entrance: Helen and Kenny, Dom and Rhys, the cloakroom girls and a clutch of semi-retired punters who usually confined themselves to the bar.

Slowly and silently, they advanced, heads bowed, perfectly in step. It was hard to tell whether they were about to expostulate on fate and mortality or instead rip into Offenbach's greatest hits.

Gray was bringing up the rear: it took me a few seconds to register that Chris was trying to hide behind him. As she was, in heels, fully half a foot taller she moved in a crouch, her eyes screwing shut as if to render her less visible.

"OK lads," I said calmly, and the bouncer loosened his grip. I got in one final kick but the only yelp that sounded was my own for that temptingly exposed kneecap was as hard as stone. Yehudi had not even blinked but when they stood him up his nose began to bleed profusely.

There was no mistaking Chris's change of allegiance. Now she was clinging to Gray's arm, pretending to shiver, pretending to weep. Although she had donned her celebrated fur-coat he had slipped off his own jacket and was trying to drape it around her shoulders. He was eyeing me with new-found resolution, daring me to do my worst. It was glaringly obvious who had won and who had lost but I was wondering whether I had done the right thing at the wrong time or just the absolutely wrong thing.

Nevertheless, I was going to play out the comedy. "I have just struck this gentleman," I announced, "For repeatedly insulting this lady."

"I didn't hear anything" – Chris wasn't looking at me – "I didn't see anything either."

"It's curtains for you, Ginger," said Gray. "You're fired."

"No, he's not," said Helen.

"Oh yes I am," I insisted but she ignored me.

"Punter and croupier were both outside the building with no other witnesses. It's a verbal warning and an unofficial one at that."

"He never hit me" – everyone turned to look at Yehudi – "I got lost in the dark and f-f-fell. He f-f-found me and helped me up."

"Oh yes I did," I said, "and oh no you didn't."

At this point the forces of law and order elected to take a hand. Deep in the shadows the door of the battered hearse creaked open, and the Police Inspector hopped out sideways like a flea. He was wearing full evening dress to impressive effect except that his flies were unbuttoned. I was relieved to see that it was merely a shirt flap that was hanging out.

"Regard the moon" – he waved at the sky – "*La lune ne garde aucune rancune . . .*" He advanced, still moving sideways. "It's nice out, isn't it?" He eyed me reproachfully when I did not take my cue. "Well" – those huge fingers adjusted his dress – "I'd better put it away before someone sees it."

He glared for a few seconds at everyone in turn – a process which, as even more spectators were arriving, took almost a minute.

"What's all this rubbish, then?" Fortunately, everyone grasped that this was a rhetorical question. "I think I'll close down this shithole, arrest the lot of you and have your licence on Mr Mayor's desk first thing Monday morning."

With head bowed and open palms Gray slowly approached him, zig-zagging as if trying to translate the snake bet into a dance. The two of them moved away to confer: their voices dropped, and their expressions were giving nothing away. Chris and Yehudi were now chatting casually, like two film-stars on set after the director has called 'cut'. They seemed to feel that their scene had gone well even though his blood was far too red to be convincing.

At last, the Inspector drew his pocketbook. After the pencil stub had dashed off a few lines he passed it to Gray who turned even paler but nodded assent. Their subsequent handshake did not look Masonic, more like the prelude to some ballet move. I was disappointed that Gray and Chris were not reuniting for a pas de deux.

"You are no longer sacked," Gray announced, "But we require you to leave these grounds immediately. Your probationary period is now over. Go home, sleep well and come in at 1pm tomorrow for your table test."

"I'm going your way," said the Inspector before I could respond, "Let me give you a lift."

He ushered me into the passenger seat. The inside of the car was immaculate with a polished walnut dashboard, green leather seats and the 'Goldberg Variations' tinkling out on some police frequency. I glimpsed the silhouette of a woman with permed hair sitting in the back. Although the face was shadowed, I had the feeling that I had met her before.

"I like your coat," I said.

"S'ocelot." This was not Lori or Lorna's mum but maybe one of their younger sisters. "Fake fuckin' ocelot." At least she had no problems with her 'F's.

The Inspector pulled a racing turn then slammed his foot down, but everyone had already legged it back inside.

"I did warn you." He sounded his horn at nothing then ran a red light. "Those people are garbage, son, lost souls. Most of them weren't even born properly and the rest have never been alive at all. I trust that you will not be going back."

"I have to take a table test."

"Forget your pride" – he squeezed my right knee – "That tart isn't worth it, you know."

"It's not about that" – I removed his hand – "If Gray doesn't sack me, I can't sign on for the next six weeks."

"What happened to all that drug money?"

"We've spent it."

"On what?"

"Books, clothes, clubs, drink, other drugs . . . the rest of it we just wasted."

The girl in the back was laughing like a myna bird but the Inspector remained silent. I had noticed that the more something amused him the grimmer his expression became.

"There are other options, you know," he said at last. "Don't forget the force. If you want to hit folk, you can do it to your heart's content.

There's a new Drug Squad starting up in North Allerton – they could use a lad like you."

"Wouldn't I need some training?"

"Don't worry – we've got Graduate Entry now."

He was taking me home all right but like Ed he favoured the scenic route. We ignored all traffic signals, driving on the pavements of one-way streets with the headlights off and all four indicators on the blink. When we passed a parked-up paddy wagon the occupants just waved. Yes, I could understand the appeal of The Force.

After finally dropping me off his head came poking out of the window: I was not sure whether he had opened it first.

"You have the key

The little lamp spreads a ring on the stair.

Mount.

The bed is open; the toothbrush hangs on the wall

Put your shoes at the door, sleep, prepare for life—"

Once again, I did not take my cue, so he finished it for me.

"—The last twist of the knife."

With its engine screeching in protest the black car exited backwards down the hill. As I had expected, the hand waving from the rear window was sporting an extra finger.

I did not need a key: the door was ajar, and the lights were on. From the front room there sounded the soaring tenor of Joseph Schmidt – 'The Midget Caruso' – doing *My Song Goes Round the World*. Either we had an echo or up on the landings the Hydra was softly joining in.

Ed was sitting at his table. Dozens of books were propped open while drafts and variant texts covered every inch of the floor.

"You're early," he said. "Where's Christine?"

"I don't think we'll be seeing her again."

He passed over his brass-bowled pipe: I thought that we had long since finished the last of the Temple Ball.

"Take a look at this." He handed me the facsimile edition of a mediaeval bestiary recently published by an American university press. BRITISH LIBRARY: REFERENCE ONLY had been stamped on the inside cover.

It was much heavier than I expected, and its laminated pages kept sticking to my finger-ends. The colours were shifting, bleeding into each other, first garish then shadowed as if occluded by passing clouds. Here was Andromeda's sea-monster carrying its own decapitated head while being consoled by a family of field-mice . . . advanced foreplay between a magpie and a fox . . . a flock of flamingos with human faces . . . a goat carrying an astrolabe . . . a black squirrel playing a harmonica . . . a lion vomiting gold . . . a tubby weasel sniffing at the tail of a tiny red bull with purple hooves and horns.

There seemed to be a narrative that I could not quite grasp – a steady progression towards some mysterious end.

"It's the lion versus the unicorn in the final," I said.

"Never" – Ed flicked a page – "If this hedgehog's drawn to scale it will roll right over the lot of them."

"We can go down the clubs if you want. I don't feel like sleeping yet."

He did not reply. After wiping Joseph Schmidt with a soft yellow cloth, he put on Ella Fitzgerald's "Wacky Dust" with Chick Webb – yet another of his midget pantheon – on drums.

"I hate to say this," he said when the record had finished, "but if I do have a soul, I am afraid that it is not a Northern one."

Within minutes I had passed out on the couch to sleep – without dreaming or rising to piss – for the next ten hours. When I awoke Ed was still in place: his back had fused with the chair and his left elbow was disappearing into the tabletop. The wire-rimmed glasses had slid down to hang precariously off the points of that great moustache. It seemed unthinkable that anyone could ever want to step outside this magical circle of light here in the dead centre of the universe.

"There's something wrong with Christine" – he spoke without looking up as if reading the words out of Langland – "I mean *really* wrong."

"You don't say," I said. "Can I borrow some socks? – I can't face these anymore."

After much rummaging and cursing he tossed me a balled-up pair, royal blue with yellow clocks on the ankles – like the ones that he had worn in court.

As always after a good night's sleep I was feeling terrible. What I needed now was a pint of Guinness and a game of pinball but less than an hour remained before my table test.

To my surprise Ed followed me into the hall.

"Don't do anything stupid," he said.

"How do you mean?"

"Sorry" – he smote my shoulder in manly fashion – "Don't do anything more stupid than you usually do."

While crossing the park I saw that someone had scrubbed the graffiti off Pomona and her sisters only to shroud them in impenetrable grey plastic mesh. I wondered whether the same might happen to Chris.

There was no sign of rain: a solitary cloud was stubbornly holding out against an ever-deepening expanse of blue. The Portland stone of the university tower was giving off a dazzling glare: I put on my shades and selected a scowl suitable for the crowds of students trudging between lectures and tutorials.

"They can't touch you." Although the wind and drizzle had rapidly returned, Kenny was waiting outside the casino. "That car park is Council property, there were no witnesses, and the security boys will swear that he followed you out."

"Well, I suppose I *was* dragging him."

"Don't you want to know what happened after you left?"

I did not answer but he carried on.

"That bloody fool – he only went back and started playing again!"

"Yehudi? I thought he'd be in hospital."

"No - when the girls cleaned him up there was hardly a mark on him."

Kenny had slapped his left thigh - the first time I'd seen this outside a pantomime.

"In less than two hours Christine had drained him dry. He crawled out of here on his hands and knees. We won't be seeing him again."

"That's what you said last time."

Together we mounted the steps. I saw that the security camera was not tracking us: it had only had eyes for Chris. Kenny had taken my arm: his body leaned against mine as if shielding me from wind and spray. He was like something out of Forrester or Captain Marryat - those tales of the seas that I had loved as a child. I was sad that I had never found an opportunity to ask him just what his own story might be.

As we breached the doors the cloakroom girls broke into applause that was not entirely sarcastic. "Big Bad Leroy Brown": they were even playing my song.

"Aren't you going to ask me about Christine?"

"No."

"She's upset."

"No, she's not," I said.

"You know what she's like - she doesn't show things."

"Has she said anything to you?"

"No" - his head shook sadly - "She's never talked to me. They say she's leaving next week."

"London? Vegas? - Or the cruise-ships?"

"I don't know. I heard something about Monaco."

I sniggered, having always found the very idea of Monaco faintly ridiculous.

"Is Gray around?"

"He's out in the Pit: he's been waiting for the last hour."

"Why?" - I checked my watch - "I'm early. I'm never late."

"You and him, you're just the same: stubborn. You won't back down and he won't either. Just bite your tongue and do the test. You could have a future in this game if you simmer down a bit" - he dug his elbow into my ribs before parting - "Just a tiny bit."

It felt odd to see the casino floor half-lit and empty once again: it looked smaller and larger simultaneously. For the first time I noticed that patches of the maroon carpet had worn away to the colour of sand.

Gray, with his back to me, was running a game on his own. Judging by the stacks he had been on a hot streak. When the ball dropped, he clapped his hands.

"17 black - 175 pieces, sir."

He went running round the table to check his winnings. I was reminded of how I had first met Ed - in the students' union where he was trying to play table tennis with himself.

"Thank you for honouring us with your presence." He spoke without looking at me.

"Sorry I'm so early: shall I come back when you've finished?"

"Christine asked me to say goodbye" - He was tucking his former winnings behind the mounting of the wheel - "She says she had a lot of fun with you and your friends but now that she's feeling more herself it's back to real life again."

"Is that verbatim?"

"Is it what?"

"Is it exactly what she said? Did she get you to memorize it?"

"Every word."

What could I say? Fun . . . friends . . . feeling . . . self . . . life: how could these people not have noticed yet?

"She finished off that fool after you left."

"Is that verbatim too?"

"He's banned - and those rugby boys too. I won't have my staff treated like that: you should have heard us laughing when they went."

"Only because they had no money left: when they've saved up, you'll welcome them back. You only bar the ones that win."

"The ones who cheat." He leaned down to reach under the table then, as quick as a snake, straightened up and threw a book at my head. I caught it backhanded, baseball-style: he was not to know how much Ed and I had practised for such eventualities.

"Christine said it was boring" - on the back cover, Céline's scowl grew even darker than before - "and she doesn't care who did it."

"Who did what?"

"Why, the murder, of course."

"It was the writer," I said, "Tell her it's always the writer who dunnit."

"You think you're clever, don't you?" - He had evidently not enjoyed my impersonating him - "When you don't know the first fucking thing."

"What's that?"

"What's what?"

"What is it, this first fucking thing?"

"That women like Christine are always in control."

"Except when they've gone mad."

"She wasn't mad: she was tired. Anyway, she's fine now."

"Did she tell you that?"

"No - you've just got to look at her." His head turned as if she was standing behind him - ten feet tall and growing.

"We were all pissing ourselves watching you trying to protect her: everything happened only because she wanted it to. She could have picked off Yehudi any time she liked. Have you ever played backgammon with her?"

"Yes," I said, "I always won."

"Only because she let you: just put a pony on the table and see what happens. She's been here for an MOT - to check that she's in proper running order, to do any fine tuning that might come up. She knows how it works: she insisted on making things even more difficult for herself."

"Was I part of this test?" I hoped that he hadn't heard that gulp before I spoke.

"No – that was just her. They say she's always had a taste for lame ducks." – He made a twisty gesture over his groin – "Still, it's good to know that her oil and anti-freeze levels are working again."

I felt my mouth opening only to shut again with a wet and pouty slap.

"I always knew that Christine was out of my league" – He stuck out his chin as if inviting me to hit it – "But you weren't even playing the same game."

My hands had gripped the table's edge as if trying to squeeze green tears out of the baize.

"You should have seen us in the old days – you'd have gone running back to mummy. We had aristocracy, gangsters, showbiz stars – the cream de la cream. When anybody ordinary came in we'd give them a no-limits tab, get some tarts to slip them a few shandies and by the end of the month they and their families would be out on the street." He reached across to keep the wheel spinning.

"Then the Gaming Board got involved. No more hostesses or drinking out on the floor . . . maximum bets that were only twice our old minimums . . . lights and cameras everywhere . . . strictly members only with a two-month waiting time: when they shipped George Raft back to America and shut the Colony Sporting Club, we knew that it was the end."

He paused, expecting some reaction. I tried to look interested, even a little impressed but this was evidently not what was required.

"You think you're so clever up on your high horse with your dirty books and nasty music. Nothing you say makes any sense . . . and you're wearing a jacket with zips up its arms: what's the bloody point of that?"

"Ventilation?" – I shrugged – "Aren't we supposed to be doing some sort of test?"

His right forefinger, blackened by nicotine, slowly rose – as if about to give a blessing – only to slash down again, scattering the chips across the table.

"Get them picked up," he said, "Then you can show me everything you've learned."

I tried to move but my hands would not loosen their grip. When I opened my mouth, no sound came. In my life so far, I had always acted or reacted immediately, without hesitation or reflection, but now I found myself contemplating the possibilities of immobility and silence. Perhaps I might never need to do or say anything again.

After a pause Gray flicked up a wooden cash-chip which struck my chest with a hollow sound. When he tried this again, I put it between my teeth then turned my head to spit it out.

"Did you swallow? Did you swallow that?"

I did not respond, just stood there and let him rave. His words came in short bursts . . . which made me wonder whether he too had been reading Céline.

"What kind of man . . . would give drugs . . . to a woman like that? She said you live like pigs in shit . . . God knows what diseases she could have picked up . . .

". . . You hate goodness . . . you hate money . . . you hate fun . . . you hate everything this place stands for . . ."

That enormous Windsor-knotted tie – more a bloater than a kipper – had come loose and a riot of paisley was spilling across his chest.

"Your lesbians . . . your lesbians . . . your lesbians . . ." – he kept repeating this as if I was the owner of a factory that was manufacturing them. ". . . Can you imagine what they might do . . . to a woman like Christine? They'll spoil her . . . ruin her . . . turn her back to front or inside out . . ."

I guessed that he was voicing some gynaecological fantasy that I could not share.

This continued for some time: I had almost succeeded in blocking it out when there came a terrible scream.

"The wheel! The wheel! The wheel!" The sound was like a dog that has just been run over. "The wheel has stopped!" His hands were clapped to his ears as if this lack of motion was somehow deafening him.

"Spin it! Spin it!"

I was surprised when my left arm reached across and set it whirling once again but anti-clockwise, in quite the wrong direction. A deep howling sound issued from its hollow bell while the spare ball flew off the spindle to ricochet away. The wheel was now generating its own speed: that blurring chassis seemed about to tear itself loose – to smash through the ceiling and resume its proper place in the darkest corner of the galaxy.

Nevertheless, I could still read the numbers, flashing past in their own weird sequence. East of zero they ran 32-15-19-4 instead of 1-2-3-4. That mysterious number four was the only one to maintain its proper position, although 29 and 35 were just a single click away. Inside the wheel three times two was no longer six but 285, while four fives wasn't twenty but 84: you couldn't count on your fingers anymore. Helen had told us that if all those numbers were kept in sequence, then no-one would ever win or lose. She had also revealed that when you added them all up – one to thirty-six – they totalled six hundred and sixty-six.

At last silence had fallen and the wheel was once again moving at a steady pace in its proper direction.

"I didn't want to do this" – Gray had produced a long brown envelope – "But you leave me no choice."

I opened it immediately. There it was, my lovely green P45, along with a sheaf of greasy banknotes, fully four weeks' wages. This was more than generous: I only hoped that Chris was not involved for then I would have had to throw the money back in his face.

"If it makes you feel any better, I'm sacking that postman and the gypsy and Dominic has just given in his notice. You've got to be tough to handle the pressures in this game. Your eyes are good, and your hands are quick but your head's all over the shop . . . I can't think of anything you might be fit for . . . unless it's social work or teaching." He made these sound the feeblest and most contemptible occupations in the world – at least we were agreed on something.

"No hard feelings." A hand offered itself, but I did not take it: long white hairs were sprouting from the fingers' lower joints. I felt bad about Gigi for she had been fast and flawless, unvaryingly cheerful: why the hell had he taken her on in the first place?

I trousered the money and walked away, determined not to break my silence. Halfway to the door, however, I heard that familiar soft wet hiss as my lips drew back from my teeth." That's the loudest smile I've ever heard," Chris had once told me – as if she possessed a machine that could precisely measure such things.

I spun on my heel and returned to the table, my hands stretching out towards Gray's neck. He did not flinch, but his face turned white and the eyes were rolling back in his head. Very softly and precisely, I refastened the top button of his shirt, then straightened his tie, adjusting its lengths and tightening its knot before passing the narrow end through the cotton back-loop . . . 'Hermes of Paris', it read – perhaps Chris had given it to him.

"There," I said, "That's better." With four over-extending strides I had regained the door: at least I could tell Kenny that until the very last moment I had bitten my tongue.

Outside, the croupiers were arriving for the early shift. Sally, the Punto Banco dealer, came over: her hair had been getting blonder by the day and now it had hit white.

"I'm sorry you're leaving." Word had evidently got around.

"It's for the best," I said, "I'm sure we'll run into each other again."

"There was never anything between me and Gray" – she was gripping my arm – "It was just for show."

"I know," I said, "It was the same with me and Chris."

"Nobody in here ever gets married, nobody ever falls in love" – she relaxed her grasp – "Sometimes I think that no-one in the world is even fucking anymore."

"So where are all these people coming from?"

She slowly turned around and shook her shining hair. "What

people?"

"We'd have got up a collection if we'd known," said a fierce-looking woman whose name I had never learned.

"We'll miss you," said a man with mismatched ears. "There'll be no-one to laugh at now."

This wasn't banter: they seemed to be genuinely upset. Instead of using the Green Room everyone was milling around the corridor: two girls were applying their make up by the distorted reflections in the fruit-machine's metal hood.

Why had I never got to know these people? Why had I thought that they all hated me? Perhaps it had indeed been all been the fault of "that Chris"?

"So, you've gone," said Helen.

"No" – I pinched myself – "Still here."

"What has Gray been saying to you?"

"It didn't make much sense." I was pretty sure that she had heard every word.

"He shouldn't have fired you."

"He didn't want to, but I persuaded him."

"What about your things?" She gestured at the Green Room. "Aren't you going to clear out your locker?"

"That's OK." There was nothing incriminating in there, just that carrier bag of rejected tapes, a denim jacket with an embroidered parrot on the back and the pale blue Converses with worn-down treads.

"I think you should go and check," she said with a heavy emphasis that confirmed my suspicion that Chris was already in there. I knew that she would not be explaining or apologizing or giving me a goodbye kiss: she was lying in wait for the sole purpose of ignoring me.

"My locker's empty," I said.

"Aren't you going to leave your uniform?"

"I'm saving you the trouble of burning it. If I was to take it off it would walk away on its own." – At this moment, for some reason, I was once again able to smell myself – "Feel it – just like cardboard!"

"What are you going to do now?"

"I'm off to the 'Newlands' to play pinball."

"No – as a job?"

"I'll become a gambler: I reckon I've got a flair for it."

"They won't let you in – once you've got a licence you're barred."

"I wasn't planning to play here."

"No – you can't play anywhere. They'll twig you the moment you pick up the chips."

"I'll fumble them."

"You'll fumble like a croupier fumbles. You've got croupier-eyes and croupier-hands – you walk and talk and breathe like a croup."

"I'll come in a wheelchair, wearing a false beard."

"They'll know you by the way you wheel," she said, sadly. "You're marked for life."

"What about bingo-calling? 'Kelly's Eye – Number One . . . Two fat ladies – Eighty-eight!'"

"There's a bit more to it than that" – at last she had smiled – "It takes a lot of training."

The five-minute bell sounded, and they cranked the music up. I thought Helen was going to kiss me but instead we bumped foreheads, Eskimo-style.

"It's a good thing you're leaving before Christmas."

"Why?"

"They make us wear antlers and little satin dresses with scarlet knickers. Gray is Santa with a cotton-wool beard and all the men are his little helpers. You need short hair to be Head Elf – we'd have been painting your ears purple and gold."

She followed the stragglers down the corridor. Why was it that everyone suddenly seems irreplaceable when you realize that you'll never be seeing them again?

"Merry Christmas!" I called but no-one responded.

I turned to face the Green Room. My right arm rose to press its palm against the door and then dropped back to my side: I had not willed either of these actions. I wondered if I should unpeel my shit-brown suit, kick off those orange shoes and then – like the businessman at the end of Pasolini's *Theorem* – go naked out into the street. I would walk through the city, then the suburbs, then the hills and moors and mountains, then the seas and the oceans until at last I reached the endless desert where, like one of the eremitical saints, I would set up my stall . . .

. . . But I didn't. I kept my clothes on, confining myself to tossing that dicky-bow tie up on to the roof before chasing and boarding the empty double-decker bus that – right on cue – came trundling past. I sat downstairs, of course . . . because there was no driver on the top.

SIX

Chris's make-up and clothing remained in the flat, but we knew that she would not be returning to collect them. I decided to leave everything in my turn when I moved to London a fortnight later. I reckoned that my talents might be in more demand down there: according to that barman I would be the only person in possession of a soul. The one question was whether I would be turned back at Kings Cross or worshipped as a God.

After waving me off at the station Ed struck up a conversation with a hairdresser from Beeston. I had noticed her earlier on the platform: she was wearing reindeer antlers that flashed alternately silver and gold. By the end of the week, he had moved in with her.

The next summer, when Ed unexpectedly appeared on my doorstep, he was wearing a bootlace tie and a midnight-blue drop-lapel jacket with matching drainpipes, topped off by a gravity-defying DA haircut. I decided not to ask why he had opted for the Batley Variety look. The monstrous moustache had vanished without leaving a scar. He had grown by almost half a foot, a phenomenon only partly explained by the thickest-soled brothel-creepers you ever did see. He no longer resembled a large midget, more a dwarfish giant.

Although he was moving in perpetual shadow, with that enormous quiff blotting out the sun, he was positively oozing domestic contentment. Fran already had two children, Ginger and Fred: in the snaps that he displayed their faces were melting together.

He had also sold his bike and was going by a different name.

"It's John now."

"How are you spelling that?"

He chuckled like the Police Inspector: "J-O-H-N."

"Why John?"

"It's my other Christian name."

Even his face looked different. "What's happened to your ears?" The lobes, previously large and pendulous, had now retracted and fused with the upper jaw.

"Nothing" – he covered them with his hands – "They've always been like this." Domesticity could evidently work miracles – if only in meaningless ones.

"What are you reading these days?"

"Nothing much – I've left college to start my own business."

"Doing what?"

"Deep-sea diving. You know – salvage, rescue, marine conservation, all that sort of thing."

"But you're sixty miles from any coast."

"That's why we're moving."

"Where to?"

"Tenby – then Crete."

"But you can't even swim."

"I can swim like an otter," he said firmly, "Now I'm straight."

"But what about your work? What about *Piers Plowman*? What about Layamon? What about Brut? What about Sweet and Skeat?"

He shook his quiff. "There's plenty of time for all that." His emphasis on the final words could only be described as contemptuous.

All through our short conversation he was consulting his new multi-dialled watch – the Hans Haas special – as if I was the one who had dropped in unannounced and at an inconvenient time.

Christine – he informed me – was now back on the cruise ships but Gray had died in the street of a massive brain haemorrhage. Apparently, opinion was divided as to whether it was she or I who had really killed him. I guessed that he must have followed my advice and – like King Pentheus in *The Bacchae* – attempted to violate the female mysteries of that back room at The Newlands'.

It turned out that Fran was doing both Lori's and Lorna's hair.

"It's a small world," I observed.

"No – I put her on to them. You should see what she's done for Lorna – proper styling can take three stone off you. As for Lori, she's gone all Space-Babe – green and purple streaks."

"What did Dom say about that?"

"He thinks it's" – he checked off the syllables on his fingers – "'Won-der-ful'."

I asked him if he fancied a pint, but he pointed at his chronometer and said that he had to go. A four-door cream Wolsey saloon had been neatly parked outside: at least there were no child-seats or nodding dogs. As he started it up, I was impressed to see that the quiff was adjusting the driving mirror.

"Well," I said, "Is everything still going to come together in the end?"

Either he had not heard, or he did not care to. After smiling without meeting my eyes he inched out – oh-so-carefully – into the city-bound traffic.

It was apparent that his hair and clothes and the children, car and marine conservation were merely attempts to make him seem interesting now that he no longer was. Even though the moustache was no more I reflected that when Salvador Dalí had attended the 1936 International Surrealist Exhibition he had almost died of suffocation inside a full diver's suit. I could think of worse ways to go.

On arriving in London, I had been neither persecuted nor worshipped: the reception had been lukewarm, at best. I was reduced to working in the oil industry – lugging crates of North Sea core samples off the Aberdeen train, driving them across the river to Waterloo then slicing them up with a temperamental saw. In compensation, however, I had encountered a woman who said she had known me at college.

Jenny's smiles were even rarer than Chris's but well worth waiting for. Love suddenly became curiously uncomplicated, almost natural. When we were not in bed, we'd be discussing politics or art or political art: we hardly ever talked about ourselves.

She had succeeded in erasing her past so thoroughly that when the phone rang every Sunday evening, I had to persuade her that she really did have a mum and dad. What was curious was she always had a substitute older couple on the go – solely, it seemed, to be able to breathe a sigh of relief when we finally got rid of them. During our years together she worked through a dozen of these unfortunates, many of whom had given the impression of being genuinely fond of her.

In those first few months I kept seeing Chris in the streets but whenever I caught up with any of these women, they had borne no resemblance. My only souvenir of her was 'Death On Credit' which – much though I sniffed – had retained none of her peppery smell. I read and re-read it on lunch breaks, sunbathing on the flat roof of the warehouse, cackling wildly. Yes, Céline was right up there with Wodehouse and Wilde – almost as funny as Kafka and Dostoevsky!

I had discovered – slanting across pages 74/75 – a single remaining hair, unmistakeably thick and red and quite immovable, as if she had super-glued it there. The passage marked – a little song by an incidental character, Mere Courtial – did not appear to be significant.

"I am the miller's daughter
I dance with all the lads!
But now I've lost my garter –
Which of you's found it, lads?"

Jenny and I went to hear Yehudi Menuhin playing Berg's *Violin Concerto* at The Proms. Looking more like himself than ever, he did not seem to notice me high up in the gallery, peeping through the railings. I thought it had been terrific until Jenny explained how thoroughly he had misinterpreted the piece. His name was no longer to be spoken so I never got to tell her about the time I had attacked him in a car park.

Music was her life. Although she had graduated from Bernard Rands' notorious composition course – 'Stockhausen and Beyond' – she had gone back to Bach and was now receding even further.

She had acquired a rebec and an unplayable shawm and was singing in baroque and early music ensembles large and small.

One Sunday she was in the chorus for the Foundling Hospital's annual performance of Handel's *Messiah* – or 'Han's Mess', as her friends affectionately called it. I did not like to admit that I had never heard this work.

My seat was at the end of the fifth row, spot-lit by a shaft of light so bright that I could not focus on the closely packed faces up on stage. What was curious was the way the sun did not shift its position for the next three hours.

Much of the music was surprisingly familiar – from television adverts, State Funerals and Investitures. At our school assemblies we used to sing along with 'Unto Us A Child Is Born' but always an agonising semi-tone too sharp: in here, however, it was sounding miraculous. After my eyes had grown accustomed to the light, I had to admit that I was crying.

"And his name shall be called" – Jenny and her chorus proclaimed – "*Wonderful!*" They had broken it into three syllables just as Dom used to do. I recognised the same tune that the waiting cleaners had been humming in the rain on the first night that Chris and I had gone to the Station Hotel . . .

"How beautiful are thy feet": I pictured the temporary corpse lying between the tracks at Lady Anne's Crossing and the black blood slowly dripping off Chris's toes . . . Suddenly a man in a brown suit – small but not quite a midget – sprang to his feet and sang in the deepest voice I had ever heard.

"The trumpet shall sound . . . and the dead shall be raised . . . Incorruptible . . . and we . . . shall . . . be . . . changed."

There above me, all the faces were trying to blur into Chris.

After the performance Jenny seemed uncharacteristically anxious.

"Don't worry," she told me, "None of us in this choir are Christians."

She obviously thought that I was being sulky and disapproving when I was merely trying to conceal my over-emotional state. I resolved that from this moment on I would never again be thinking about Chris.

This turned out to be surprisingly easy: for a long time, nothing happened to jog my memory. Ed had vanished along with almost everyone else from the old days. Perhaps he had signed them up and they were all now a-roving the Spanish Main, fighting with ghost-pirates and giant squid, like Scooby Doo on angel-dust.

Whenever we drove up to visit my parents, I wondered whether a stack of mail would be awaiting me: I was not sure whether I felt relieved or disappointed when there wasn't. I did not receive a single mas card – but then I hadn't sent any either.

Jenny and my 'endless conversation' had gradually modulated into perpetual rows punctuated by ever-deepening silences. We got trapped inside the Schumann Question: she insisted that Robert's entire career had been solely intended to stifle and negate Clara's superior talents.

"He maimed his own hands because she played the piano better than him."

"Didn't that happen before they met?"

"He forced her to have children. He laughed at her operas."

"What operas?"

"That's just it: he made her destroy them all."

"He was mad, poor devil: he threw himself into the Rhine."

"He didn't drown, did he? It was just attention seeking. I bet he was a champion swimmer."

I didn't give a damn whether the Schumanns had sunk or swum and neither, of course, did she.

One night I returned from work to hear screaming and wailing coming from the front room. Jenny was lying on her stomach, eating crumpets, watching the TV news.

"What's happening?"

"There's more rioting up North." She made it sound as if I was somehow responsible for this.

Flames and smoke with crowds surging in front of a large burning building: there was indeed something oddly familiar about these pictures.

"It's 'The Newlands'!" I exclaimed. "We used to drink in there!"

"Who's we?"

"Me – and friends of mine."

The reporter was ducking as various missiles flew over his head. Behind him a ghostly form slowly passed, punching itself in the face: unlike me, the youngest of the Luria Boys seemed not to have aged at all.

"Why are they burning down their own pub?"

"I don't know," I said. "I suppose they've got their reasons."

Now two more figures were wheeling something along. It could have been a casualty on a gurney, but I was sure that it was the father and eldest son rescuing from the inferno that irreplaceable pinball machine. It was a moment that should be preserved and celebrated by art, like *The Oath of the Horatii* or *The Charge of the Light Brigade*. A looming figure was watching them approvingly: the Police Inspector was evidently on the wrong side of the barricades.

"What a horrible place." Jenny's buttery fingers turned off the set.

"Everywhere looks the same when it's on fire." Even as I spoke these words, I realized that this was the best exit line I would ever come up with.

⁂

When I turned up alone at Christmas, I watched my parents taking in my renewed pallor, weight loss and trembling hands. They had, of course, thought the world of Jenny but of me they were no longer quite so sure.

"Any mail?" I asked as usual.

"Lots." – I knew that my mother took such matters too seriously to be having me on.

Could it be that my old friends had not forgotten me after all? Had they somehow learned that Jenny and I had broken up? Would we be trying to rebuild 'The Newlands'? Would Ed be returning to his studies? Was everything at last starting to come together?

As my father handed me the bulging Jiffy-bags I recognized Jenny's writing. She had mercilessly forwarded the circulars and flyers of pizza-parlours and minicab firms and the laminated calling-cards of half-naked women with four letter names and Bayswater telephone numbers. There were overdue notifications for books I didn't recognize – Jenny was evidently using my British Library ticket – and recent issues of *The Watchtower* and *Peace News* . . . And here were *Ambit, Stand* and *The London Magazine*, my literary periodicals: I never read them but would continue to subscribe until they finally deigned to publish some of my own stuff.

Along with the junk I had initially discarded a large picture-postcard until the name 'Dean Martin' caught my eye. The image was of Las Vegas under a blood-red sunrise or sunset with he and Jerry Lewis headlining in neon while, beyond, the featureless desert was stretching away towards infinity. Dino had died just last week: if someone put up enough money maybe he would rise from the grave to take a piss?

The card was undated, but the franking revealed that it had been posted this year.

"HAVING WONDERFUL TIME. WISH YOU
WERE HERE."

This could only have come from Chris: how she had loved her felt-tipped Berol pens! The signature – reduced to a 'C' – and two attendant kisses looked to have been limned by an index finger dipped in blood which had now dried to russet and flaked off at my touch. When I sniffed at it there was no smell of pepper, not even the faintest tang of ". . . Connect."

It had been posted on a UK stamp but the franks on the Queen's face had blurred to 'WEST' – something. Could she be in West Hampstead, just across the Heath from my current tawdry gaff?

Or had she glimpsed me inching my van through Westminster and dashed off a card to post in the huge tourist double-box on the Bridge Approach? Or was she in West Grinstead, from whence Jenny had escaped? Or even West Yorkshire, at the very heart of which I was presently standing?

No: that first letter was definitely an 'H' and the last an 'L' – but it was too long to be 'Hull' or 'Hell'. I had to face it: at last, unimaginably broken and defeated, she must have crawled back to that abhorred place where it all began – to be swallowed up by West Hartlepool's endless night . . .

. . . But suppose the message had not come from Chris at all? It was only eight words long – more like a telegram – and that blithe tone was completely out of character. Hadn't there once been a Cathy who had threatened never to forget me? – Or had that been Charlotte?

Only now did I register that the 'F' – that fateful, looping letter – had been written in a different hand, cruder and sloping the other way. With someone's help Chris had lost – or was losing – at least one of her fears. Her father was dead, and she had never mentioned her mother: if she was with a man, I hoped that he would be kind and that she would be making him a lovely tea.

Although she had wished me there, she had not included an address: evidently this was a wish that could never come true. For me to set a North-Easterly course and search for her would be pointless: I had the feeling that if we ever met again, we would be quite unable to touch or even speak.

Had she discovered that wherever you were and whatever you did it made no difference? That being in West Hartlepool was the same as being in London or Vegas or on the gambling ships? I supposed that when she had finally returned a door had opened and she had stepped inside – but it would have been her own door, through which I could not follow.

"Wonderful": the word that had threatened to shatter the windows of the Foundling Hospital . . . "Having wonderful time"

- but wasn't time supposed to be all-devouring? This sounded as if Chris might be consuming it rather than the other way around.

Perhaps . . . one day my own door would open, and I too would step through to find that Chris had waited for me on the other side. We would both look and act just the same, of course, except that we would be changed.

When I rejoined my parents, they eyed me as if I might be turning into a timber-wolf.

"Auntie Doris and Auntie Mary are coming over," said my father, dolefully. He disliked them even more than I did. ". . . And Uncle Bert is bringing . . . some games for us to play . . ."

"That sounds wonderful," I said and – at least in that moment – I meant it.

Acknowledgements

To my agent, Annette Green. To Emily and all at Beck Mills for Office Space. To The Royal Literary Fund for financial support – and more!

This book has been typeset by
SALT PUBLISHING LIMITED
using Neacademia, a font designed by Sergei Egorov for the
Rosetta Type Foundry in Czechia. It has been manufactured
using Holmen Book Cream 65gsm paper, and printed and
bound by Clays Limited in Bungay, Suffolk, Great Britain.

CROMER
GREAT BRITAIN
MMXXVI